MY WEEK*

MY WEEK*

THE SECRET DIARIES OF ALMOST EVERYONE

*ACCORDING TO HUGO RIFKIND

The Robson Press

First published in Great Britain in 2013 by
The Robson Press (an imprint of Biteback Publishing)
Westminster Tower
3 Albert Embankment
London SE1 7SP
Copyright © Hugo Rifkind 2013

These columns were originally published in *The Times*.

ISBN 978-1-84954-551-8

10 9 8 7 6 5 4 3 2 1

A CIP catalogue record for this book is available from the British Library.

Set in Sabon

Printed and bound in Great Britain by
CPI Group (UK) Ltd, Croydon CR0 4YY

CONTENTS

MY INTRODUCTION*

In 2006, slightly to my surprise, I ended up as the gossip diarist for *The Times*.

It's not a healthy job, being a gossip diarist. I mean, it's not like going down the mines, or anything, but it's still a pretty dispiriting way to spend your time. Your days are full of phone conversations with the representatives of household names who don't want to speak to you (or sometimes, and somehow so much more depressingly, do want to speak to you because they've got a book out). Then, in the evenings you go to aggressively horrid parties and bother the same people directly, until they snap and tell you to go away.

At least, usually. I've a friend who, on his first ever diary outing, spotted Martin Amis at the other end of the room. 'Could I just have one word, Mr Amis?' he said. 'I'll give you two words,' said Amis. 'F*** off?' anticipated my friend, at which point the greatest novelist of his generation looked terribly crestfallen, and walked off.

Heavens, but it's bleak. And because of this, while deeply valuing the career boost that a daily column in *The Times* had given me, and the trust which it betokened, and suchlike, I was also keen from the outset to spend as many days as possible doing something else.

So, after a few weeks in the job, I wandered along to see the Saturday editor – then the mighty George Brock – and asked him if I might, one day a week, do something slightly different.

'Anything you like,' said George. 'As long as it's not another one of those columns in which people drone on about how they've spent the week. Because there are enough of those in newspapers already.'

'Hmmm,' I thought.

Then I thought about all those people who had spent the past few weeks refusing to speak to me, and about how much easier it would have been if I'd just been able to make it all up.

Then I thought, 'hmmm' again, and this column was born.

I moved on from the gossip diary after a few years, but *My Week* remained. Since then, I've written roughly one a week for seven years, which makes for ... oh, I don't know. Lots.

You won't find them all in here. Rather, this is a collection of what I consider to be the best ones, which tend to be the most recent, and a handful of others that stuck in my mind. Where you might not have a clue what I've been on about (because jokes age, like cheese) I've tried to explain. They're not ordered chronologically, because then all the best ones would be at the back, which makes no sense for a book. Nor are they necessarily ordered by person, because then it would be far too obvious how often I recycle my own jokes.

Among this lot, anyway, you'll find one that made its way into *Private Eye*'s Pseuds Corner (because they didn't realise that I wasn't actually a Spice Girl) and two that I'm reliably informed now hang in the toilets of former Cabinet ministers. And one that Mohammed Al Fayed wrote about me. Funny old job.

*according to Hugo Rifkind
Summer 2013

PART I
BRITISH POLITICS

ED BALLS
22 JANUARY 2011

Ed Balls has just been made Shadow Chancellor, after the resignation of Alan Johnson, his predecessor. His wife, Yvette Cooper, is often talked of as the next Labour leader. Meanwhile, David Cameron's press spokesman (Andy Coulson) has also just resigned, and Tony Blair (you remember Tony Blair) has appeared before the Chilcot Inquiry into Iraq.

MONDAY

'You're looking cheerful,' says Yvette, my wife, looking up from her laptop. 'Did somebody die?'

It's better than that, I tell her. Alan Johnson has embarrassing marital difficulties.

Yvette frowns. 'I didn't realise he was on the list,' she says.

'Of course he's on the list!' I shout. 'How many times do I have to tell you? Keep up to date with the list!'

My wife sighs. It's true, she admits. She hasn't been keeping up to date with the list. She has been busy fine-tuning the complicated spreadsheets that we require to get our children to school each day, while simultaneously both giving 110 per cent to the Glorious Labour Recovery. She has also been taking smiling lessons. And being Shadow Foreign Secretary.

'He's been on the list for ages,' I say. 'Quite far down, admittedly, No. 37. Between Eric Pickles and that binman who wouldn't take our loose egg boxes. He'll get his. But Johnson will probably resign. And I'm the only plausible replacement!'

'Aside,' notes Yvette, 'from me.'

For a moment I just stare. Then I go upstairs, and put her on the list.

TUESDAY

Ed Miliband isn't on the list. Never really got the point. He's at his desk when I arrive, eating a banana. I make him give me his chair. He sits on the bin.

'You do respect me?' he says, settling down with his knees in the air.

'Course I do, Ed,' I say. 'Now give me your banana.'

Ed says he's been thinking about our problem.

'The way you aren't up to the job and don't understand anything?' I say.

Ed blushes. 'Our other problem,' he says. 'Alan will be gone in a few days,' he muses, 'and I just can't think of any plausible replacement. I wonder if David might come back? Or Harriet?'

'I'll kill you,' I breathe.

'You said that out loud,' says Ed.

'I meant to,' I say.

WEDNESDAY

Johnson didn't know anything about the economy. If he'd caused a deficit it would have been tiny. The amateur.

'Shhh,' says Yvette. She's standing in front of the mirror, trying to smile.

'It's not hard,' I tell her. 'Just imagine somebody who has marginally different politics to you, being hit by a truck.'

'I'm tired,' says Yvette. 'Maybe I'd find it easier to smile if we had an au pair.'

'What are we?' I shout. 'Tory scum?'

'I just want someone to come in and help out with the children,' she sighs.

'Why didn't you say so?' I say. 'We can certainly get one of those.'

THURSDAY

Back in to see Ed Miliband. With Yvette this time.

'Well,' he says. 'It's happened. I've lost my Johnson. So now I need to rearrange my Balls!'

There's a pause.

'But that was a great joke,' he says, plaintively. 'Why aren't you smiling?'

'Yvette doesn't know how to,' I tell him. 'And I just didn't find it very funny.'

FRIDAY

'What a week!' I crow. 'Johnson resigned! Coulson gone! Blair humiliated in front of the Chilcot inquiry! Those suckers on the list are dropping like flies!'

Yvette says she saw the binman fall over in a puddle. 'If that helps,' she adds.

'It really does,' I tell her. 'And to cap it all, I'm the Shadow Chancellor! And Miliband won't last long. So, realistically speaking, there's only one more person I need to grind brutally into the dust to have a clear path to Downing Street!'

'Do you mean David Cameron?' says Yvette. 'Or do you mean me?'

'Fair point,' I say. 'Two people.'

DAVID CAMERON
9 OCTOBER 2010

It's the week of the Conservative Party conference. Party conference weeks are always easy because a speech is fresh in your mind, and all speeches are always absurd. Not much more you need to know for this one, except for the way that Liam Fox, the Defence Secretary, was in near open revolt at the time.

MONDAY

Let me tell you something. This week I'm at our party conference.

I'm practising my speech. I've a new speaking style. Lots of very short sentences. Even shorter than Tony Blair's sentences. Is it possible? Yes. See? Sometimes it might sound like I'm rapping, but only until they start clapping. Rhyming bits, but just in fits. And then I start talking normally again, in a manner that feels curiously jarring and suddenly quite incongruous, perhaps.

Don't just stand there, let's get to it, strike a pose, there's nothing to it. In the national interest.

It's early. George Osborne has come to talk about his own speech.

'No time,' I tell him. 'My new, uplifting, slightly forced manner of speaking isn't just going to craft itself, you know. Say whatever you like.'

George leaves, and I get back to work. Tucking, toning, periodically moaning. Making it longer, making it stronger. Drinking coffee, drinking Coke. Feeling wired, increasingly tired, practising my rapping, no breaks for my crapping. Not even for breathing, in fact slightly wheezing, feeling dizzy, in a tizzy, start to frown, falling down, bumping head, go to bed.

TUESDAY

Tuesday morning, I'm still yawning. Papers cross at child benefit loss. Angry mums, George's dodgy sums. And worse, I'm sneezing, because of the window's all night breezing. Andy Coulson issues. A box of tissues. But it's going well. I can tell.

Sentences – getting shorter. Phrases – getting tauter. Although it would be better if they didn't rhyme. Seems to be happening all the time.

'Fakkin 'ell, Dave,' says Samantha, my lovely wife, who has come in with little baby Florence. 'You're sounding fakkin mental, innit.'

Can't stop. Won't stop. I'm a new leader. It's a new day. And I have a new way. To say. Hey. We're all in this together.

'That last bit is rubbish,' says Andy Coulson.

'Maybe I'm not doing it fast enough,' I say.

WEDNESDAY

Big day. Speech day. Feeling the power, practising in the shower.

'Choose life. Choose a job. Choose a family. Choose a f***ing big television.'

Maybe I didn't write that. Maybe I shouldn't recite that. Might be losing my mind. Hope for the best. Need a rest.

A few members of the Cabinet drop by, to see how I'm getting on. George and Michael Gove think it all sounds pretty good, but that I should probably take more pauses, in order to breathe.

'Otherwise you'll possibly suffocate,' says Michael.

'Although that really would be in the national interest!' points out Liam Fox.

'I don't think he should be here,' says George.

THURSDAY

Speech – done. Party conference – over. Audience – spoken to. Standing ovations – earned. New baby – waved about. Child benefit fuss – survived. Liam Fox – not sacked. Ed Miliband – mocked. New speaking style – established. Weird story about little girl sending in tooth-fairy money – told. Big Society – gibbered about.

Blood pressure – going down. People still in Birmingham – coming down. Tory mums – calming down. Newfound tendency towards rapping – occasionally curbed. But only when I do this weird listy thing.

FRIDAY

In the morning, I wake up. From the bed, I get up. At the kettle, I brew up. My tea, I drink up.

'Mate,' says Andy Coulson. 'I'm worried about you. You're genuinely sounding like a lunatic.'

Hypodermics on the shore, China's under martial law. Rock and roller cola wars, I can't take it anymore. He might have a point.

NICK CLEGG
26 FEBRUARY 2011

David Cameron has gone to the Middle East to sell weapons. Coalition still being quite a new concept, Westminster is convulsed with the usual story about who has been left in charge. Meanwhile, Libya is in meltdown and British personnel are being evacuated. William Hague (the Foreign Secretary) has just announced that Colonel Gaddafi has sought sanctuary with Hugo Chavez, only for him to turn up, that night, on telly, very much still in Tripoli. Oops.

MONDAY

Dave's away so I'm in charge. We're having an emergency inner Cabinet meeting, even though it's half term.

'The situation,' says William Hague, 'is dire.'

'No snow?' I say.

William, George Osborne, Michael Gove, and Danny Alexander all turn and stare at me, as one.

'We're going to Davos later this week,' I say, 'and apparently there hasn't been a fresh fall in days. It's a terrible worry.'

George says they aren't talking about Davos.

'Courchevel?' I say.

Quite politely, William tells me they're actually talking about Libya.

'I didn't even know you could ski there,' I say.

'Amazing, all these new places they're opening up. We went to Croatia the other year. Marvellous.'

'Of course you can't ski there!' shouts William. 'It's in the bloody desert! And it's blowing up. Benghazi is on the verge of falling to the uprising, Gaddafi's son is threatening civil war, and somebody just told me that the man himself is going to Venezuela!'

'Well that's probably very wise of him,' I say. 'The mountains are extraordinary.'

TUESDAY

Apparently Gaddafi didn't go to Venezuela after all, and everybody is furious for William going on the telly and suggesting that he had.

Now William is trying to get out of it by pretending that 'going to Venezuela' is a well-known figure of speech, frequently used about people who are just behaving strangely.

'I can't believe Dave has taken all those arms traders on his trip,' says William. 'Anyone would think he was going to Venezuela!'

George tells him he's not fooling anybody.

WEDNESDAY

Thank God for half term. Off soon. All packed. Can't wait. I used to be a ski instructor, you know. But I keep feeling like I've forgotten something, though. But what? Goggles?

'Bad news,' says William, as I stare idly out the window and dream of black runs. 'Lots of British people are stranded and we have absolutely no way of bringing them home.'

'Sledges?' I say, looking up. 'Snow cats?'

'What?' says William.

'I always quite liked the idea of those dogs,' I say, dreamily. 'With the barrels of brandy around their necks.'

Michael Gove says that might be considered a bit offensive in the Middle East, all in all.

William says I've been useless all week, and he's starting to think I'm going to Venezuela.

'For God's sake, William!' shouts George. 'Stop accusing people of going to Venezuela!'

THURSDAY

In a tiny train, winding up the mountain. The snow doesn't look too bad, actually.

'¿Happy, Neeck?' says Miriam González Durántez, my beautiful Spanish wife.

'Broadly,' I say. 'Except I can't escape this nagging feeling there's something I haven't done.'

Miriam says she doesn't know what it could be. Obviously, we have our passports, otherwise we wouldn't be here. We have all the children. We have our goggles, hats and gloves. We cancelled the milk, left out food for the cat, and put fresh straw in the underground cage in which we've lately taken to keeping Vince Cable.

'Other than that I can't theenk of anytheeng,' she says. 'Except for maybe the way that you're supposed to be running the country while David ees in the Meedle East.'

'Oh f***,' I say.

FRIDAY

Back in London. Didn't ski at all. Dave is back, too, and furious.

'I know it's half term,' he says, 'but this week has been a shambles. William, I'm particularly disappointed in you. Broken aeroplanes? No boats? And I can't believe you said that Gaddafi was on his way to Venezuela!'

'You think he isn't?' says William. 'You're as bad as Tony Blair!'

George hisses at him. I'm looking out of the window, dreaming of powder and schnitzel.

'Stop it,' says Dave. 'You've all been hopeless. I mean, honestly, Nick. I leave you in charge of the country, and you go skiing? Skiing? And after all that stuff about you knocking off early all the time? Get a grip, man, for God's sake. You're on a slippery slope.'

'I wish I was,' I say.

BORIS JOHNSON
13 AUGUST 2011

London is engulfed by riots. The Mayor is on holiday.
That's about it.

MONDAY

Preposterous. Damnable disingenuous drivel. I cannot be expected to cut short my family holiday in North America simply *ad captandum vulgus*, can I? It's only Tottenham. Nobody votes for me there, anyway.

I think that's the right decision. I'd phone the Commissioner of the Metropolitan Police to make sure, but we've gone through so many lately I can't remember who it is.

Dave calls, from Tuscany. 'I'm staying put,' he says. 'It's only Tottenham.'

I tell him that's exactly what I thought.

Then I tell him that it can't be a proper riot because nobody is in a tailcoat.

'No, no,' says Dave. 'I had a briefing. These sorts of riots are apparently much more casual.'

'Blazers?' I say.

'Maybe sports jackets,' says Dave.

TUESDAY

So yes, I'm back in London. Deputy Mayor for policing called late last night. Who even knew I had one?

Turned out it was, in fact, quite bad. Fires and whatnot. Muggings. *Periculum in mora*, and all that.

Don't want *hoi polloi* getting all fierce. Time to show the old beaming face, and reintroduce the old *Pax Boris*. First stop is Clapham Junction, where the mob made off last night with all manner of proletariat footwear and entertainment systems. Today, an army of well-meaning fellows with brooms have assembled, to make all spotless. Fine people! Born Conservatives! The very bedrock of my natural support!

'Wanker,' says one old lady.

'Jolly good,' I say. 'Boris to the rescue! What ho!'

WEDNESDAY

Into No. 10 last night, for a meeting with Dave and the Home Sec, who was late. Dave had the telly on, and was doing the old tight-lipped manoeuvre. You know. Makes him look like he's trying to catch drool.

'Take you back, old boy?' I say.

'Hmmm?' says Dave.

The crash of broken glass, I say, quietly. Heart beating like a drum. Shopkeepers running for cover. Claret and port all over the pavements. Good times.

'I think that's actually blood,' says Dave, peering at the screen, and then we both stop talking suddenly because Theresa May has arrived and she went to a girls' college.

'So anyway,' I say, 'who is in charge of the Met these days?'

The Home Sec looks startled. 'I thought it was you,' she says.

'I thought it was you,' I say.

'Somebody really has to Google this,' says Dave.

THURSDAY

In Hackney today, I meet a collection of what some would colloquially call 'da youth'.

Dave thinks we should hug these chaps, but I think I'm a touch more adept at speaking their language.

'*Carpe diem*!' I say. '*Illegitimi non carborundum*!'

The boys in hoods all scowl, and ask each other if I'm talking about spaghetti.

'Fing is,' says one, after a while, 'me an ma bredren doan gatt no prospects, nahut I mean?'

'Strictly Latin and Greek, old chap,' I tell him. 'I don't know that one. Is it Phoenician?'

FRIDAY

Back into Downing Street to see Dave.

'Time to stop dissing the Feds, old chap,' I tell him, as we crack open a bottle of wine.

'What?' says Dave.

It's Phoenician, I explain, and I tell him he should be nicer to the police. Then I show him a helmet I nicked off a community support officer when his back was turned and we reminisce about that time, with the Buller, when somebody threw a pot plant through a window.

'Do you feel old?' says Dave. 'I feel old.'

'You've got a pot plant on your desk,' I say, and Dave looks scared for a moment, and then nods.

Then there's a thud.

'Bulletproof,' says Dave.

'I'll get a broom,' I say.

BORIS FOR PM: TO DO LIST
(NOT FOR CIRCULATION AMONG PEOPLE
WHO AREN'T CALLED JOHNSON)

*Oh, and while I'm on the subject of Boris Johnson,
here's a thing I wrote for GQ magazine about his plan to
become Prime Minister.*

1. FIND SEAT
Back in the old days it was far more simple. Strike a deal
with the Praetorian Guard, march upon Downing Street,
bish bosh, Dave's head on a spike, casseroled cat for dinner
and impose the old *Pax Boris*. Deploy the family. Sis could
have Cornwall. Put a Johnson in charge of the North, and
another in charge of Wales. Buggered if I know how many
brothers I've got, but it's bound to be enough to go around.
Father could have Northern Ireland. Blond revolution.

Not now. I need a constituency. But where? Somewhere
I haven't offended and apologised to, for starters, which
narrows it down.

Probably I could find some London Tory MP prepared
to hurl himself under the campaign bus in exchange for
a peerage, but is that really what I'm after? Whither,
as a London MP, the kitchen suppers? Also, quite a lot
of Tory London is quietly ghastly. Especially the Zone 6
bits. I'd have to live there. Or, at least, go there. Problem.

2. BE EXCELLENT MAYOR
I've got another four years of this dross. I don't know

what the hell I was thinking. There was the first term, then the election, then the Olympics and now ... what? Until 2016? More bloody bicycles and bus lanes? I'll be climbing the city walls. Do we even have city walls? I'll be building some, and climbing them.

Can't go losing interest, like Sarah Palin in Wasilla. Real blot on the copybook. So the only option is brilliance. But dammit, how? What's mayor for, anyway? Always thought I'd have figured it out by now.

3. LOSE WEIGHT

Down with pudding. Down with girth. The public may love a fat Boris, but they shall not respect a fat Boris. Be still, mine spoon hand.

4. NO BUNGA-BUNGA

Fewer affairs. Ideally, no affairs. Granted, the public don't seem to mind me sleeping with extra people, but the people I sleep with do. And, unchecked, there's a real danger that they could start to represent a significant proportion of my potential vote.

5. DISCREDIT GEORGE OSBORNE

Nobody else worth worrying about. Jezza Hunt made a fool of himself by wanging off his bell-end, and Govey says he doesn't want it. Mitchell's history, Fox went postal and Hague doesn't have the bottle for another crack. Hammond, May and Grieve all look uncannily like undertakers. It's me or George. *Mano-a-mano*. There can be only one.

Right now, to be fair, the old chap is doing a cracking job of discrediting himself. But it might not last. Economic upturn means Boris downturn. Our best hope is that he shags someone. And not in a good way, like I shag people. In a bad way, like John Prescott shagged people.

6. ~~HAIRCUT~~
Actually, strike that. Bad idea. Remember Samson.

IAIN DUNCAN SMITH
6 APRIL 2013

After months of preamble and debate, this was the week that coalition cuts to benefits, including the infamous 'bedroom tax', came into force. Meanwhile, George Osborne gave a speech in an accent which puzzled everybody.

<u>**MONDAY**</u>

After I come off the radio, the Prime Minister calls with an idea.

'April fool?' I say.

'No,' he says. 'I'm deadly serious. I think you should live on £53 for a week. Like you said you could. In fact, I think the whole Cabinet should. To show how easy it can be.'

'It's not supposed to be easy,' I say. 'It's supposed to be very, very hard.'

'Not at Chequers,' says Cameron. 'Sam's already done Ocado, and there aren't any shops.'

Look, I tell him. It's do-able. For I have also already done Ocado. But I don't get the point. Frankly, the last thing we want to be doing is sending out the signal that it's easy to survive on benefits.

'What you have to remember,' I point out, 'is that we're not cutting benefits because we want these people to be poorer. We're doing it because we want them to be richer.'

'April fool!' shouts Cameron.

'No,' I say. 'Really.'

TUESDAY

Bought the papers and got a cab to the office before I remembered what week it was. So that's me down to my last £20 already.

Apparently there's an online petition calling for me to live on £53 a week for a whole year; 100,000 people have already signed it.

'I know,' says the Prime Minister, when I call Chequers to tell him about it after lunch. 'I'm one of them.'

'It's a stupid gimmick!' I shout. 'It proves nothing! You might as well ask me to justify disability benefit by spending a week walking on one leg!'

'Could you?' says Cameron.

If I had to, I tell him.

'What if you also had to close one eye?' says the PM.

'I would cope,' I tell him. 'But this is getting ...'

'What if you had to close both eyes,' says the PM, 'and put a finger in one ear?'

'You're drunk,' I say.

'Tipsy,' admits Cameron. 'But it didn't cost a penny. Excellent cellar.'

WEDNESDAY

I've gone round to No. 11 to see George. Plus, you get free biscuits there. He's been defending all of our benefit changes by giving a speech at a supermarket in Kent.

'I wish you'd told me,' I say. 'I'm out of milk.'

'Buy your own milk,' says George. But I can't, because Ocado has a £40 minimum.

I saw it on the news, I tell him. The only thing I didn't

understand was why you did that silly accent. You sounded like the chimney sweep in *Mary Poppins*.

George says that Dave told him to, because if people on benefits can survive by talking like the chimney sweep in *Mary Poppins*, then he should be able to, too.

'We're orl innit togevver,' he points out.

'Didn't catch that,' I say.

THURSDAY

A bunch of us meet up in a Westminster café to pool the last of our money and see if we can afford a plate of chips.

'I'm not enjoying this week at all,' says Eric Pickles, eating most of them.

'It's grim,' agrees Nick Clegg. 'I'm having to eat British cheeses.'

Theresa May has been seen wearing gym shoes and William Hague isn't getting out of bed.

Vince Cable has been dancing alone, at night, on empty streets. And Ken Clarke looks like he's been sleeping on a bench.

'I don't even know what you're talking about,' says Ken. 'I'm only here for the chips.'

FRIDAY

The Prime Minister is back in London. Having no money left for the bus, I cycle in to see him.

'I'm not sure how you managed that,' he says. 'What with the way you're supposed to be only using one leg and no eyes.'

This needs to stop, I say. And also, I need to borrow a cup of sugar.

Dave says he still hasn't spent a thing.

'Aren't you finding this really easy?' he says. 'All the fun you can have for free! Haven't these people got anybody to borrow a horse off?'

But it's not meant to be easy, I remind him. It's meant to incentivise them to find new work.

'Never really understood that,' says the PM.

'Look at it this way,' I say. 'It's certainly incentivising me.'

NIGEL FARAGE
4 MAY 2013

UKIP has done stormingly well in local elections, even after Ken Clarke called them a 'bunch of clowns' and newspaper reports suggested a preponderance of freaks and borderline Nazis.

MONDAY

Let's be honest, I say to the journalist. Clearly, there are a fair number of eccentrics among our candidates. Can't police thought, can you? But here in UKIP HQ it's a different business. This is the inner circle. Sober, credible fellows, one and all! Such as Geoff. Has he met Geoff?

'In the, uh, helmet?' says the journalist.

'Yep,' I say. 'With the spike on top. What of it?'

Next to Peter, I add. In the sandals. And Neil. With the beard. Yes. The very, very big beard.

'Amazing,' says the journalist.

'Don't be fooled by Ken Clarke, old bean,' I tell him. 'Bunch of clowns? We've got the blighters rattled! No clowns in here!'

There's a parp from over by the phone bank.

'Except for him,' says the journalist.

'He's just got a cold,' I say. 'And baggy trousers. And very big feet. Damn. Come on. Let's go.'

TUESDAY

We're a party of normal people. Not like those aloof

Westminster elitists! Somehow, though, the rest of the
party just doesn't come across like that on telly.

Which is why I have to do everything. Which is why
I've come to the pub to meet one of our young, photo-
genic candidates from up North, to see if he can be
trusted to take some of the load.

'Hello, Mr Farage!' he says, giving me a big wave.

'Do you always wave like that?' I ask.

'Like what?' he says.

'I'd better go,' I say.

WEDNESDAY

Today I'm holding a campaign meeting in a suburban
school. I'm explaining to a group of floating voters that
UKIP believes in freedom.

'You mean the freedom for me to marry my boyfriend?'
says a man.

'Different sort of freedom,' I say.

'What about the freedom for my community to build
a new mosque?' says another.

'Again,' I say. 'Slightly complicated.'

'Personally,' says one young woman, 'I'd like the freedom to live and work in France.'

I slump a bit.

'Look,' I say to one of the pupils. 'I don't suppose
you're allowed to smoke in here?'

'No, Mr Farage,' he says.

'Well, that's precisely what I'm talking about,' I say.
'Vote UKIP and all that could change.'

THURSDAY

Polling day. The Prime Minister calls.

'I don't even know who you are,' I say. 'I literally cannot

remember if you're in charge of Labour, the Tories or the Lib Dems. You're all exactly the same.'

'Come off it,' says David Cameron. 'This has to stop. You'll be putting Miliband into Downing Street at this rate.'

'Well,' I say. 'He is your brother.'

Cameron says he thinks we should meet. Venue of my choosing.

I suggest a lap-dancing club.

'Look,' sighs Cameron. 'We're not enemies. In fact, we've actually got quite a lot in common.'

'Really?' I say. 'Leg man, myself.'

Cameron hangs up.

FRIDAY

What a day! UKIP has stormed the polls. I'm giving a victory address at UKIP HQ.

'In a minute,' I tell them, 'I'll obviously be locking the doors and banning any of you lot from leaving the building until after the bank holiday, in case anybody tries to take your picture or ask you any questions about anything. But first, I just wanted to say, well done!'

There's a big cheer. People are celebrating with English wine and fruit cake.

'It's a great day for England,' I say. 'The Westminster elite has been shaken to its core! Across this country, we have literally done considerably better than the Liberal Democrats!'

Everybody goes wild. Coco is crying so hard he's had to take his nose off.

'And best of all!' says Geoff. 'We now have an opportunity to spend the next few years getting significantly involved in local politics!'

'Bugger that,' I say. 'I'm off back to Brussels.'

ED MILIBAND
1 OCTOBER 2011

Another party conference one. Ed Miliband's big speech has been about 'predators and producers' which might mean 'nice capitalism and nasty capitalism'. Although might, let's be honest, mean f*** all.

MONDAY

I'm not Tony Blair. I'm not Gordon Brown, either. I'm my own man. I'm David Miliband. That's just who I am. Oh wait. No it isn't. Bugger. I keep doing that.

I'm in Liverpool. Me. My feet. My hands. My other bits. That's just where I am. I'm here for the Labour Party conference. Not the Conservative Party conference. That would be wrong.

You know, I'm here with Justine. In Liverpool. She's my wife. She didn't used to be my wife. We weren't married. That just wasn't something that we'd done. I make no apology for that. But I am sorry. That might sound contradictory. But I'm not interested in things that sound contradictory. I'll tell you what I'm interested in. But later.

TUESDAY

I'm walking through conference. About to give my speech. In Liverpool. I'm with Ed. And I am Ed. But this is another Ed. Ed Balls. My friend. No. My colleague.

Yes. That's just who he is. People are kicking me. In the bottom. And I'll tell you what I don't know. Why.

'Search me,' says Ed. 'It's not like I've stuck a sign on your back which says "kick me", or anything.'

I believe you, I say. Then I say ouch. We've come from a hotel room. Not somebody else's room. My room. And conference, I am so proud. That I have a room. And nobody has taken it from me. And made me sleep in the bath. Like Ed did last year. The git.

WEDNESDAY

So I did the speech. My speech. Using my tongue. Not Tony Blair's tongue. Not Gordon Brown's tongue. Great men. With great tongues. We must assume. But I'm my own man. I have my own tongue.

It didn't go brilliantly. Conference, I know what you are thinking. But that's just not how it went. At one point, all the TV cameras cut out.

But I'm not interested in TV cameras. I'll tell you what I'm interested in. I'm interested in the fact that, when they did, I finally realised that I did have a 'kick me' sign on my back. After all. And conference, I am proud. So very proud. That this bit wasn't on telly.

THURSDAY

Justine thought the speech went well. But I'm not interested in what Justine thinks. I'll tell you what I'm interested in. I'm interested in what everybody else thinks. The people I'm not married to. And have no intention of marrying. They're the people who matter.

Conference, I am not anti-business. I am pro-business. But being pro-business today means being anti-business. The predators. Versus the aliens. Which side are you on? That might sound confusing. But so was the film. With all that stuff about pyramids.

But I'm not interested in pyramids. I'll tell you what I'm interested in. Social justice. There were riots. Near my house. Well. One of my houses. Something for nothing. That's what predators want. I support the aliens. Who just want to lay eggs. In your face.

FRIDAY

Back in London. Ed Balls comes round. And kicks me. I didn't even know there was a sign. Must have been the kids.

'Great speech,' he says. 'Exactly what we wanted to hear. Yvette and I were laughing all the way through.'

'Thanks,' I say. 'I was quite proud of some of the jokes.'

'There were jokes?' says Ed.

ED MILIBAND
6 OCTOBER 2012

And another one.

MONDAY

It's party conference week. I'm in a hotel suite with Ed Balls.

'It's all changed, Ed,' says Ed. 'You've won my respect. Now you just need to give a speech that wins the country's. Or else,' he adds, 'I'll give you a Chinese burn.'

No need, I say. For I have a plan. That's just who I am. A man with a plan. Not a man without a plan. That's just not who I am. No.

'Go on,' says Ed.

My plan, I continue, is to boldly appropriate a famous Tory slogan, thus indicating that I have moved to the centre ground. I was thinking of Get On Your Bike. Channelling Norman Tebbit. Good, eh?

'Are you,' Ed wants to know, 'on drugs?'

Well, I say. It doesn't have to be that one. Just something that shows, bravely, that we aren't the enemy of the middle classes. I want people to realise that Labour can be for everybody. We are the children. We are a banker and a miner. We are a grandmother...

'Oh!' I say.

'No,' says Ed.

TUESDAY

Still locked in. The speech is pretty much written. I just

still need that slogan. Then I can drop it in, subtly, about once every seventeen seconds.

'We're running out of time,' says Ed. 'Would it help if I gave you another dead arm?'

I need to show we've changed, I say. Although not in a manner which suggests a U-turn.

'U-turn if you want to,' yawns Ed.

'Actually...' I say.

'That was a joke,' says Ed. 'And this is a terrible idea. You'll never find a Conservative slogan which says exactly what a Labour leader wants to say, without sounding entirely crazy.'

'I've got it!' I shout. 'Labour Isn't Working!'

Ed says it's amazing that I'm his boss.

'Literally,' he adds. 'Amazing.'

WEDNESDAY

One Nation! Of course! And today, my brother David calls.

'Hey,' I say, touched. 'Were you watching?'

'Sort of,' says David. 'I mean, I had it on in the background while I was, like, worming the cat or something.'

David says the best bit was the section about going to a tough comprehensive as the political geek son of an obscure Communist who was friends with Tony Benn.

'I bet lots of people could relate to that,' he says. 'At least, I know I could.'

'Thanks bro,' I say, and I tell him that I'm annoyed that I spoke without notes, because it meant I forgot all about my big idea for a tax on cheap immigrant builders. I was going to call it the Pole Tax.

'But David,' I add. 'Are you crying?'

David says it's the cat, who has got a hairball. But he says it quite tightly.

THURSDAY

David Cameron calls. This is unusual.

'Clever,' he says. 'But you've given me an idea. I'm going to come on stage to "Things Can Only Get Better".'

'Huh,' I say, impressed.

'Or,' he adds, 'I'm going to pledge to be Tough On Crime, Tough On The Causes Of Crime.'

'I thought that was yours anyway,' I say.

Cameron says he suddenly isn't sure. But he'll check.

FRIDAY

Ed and I are getting changed after a game of squash. He won. Quite convincingly.

'Look mate,' he says. 'I just wanted to say. You've done it. You've proved them all wrong. And I for one am now proud to say that you are my leader.'

'Does that mean you'll tell me where you've hidden my trousers?' I ask.

'See you back at the office,' says Ed.

KEN LIVINGSTONE
14 APRIL 2012

There's a mayoral election in London. Ken Livingstone has been attacked for his cleverly constructed tax affairs (after having criticised bankers for their cleverly constructed tax affairs), and for saying that Jews wouldn't vote for him anyway, because they're too rich. Yeah. He's also generally being a bit weepy and histrionic about everything.

MONDAY

I'm having a coffee and biscuit break with my campaign team.

'These greedy bastards just don't get it,' I say. 'Nobody should have a second biscuit! Never mind a third, fourth or fifth!'

My press officer blinks at me. 'But you just took five biscuits,' she says.

'Smears!' I shout.

'You're holding them in your hand,' she points out. 'Right now.'

This is a completely different situation, I tell her. I have staff. It is my responsibility to gather additional biscuits in order to distribute them fairly to those who rely on me.

Everybody does this. You can certainly bet that bloody Boris does.

'But you aren't going to distribute them,' she says. 'Are you?'

'Can't hear you,' I say. 'Mmmm. Crunchy.'

TUESDAY

I'm the guy this city needs, and the people in this city know it. All of them. Even the Jews. Well, most of the Jews. I am London. I have Thames water in my veins and Trafalgar Square pigeon in my belly. Mayor's prerogative. Like the Queen and swans. Feel a bit queasy, actually.

Of course, I'm not technically mayor at the moment. Only morally. That bastard Boris stole my job. I can't bear the thought of him sitting in my secret lair under City Hall, stroking my white cat. If he ever found the lair, that is. I wonder who's feeding the cat, otherwise? Damn.

We had an argument last week, about my tax affairs. I said he did what I do. He denied it. Since then, he's been sending me text messages.

'UR A F***ING LIAR,' he'll say.

Remarkable, how some people think a childish buffoon like that should be in charge of the greatest city in the world.

'NO, UR A F***ING LIAR,' I'll usually reply.

WEDNESDAY

My campaign officially launches today, with a snazzy reception. Some people say I'm old and past it, but a lot of my supporters are actually quite young.

'And what's your name, sonny?' I say to one bright-eyed kid who comes up to shake my hand.

'Ed Miliband,' he says. 'And don't call me sonny.'

After that, we watch a video of lots of ordinary Londoners pleading with me to save the city from the Tory clownman. I'm moved to tears.

'Ken?' whispers Ed, leaning in. 'Why are you crying? These people were paid by an ad agency to read a pro-Labour script.'

'But isn't it quite moving that there are people who are still prepared to do that?' I say.

'Fair point,' says Ed.

THURSDAY

OK, says my campaign manager. We're getting hammered on the doorstep over two things. The tax thing, and the Jews thing.

'It's funny,' I muse. 'You'd think the one would cancel out the other. Because if there's anybody who's really good with money...'

'Let's agree that you didn't just say that,' says my campaign manager.

Boris has stopped texting and started calling. I'm not answering. Bloody usurper. It makes me sick to think of him doing all the things I once did. Wandering around my city as if he owns the place. Nipping into the Tower at night to try on the crown. Chiselling his own face on to the top of Nelson's Column.

'Tell me you didn't really do that?' says my campaign manager.

'Of course I didn't do that,' I say.

I totally did that.

FRIDAY

Still not answering my phone. But this morning, I run into him knocking on doors in Tower Hamlets.

'I want a word with you,' he says.

'Bugger off,' I say. 'We've nothing to talk about. I'm taking back what's mine. This city is mine. I'll be turning Boris Bikes into Ken Bikes and sinking your stupid bloody buses into the Thames. You just see if I don't.'

'Never mind all that,' says Boris. 'Can I have the number of your accountant?'

JACK STRAW
10 NOVEMBER 2007

Old one. I wrote this shortly after Jack Straw became Lord Chancellor, I think. Quite a while later, I was writing an editorial about, I think, the desirability of closed civil trials involving terrorism suspects who alleged mistreatment, and I gave him a call. 'I loved that thing you wrote about me wearing tights!' he said. 'Thank you!' I said. And then we talked about torture for a while. Bit odd.

Oh. Also. There used to be a man called Des Browne, who had big hair. Vital.

MONDAY

I am in the bathroom. My wife is banging on the door. 'Jack?' she says. 'Are you OK? What are you doing in there?'

'Just a minute!' I call, and I very slowly straighten my lacy cravat. I am a modest man but some things are undeniable. I look magnificent. I should be on a £5 note.

Tomorrow is the Queen's Speech. I am trying on my costume. Again. Look at me. This is dignity. This is gravitas. This is how a man should look.

'Jack?' calls my wife. 'I'm going to be late. Have you seen my tights?'

I ignore her. I have to get this right. The Queen will be there. She has jewels. I do not. I will not be outshone.

TUESDAY

Just before the Queen's Speech, I attend a hurried
meeting of trusted lieutenants in Gordon's office in the
Commons. Cabinet ministers flutter around me, cooing
like bridesmaids. I fancy I may be pouting slightly. Gordon
is at his desk. He might be pouting, too. But then, he
always is.

'I mean ... wow!' says David Miliband. 'You look ...
amazing.'

I wink at him, like Humphrey Bogart in *Casablanca*.
He's not wrong. I really do look amazing. They have to
put me on fivers.

'Where's the wig?' says Gordon.

I explain. Only Lords wear wigs.

'But you're Lord Chancellor,' says Ed Balls.

'But not a Lord,' I explain.

'Just a Chancellor,' says Des Browne.

'Just?' says Alistair Darling.

'Not yet,' says Gordon.

WEDNESDAY

These shoes don't just have buckles. They also have
heels. They make me swing my hips slightly, like Marilyn
Monroe. I'm just sashaying into the office when David
Miliband calls.

'Seriously,' he says. 'You looked really good. I mean,
wow. Really, really good.'

I am not sure where this is going.

'I want one,' he says, eventually. 'A costume. Although
I'd want mine to have a wig, too.'

I adopt a regal tone. 'Only I get a costume,' I tell him,
haughtily. 'For I am the Lord Chancellor. And no wig,
certainly. Only Lords get wigs.'

'Rubbish! What about Des Browne?'

'Des doesn't wear a wig,' I say.

'Doesn't he?' says David.

THURSDAY

'I don't think Des Browne does wear a wig,' says my wife, reaching over to turn off the bedside light. 'I think it's just really big hair.'

I think so, too. 'Nobody else deserves a costume,' I add. 'Only the Lord Chancellor has the gravitas.'

'Yes, dear,' sighs my wife.

'I'm surprised they don't put me on fivers,' I continue. 'Looking as dignified as I do. Whoever would have thought I could be so comfortable in tights?'

My wife rises up on her elbow. 'You have taken them off?'

'Of course!' I say. I squirm away slightly, towards my side of the bed.

FRIDAY

Another crisis meeting in Gordon's office. Tempers are frayed.

'I'm Lord Chancellor,' I remind Alistair Darling. 'You're just a chancellor. So do as you are told. Put me on fivers.'

'No,' says Darling. 'Anyway, why are you still wearing all that? You look absurd.'

I stamp my buckled foot. 'Is it because I won't wear the wig?'

'Don't be ridiculous,' says Darling. 'I wouldn't put Des on fivers either.'

'It's not a wig,' says Des.

ALISTAIR DARLING
<u>27 OCTOBER 2007</u>

Even older. This was one of those many, many weeks when the government of Gordon Brown seemed to be falling apart.

<u>MONDAY</u>

We are in Gordon's office, which looks an awful lot like my office. Although bigger. Gordon is pacing around, and I am practising looking at myself in the mirror and not noticing that I am there. The eyebrows are a problem. Not noticing yourself is the first step to actual invisibility.

'So what do you think?' grunts Gordon.

'I think what you think,' I grunt back.

Gordon chuckles. It's a new thing of his, the chuckle. I must master it. Although I can't pretend I get the joke. I really do think what he thinks. I don't think anything else. I wouldn't remember how to go about it.

As a general rule, it is best never to think things that nobody else thinks. If you do, people might notice you thinking it.

'We're suddenly on the back foot,' Gordon grunts now. 'Don't you think so?'

'I do think so,' I agree, allowing myself to fade in and out of view.

'Fancy,' says Gordon.

TUESDAY

Today, I may think about rethinking what I think about capital gains tax. Perhaps I should try thinking what George Osborne thinks. I think Gordon thinks I should.

I ask my wife. Usually, I call her 'darling'. Also, she calls me 'darling'. This is something we have never discussed.

'Darling?' says my wife. 'Run that past me again?'

We are in our apartment in Downing Street, which we have had decorated in very neutral tones. We may be in the living room, we may be in the bedroom. There is no difference. Not being different is the second step towards actual invisibility.

I explain about being on the back foot. 'I must also change my voice,' I add. 'I must be posh and squeaky, like George Osborne. Not Scottish, like Gordon.'

'But darling,' says my wife. 'You are Scottish, too.'

I had forgotten this. Distinguishing characteristics pain me.

WEDNESDAY

They say I am a boring man. Good. Boringness is the third step towards actual invisibility.

Perhaps I was unclear. Although Darling is my name, it is also a term of endearment. When used by myself or my wife, both meanings apply. Do you follow?

Some people consider this concurrence humorous. I consider it efficient. My name, like my face and beliefs and voice and everything other than my accursed eyebrows, is neutral. When somebody says it, nobody thinks of me.

Yet suddenly, I think people are thinking of me. Ever since my Pre-Budget Report, I am a man about whom people have views. It is almost intolerable. People are saying my name and meaning me. Why? It makes no sense to mean me. It is inefficient. One might as well mean Gordon Brown or George Osborne, and save time.

Maybe, tomorrow, I will call Gordon 'darling' to clarify matters. Or maybe not.

THURSDAY
A terrible morning. I give evidence to the Treasury Select Committee about Northern Rock and I am studied, remorselessly.

A better afternoon. They say that a white polar bear, on the white ice, covers his black nose with his paw in order to conceal himself from seals. This afternoon, I am like that. With my hands over my eyebrows I float around Westminster like a wraith.

FRIDAY
If only every day could be like yesterday afternoon. Last night I shaved off my eyebrows. Now, I am waiting in Gordon's office with my head in my hands. He wanders in, scowling, and sits down at his desk. After a while, I clear my throat.

'Hello?' I say. 'Gordon? Darling?'

Gordon says nothing. He doesn't even look my way. Eventually, I let myself out. Nobody sees.

DAVID MILIBAND
2 AUGUST 2008

*No idea what was going on this week. Not sure it matters.
I suspect David Miliband was almost but not quite rebelling against Gordon Brown, again.*

MONDAY

Let me tell you a secret. A lot of people think that there
are only two Milibands, David and Ed. Actually, there are
eight. Five of me and three of him. And we are planning many more. We all live together in a big house in
Primrose Hill.

Today my wife finds a few of me sitting at a table in
our apparently fashionable kitchen, holding spoons and
staring at a boiled egg.

'David?' she says, to all of us. 'Are you going to eat
that?'

There is some disagreement. We have always wished
to support this egg. This egg is a fine example of an egg.
No doubt we will enjoy the egg, when the time is right.
As yet, it may not be. We have made our position clear.

My wife just sighs. After a while she takes the egg
away and makes us a plate of sandwiches.

TUESDAY

Once, there really were only two Milibands. One David,
one Ed. We had a plan. We wanted to be in the Cabinet.

We knew we would be good in the Cabinet. We knew we would be better than anybody else.

So we came up with a new plan. A Miliplan. We built a machine to make more Milibands. We keep it in a Ford Transit in the garden, otherwise known as the Milivan. We have some way to go. One day, there will be a Cabinet made up entirely of Milibands. And maybe Geoff Hoon, just for a laugh.

WEDNESDAY

We are David Miliband. We are five times as clever as normal people and one and two-thirds times as clever as our own brother, even though he has better hair. His hair can go in several directions. Our hair can only go in one direction. Despite this, we believe ourselves to be the more versatile politician.

The Eds are angry. They feel we have been premature. This morning, one of them pays us a visit.

'Tea or coffee?' he says grimly, heading for the kettle.

There is some disagreement.

'Yes,' we say, eventually.

The Ed throws a mug into the sink, in a fury.

'You're impossible!' he shouts. 'Listen, I need to know. The article in *The Guardian*! Is this a leadership bid or not?'

Some of us feel that it is. Some of us feel otherwise. Some of us feel that we haven't entirely thought the whole thing through.

THURSDAY

One day soon, all of our Milibands shall be unleashed. A full Cabinet will require around twenty-five of us, probably at a David:Ed ratio of 3:2. That will take a couple of years. Thereafter, we intend to produce one giant

Miliband to take the place of the British Army. We shall call this the Godzilaband.

We aren't going to stop there, either. Finally, we will need an extra five Milibands to fulfil our secondary dream of creating a musical group devoted to the guitarist behind the 1973 smash hit 'The Joker'. We intend to call it The Dave Miliband and Ed Miliband Steve Miller Band Tribute Band.

It's not politics as such, but we feel it would be rather droll.

FRIDAY

It's not surprising that the Eds are annoyed. They are all very close to Gordon Brown. Occasionally, he will burst into their office, unannounced. Usually, they will stand in single file and take great pains not to move their arms. Gordon suspects nothing.

For now, we Davids are keeping a low profile at home, waiting to see how the situation develops. This afternoon, we go out into the garden.

We sit, side by side, on the fence. It is the only place we feel comfortable.

JAMES PURNELL
6 JUNE 2009

A year later, lots of other people did resign, and David Miliband still didn't. Damian McBride, Gordon's bruiser press aide, has recently left in disgrace after some sort of e-mail-based smearing scandal. The election referred to here is one for the European Parliament. Apparently we have those.

MONDAY

So we're in No. 10, most of us, in the small waiting room outside Gordon's office. Ed Balls and Peter Mandelson have already gone in to light some candles and see whether Gordon will be speaking to us face to face or from behind a curtain, as has become normal. The rest of us are on sofas and armchairs, around a coffee table.

'Who,' I say, 'would like a biscuit?' And everybody freezes.

'Yeah, Jack,' says Alan Johnson, fixing the Justice Secretary with a powerful stare. 'Why don't you have one of Gordon's biscuits?'

Jack Straw narrows his eyes. 'Oh no,' he says. 'After you. Or maybe the Foreign Secretary would like a biscuit? Or maybe James would like a biscuit himself?'

I can feel myself start to sweat. I do really want one. But you can't just go taking a biscuit. David Miliband did once, last summer. It was obvious that he expected everybody else to start taking them too. But nobody did.

Then Gordon came out. He didn't say anything. He just fixed David with a terrible stare, bent down, picked up the plate of biscuits and gave it to Ed Balls. Who ate them all. It was brutal.

Ed comes out now to say that Gordon is ready for us but we might want to open a window. And, as we move inside, Jacqui Smith reaches down and grabs a biscuit.

'But I'm hungry!' she says as we all stare at her.

Wonder if she really gets the whole biscuit thing. I'm guessing not.

TUESDAY

Or maybe she does. Because today she's resigned. I can't help thinking what would have happened if I'd just taken a damn biscuit. Maybe it's time to take a stand. Steeling myself, I head back to Downing Street.

David Miliband and Alan Johnson are already there, outside Gordon's office. Alan nods at the door.

'I'll follow you,' he says.

'No, no,' says David. 'I'll follow you.'

'Oh for God's sake,' I say, and I open the door.

It's dark in there. Windy. Too dark to see any sign of Gordon. For some reason, I find myself thinking of Damian McBride. Did anybody ever see him leave? What would he smell like, now, if he … if he…

'We'll be right behind you!' calls Alan.

'Really?' I say, and I turn around, and they're gone. And I'm alone. Maybe tomorrow.

WEDNESDAY

PMQs today. It's very tense. Partly this is because Hazel Blears resigned this morning. Partly it's because Gordon turned up wearing odd socks and no shoes. Geoff Hoon says Ed had to give him Damian McBride's shoes. Geoff doesn't know why Ed had Damian McBride's shoes. He says it's probably best not to ask.

THURSDAY

Election day today, and my mind is made up. When polls close, I'm going to resign. Officially I don't tell anyone, but unofficially I ask around. I'm very worried about it all. I'm prepared to make a stand but I don't see the point in just throwing my career away. I just keep remembering that time when I asked the whole government to grow ludicrous sideburns for Comic Relief. Nobody else did. I was mortified. I haven't had the courage to shave them off yet.

'Don't worry,' says one colleague, 'I'll follow you.'

'Will you?' I say.

'Absolutely,' he says. 'Provided that everybody else does.'

FRIDAY

'We're all really sorry,' says one of my old colleagues, who calls after lunch.

He says that everybody knows that they've let me down.

'But maybe it'll be different now,' he adds. 'Rock bottom, and all that. Gordon called us into his office. The lights were on. He looked washed and everything. There wasn't anything that could have been a bit of Damian. Not even a belt. And so we all decided, well, maybe it's time for one last heave.'

Bunch of cowards. So here I am. Stupid sideburns and no job. And I didn't even get a biscuit.

DAMIAN McBRIDE
18 APRIL 2009

Looking back, it turns out I chronicled the Damian McBride affair as well. Huh. Didn't remember that at all.

MONDAY

I'm texting, furiously. 'UR DED TO ME,' I write. 'U THINK IM JOKING? EVRYBODY WILL KNO UVE GOT HORRIBLE DISEESES & THT U DO THT THING WHERE U LET UR DOG LICK UR TONGUE EVEN IF ITS JUST BEEN [message continues] LICKNG ITS OWN JCKSIE. U WNT ACCESS TO GB? NO CHANCE. U WNT TO SPK TO GOVT MINISTRS? NEVR AGAIN. UR FINISHED IN THS TOWN & DNT THINK I DNT [message continues] MEAN IT BCOZ I DO.'

'Your threats don't work on me,' says the shopkeeper. 'If you haven't got any money, you can't have a pint of milk. And stop texting me. I'm right here. It's weird.'

TUESDAY

This shopkeeper has to be ruined, for Britain. So I e-mail Derek Draper straight away and tell him about the dog-licking accusation. 'Absolutely totally brilliant Damian!' he replies, almost instantly.

It's a start, but I'd like to take it further. Annoyingly, though, none of my old government colleagues are getting back to me. I can't think why.

I know this e-mail smear business looks bad, but we've

got a history, forged over pizza and beer. Me, Gordon, Ed, Tom and Charlie all put on our sixteenth stone together. It was an emotional moment. In Gordon's flat above No. 11, all boys together, taking turns on the scales. I remember it well.

I withhold my number, and call the office.

'Hey,' I say. 'What's happening, guys? Listen, there's this Tory shopkeeper, right, and he...' A squeaky voice tells me I must have a wrong number.

'Tom?' I say. 'Mate? Are you holding your nose? It's me. Damo!'

There's a pause.

Then the person with the squeaky voice tells me that he has no idea who I am, and if I think differently I can speak to his lawyers. Then he hangs up.

WEDNESDAY

Fine. I'm going to smear them, too.

You think I can't? They're all going down, Brown, Balls, Watson and the rest.

And that bloody shopkeeper. They don't know who they're messing with. I'm going, right now, to my Hotmail account and I'm going to tell people that Gordon has a wooden leg. And that Tom Watson believes in UFOs. And that Charlie Whelan moonlights as a chorus girl called Tallulah. And that there's a photo of Ed Balls at university, dressed as a Nazi.

'Absolutely totally brilliant Damian!' writes Derek Draper, but nobody else replies. Not one of my top press contacts.

It's bloody unreasonable. It's not like I ever actually did blind any of them with acid, or behead any of them with an axe, or maim their kids, or find out where any of them lived and leave photoshopped pictures of them cavorting with prostitutes on their wives' bedside tables. It was all talk. Just friendly banter. Between mates.

THURSDAY

It's a fact, anyway, that most political journalists have syphilis.

'Absolutely totally brilliant Damian!' writes Derek Draper, who I'm e-mailing about all of this.

Also, I add, the bloke in the shop at the end of my road is clearly a paedophile.

'Absolutely totally brilliant Damian!' writes Draper, again.

And, I continue, Charlie Whelan once kicked a kitten to death. Probably. And Tom Watson was secretly born as a girl. And Ed Balls has a really furry tongue. And isn't it interesting the way that Gordon has never publicly denied being a Muslim?

'Absolutely totally brilliant Damian!' writes Draper. He can be a rather tedious correspondent, to be honest.

FRIDAY

Derek Draper calls to say that he hasn't been checking his e-mail this week. 'Absolutely totally brilliant Damian!' has been his automatic out-of-office reply for months.

He wanted to make sure he stayed on my good side, he says, but he's not so bothered anymore.

I'd smear him, only he seems pretty well smeared already. But I've got to smear somebody. It's all I know. I sit and think for a while and write another text.

'EVRYBDY KNOWS UR FNSHED IN THS TOWN,' it reads.

Then I send it to myself. I should never have put myself in this situation. I should have known better. I'm a very dangerous enemy to have.

SARAH BROWN
3 OCTOBER 2009

*Conference again. Labour has just revealed Sarah Brown,
Gordon's wife, as their new secret weapon. She's big on
Twitter and he's her hero. Meanwhile, Gordon is dogged
by various phone-throwing rumours. Remember those?*

MONDAY

'He's messy,' I say, practising, 'and he gets up at a terrible
hour. Plus, he plays with his own earwax, has loads of
verrucas and picks off little bits of dead skin from his
elbows and keeps them in a jar. But I love him.'

Ed Balls looks quite green. We're in Brighton for the
Labour Party conference. I'm going through my speech
with him and Peter Mandelson, while Gordon sponges
some phlegmy gruel off his own lapels.

It's very exciting. This year I'm going to mention all
of my husband's endearing faults. Just like Michelle
Obama did.

'Does he have any nicer faults?' asks Peter.

After all, he adds, politely, we don't want delegates to
vomit into their own cupped hands.

'What about toilet habits?' I ask.

Best not, reckon Peter and Ed.

'Temper tantrums?'

Again, say Peter and Ed, no.

'What about,' I ask, 'the way he sometimes belches his
food up while he's eating it, and then eats it again?'

Peter shakes his head. Ed excuses himself and goes off to the bathroom. I must say, they aren't leaving me an awful lot to work with.

TUESDAY

This morning, before the big speeches, there's a quick Cabinet meeting.

Gordon says I ought to go in first, even though I'm really busy telling my Twitter followers that I've just eaten a yoghurt.

'My husband!' I announce, lowering my BlackBerry. 'My hero! Gordon Brown!'

Andy Burnham says they know who he is perfectly well already, thanks.

Gordon sweeps in, beaming and waving. 'I didn't know what she was going to say,' he tells everybody. 'I had no idea. We didn't even discuss it.'

David Miliband sighs. But I always say that, he points out. Every time.

Gordon glowers.

'He's very messy,' I tell Miliband, sharply. 'And he gets up at a terrible hour. But I love him.'

Miliband says this isn't relevant to anything at all.

'We need to talk about Iran,' he adds. 'This government is descending into a farce.'

'My husband, my hero, the Prime Minister,' I announce, 'is probably about to throw a BlackBerry at your face.'

David Miliband drops to the floor.

'It's actually very good that you're here,' remarks Peter.

'Thanks,' I say, over the sound of shattering plastic.

WEDNESDAY

There's a rumour, actually, that Peter Mandelson isn't

even staying in the hotel. Some people reckon he's got a friend with a yacht, moored off the coast of Hove.

I think it must be true. Late last night he came running in, ashen-faced and wet from the knee down.

'*The Sun* is backing the Conservatives!' he roared, and there was pandemonium. We were all up half the night worrying about it.

'This is awful,' sighed Peter, when somebody finally got hold of a first edition at about 5 a.m.

Could be worse, I said, peering over his shoulder.

'It's not that,' said Peter. 'I've missed the tide.'

THURSDAY

Yesterday was horrid. Back to London today. It took ages. As I told my Twitter followers in detail, Gordon had far too much coffee so we kept having to stop at service stations.

Quite exhausting, actually.

'My husband, my hero, Gordon Brown!' I kept having to say.

'You wouldn't want to share a bed with him after he's eaten eggs!'

Then he'd come in smiling and shaking hands, and telling everybody that he hadn't been expecting me to say any of that at all. Only, with all the hand-dryers and flushing, I'm not actually sure that anybody could hear us.

FRIDAY

'You know,' I say. 'None of this would ever have happened if I'd been allowed to tell the conference about Gordon's verrucas and earwax. Maybe I'll put it on Twitter. Where's my BlackBerry?'

'Don't blame me,' says Gordon. 'I didn't know what you were going to say until you were up there. Famously.'

Ed Balls frowns. 'But you were right there,' he says. 'When we wrote it. In the very same room.'

There's a sound of breaking plastic.

'Has anybody else got a BlackBerry?' I ask.

TESSA JOWELL
4 MARCH 2006

In 2006, the big political fuss concerned Tessa Jowell, then the Culture Secretary. Her husband, a tax lawyer called David Mills, was under investigation by Italian tax authorities due to his links with Silvio Berlusconi. This week, she was revealed to have co-signed a mortgage application which he (Mills) was alleged to have used to conceal payments coming in from elsewhere.

(To keep the lawyers happy, I should probably mention that after a vast number of appeals and counter-appeals, and the expiration of the Italian statute of limitations, he was found not guilty.)

MONDAY

I wake terribly early because, on top of everything else, I'm worried about the bill from the window cleaner. It seems an awful lot. Still, what do I know? I'm hopeless with figures.

'Morning, m'dear!' says my husband, David, swishing down the stairs in a platinum-coloured dressing gown made from real pressed platinum, with buttons made out of platinum. 'Why the long face?'

'Oh, David,' I say. 'It's everything. Nobody seems to realise how hard it is being a committed socialist in a house worth three quarters of a million that we managed to buy without a mortgage when I was a 32-year-old social worker. And I'm a bit worried about this bill from the window cleaner...'

'Never mind that,' says my husband. 'We're out of milk. I'm going to buy a pint and you will probably drink half of it, which means you owe me 21p.'

'I'll get my purse,' I say, because our finances are entirely separate.

TUESDAY

My private secretary sticks her head around the door of my office at the Department for Culture, Media and Sport, and tells me that the Prime Minister is on the line.

'Hello, Tony,' I say.

'Tessa, hi,' he says. 'All this business with Berlusconi? I just wanted to let you know that you have my...'

I slam the phone down and leap out of my chair. 'Lalalalalalala,' I say to myself, brightly, pacing around the office.

Within seconds, it is ringing again. I snatch it up.

'Look, Tony,' I say. 'Please don't tell me that ... oh. It's you. Hello, David.'

'Hello dear,' says my husband. 'Listen. I'm sorry to bother you at work. Could you call the bank and have 60p transferred from your account into mine? I need to buy a copy of *The Times*.'

'Don't you have 60p of your own?' I ask, tentatively. It doesn't sound like an awful lot of money, but what do I know? I'm hopeless with figures.

'Of course I do,' he says. 'But if I use your 60p instead of my 60p, that means that I can call your 60p a gift, invest mine as part of a high-yield bond deposit in the Cayman Islands, take it out again, reinvest it in a doomed yet tax-efficient short film project in the Outer Hebrides, sell you a share for 1p and return the other 59p in the form of a dividend. It's just common sense.'

WEDNESDAY

'We've just had a fax,' says my private secretary. 'Next year, the Treasury wants to allocate us 94 per cent of the budget we had this year.'

'Splendid!' I say, nibbling a biscuit. 'What a lot of per cents that is!' My private secretary stares at me. 'It's less money than we get now,' she says.

'I don't understand,' I say.

THURSDAY

I'm in the office so early that the cleaners are still wandering around with brooms. There is a note from Tony on my desk. 'Dear Tessa,' it reads. 'These allegations aren't going away, but I wanted to let you know that you have my full and...'

I screw it up and throw it into the bin. 'Lalalalaaa,' I say to myself and pull out that troublesome bill from the window man. I mentioned it to David last night.

He told me that it might be more than usual, because he had technically married and divorced the window man in civil ceremonies in Guadeloupe, so that he could pay him in the form of a tax-reduced maintenance payment.

Out in the hall, I find a passing cleaner. 'Excuse me,' I say. 'I'm hopeless with figures. Does this seem a lot to you?'

'Twelve pounds ninety-eight?' says the cleaner.

I study the bill. 'I thought it was over a thousand,' I say.

'There's a decimal point,' says the cleaner.

'What's a decimal point?'

FRIDAY

In the evening, the Prime Minister catches me in the lobby of Portcullis House.

'I can't stop,' I say, pushing past him.

'Tessa!' says Tony, and catches me on the arm. 'You poor thing. You must be frantic. I just want you to know...'

'Lalalala...' I whisper.

'... that you have my unqualified confidence and support.'

I sag. 'Well, that's it,' I say. 'I'm doomed. Can I borrow eleven hundred pounds for a taxi back to Kentish Town?'

CHRIS HUHNE
21 MAY 2011

Chris Huhne (the Climate Change and Energy Secretary) has been accused of swapping speeding points with his wife, which he denies. Meanwhile, Ken Clarke (the Justice Secretary) has been on the radio and said something daft about rape.

MONDAY

The PM was in a frightful mood at Cabinet this morning, because somebody's phone kept ringing. Vince Cable is going to say it was his. Good old Vince. He's a pushover.

'Now Chris,' says Cameron, just before we finish. 'This stuff in the papers. I need to know you didn't do it.'

I tell him these stories are completely inaccurate.

'Seriously,' he says. 'I don't mind the other stuff. Own eight houses, if you must. Leave your wife for a woman who used to have a girlfriend. Smile all the time, despite being basically poisonous. That's all fine. These things are all to be expected. Because you're a Lib Dem. But I won't have my Cabinet ministers fobbing off their speeding points on to other people.'

'And rightly!' says Ken Clarke, as he heads out the door, 'because that's worse than rape!'

'Did he just say what I thought he did?' says Dave.

'He can't have done,' I say.

TUESDAY

Liam Fox corners me, and says he wants my ex-wife's phone number.

'Don't take her dancing,' I say. 'She gets angry, and kicks.'

'I don't want a date,' says Fox, and he explains that he has a problem, in that a letter he sent to the PM has leaked, and everybody thinks he's responsible. So he needs somebody else to take the rap.

'I can't imagine why you think she'd be suitable,' I say, gravely.

Fox just stares at me.

'Try Vince,' I say. 'And I doubt you'll even have to buy him dinner.'

'Like I said,' says Fox. 'It's not a date.'

'Shame,' I say. 'Great dancer.'

WEDNESDAY

I made a statement in the Commons today, and MPs kept asking questions with puns about driving offences in them.

'It's not as though I'm giving them licence!' says the Speaker. Bastard.

Afterwards, Ken collars me. He's having a bad time, too, because he was on the radio and made a rape gaffe.

'Listen here,' he says. 'There's a rumour going round that somebody made another rape gaffe in Cabinet the other day. I need somebody to take the rap. You know about this sort of thing.'

Vince, I tell him. Pushover.

Ken says he's really grateful. Or possibly wheely grateful. I'm not sure.

THURSDAY

'Listen,' I say to Danny Alexander. 'Vince has found out that somebody has been saying he's a pushover. It was me. But I wondered if you might do me a favour and say it was you.'

'I don't get the point,' says Danny.

He covered for me, I explain. About that phone in Cabinet the other day. I can't afford to get his back up.

'No,' says Danny. 'The point!'

'Right,' I say. 'Yes. Very funny.'

FRIDAY

Another Cabinet meeting. The Prime Minister says it's been a bad week, and we ought to put it all behind us.

'Get back in the driving seat,' agrees George Osborne. 'Put our feet down. No more passengers. Full speed ahead.'

'Are you doing this on purpose?' I say.

'Chris is probably finding it all really tyre-ing,' chortles Theresa May.

'He's been having a bumpy ride!' says Nick Clegg, and everybody sniggers.

'Now stop this,' says Cameron, drying his eyes. 'Chris, I'm sorry. People just can't help themselves.'

'It's automatic!' guffaws Osborne.

'Right,' I say. 'I've had enough of this. This is childish, and frankly offensive.'

'Worse than rape?' frowns Ken. 'Or not worse than rape?'

'You,' says Cameron, 'are a whole different problem.'

NICK CLEGG
2 MARCH 2013

And, of course, eighteen months later Chris Huhne was detained at Her Majesty's pleasure. Lucky Ma'am. Here's the one I wrote during the week of the by-election in Eastleigh, created by his departure. At the time, Nick Clegg was under fire over what he had or hadn't known about allegations of sexual misconduct levelled at Lord Rennard, formerly the Lib Dem's Chief Executive, and had hit out at the 'self-appointed detectives' in the press who were trying to figure it out. Essentially, his position was that he didn't know, but sort of did, but only vaguely. Oh, you get the idea.

MONDAY

Off down to Eastleigh to campaign for this week's by-election.

'Has anybody offered you a drink, Nick?' asks one of the women in the constituency office.

No, I tell her. Well, yes. But only in an indirect and non-specific way.

'Wuh?' she says.

I can only act upon an offer of a beverage, I point out, if that offer is made and lodged and registered in a suitable way.

'So you do want a cup of tea?' she says. 'Or you don't?'

I cannot provide a running commentary on every shred of speculation, I say, miserably. These things have to happen in the appropriate way, through the appropriate channels. There are actually some brands of tea I'm very fond of. This is an issue which concerns me enormously.

'I think you should probably go back to London,' she says.

'I think you're probably right,' I say.

TUESDAY

Back to London. This latest sex scandal has knocked me sideways.

I mean, I always knew this was a party made up of sexually experimental philanderers who leave their wives for people who used to be lesbians, do unspeakable things with rent boys, have secret relationships with their landlords, ridicule gay people before turning out to be gay people, shack up with weather girls and Cheeky Girls, have affairs with people who are accused of spying for the Russians and get accused of conspiring to murder their former gay lovers' dogs. But I thought that was as far as it went.

'If you don't mind me saying so,' says my bodyguard, as he opens the car door, 'you're making a bit of a palaver out of this. Either you knew or you didn't know. Simple as that.'

'I'm sick of all these people acting as self-appointed detectives!' I shout.

'In fairness, sir,' says the bodyguard, 'I'm an actual detective.'

'Yes,' I say. 'You would be. Sorry.'

WEDNESDAY

Today I'm doing a radio phone-in for a London station. Danny Alexander insists on coming with me so I don't get into trouble.

Last time, you see, 'Boris from Islington' called up, and

I ended up getting a humiliating dressing-down from the Mayor of London.

This time it's 'Cathy from Dulwich', who turns out to be a reporter for *Channel 4 News*.

'You're a disaster waiting to happen,' says Danny, once she's rung off. 'And you're not doing this again.'

'Be fair,' I say. 'Cathy and Boris are both really common names. Who's next? Oooh! Lembit from Wales!'

'Seriously?' says Danny.

'What?' I say.

THURSDAY

Vince turns up unexpectedly while I'm having breakfast with my wife.

'¿Tortilla?' says Miriam. '¿Peeg?'

'Bacon,' I clarify.

'No,' says Vince. He's glum. He says he's eighty-seven years old, or something, and he's never been embroiled in a sex scandal at all. He says it makes him wonder what the hell he's been doing with his time.

Nor me, I say. I've only slept with about thirty people.

'Only?' says Vince.

'So far,' I say.

'Peeg!' shouts Miriam.

'Bacon!' I shout back.

'No,' says Miriam. 'Peeg.'

FRIDAY

Very early in the morning, David Cameron calls.

'Eastleigh,' he says. 'You have heard the result?'

Only non-specifically, I say. I may or may not have had some indirect information brought to my attention. Through irregular channels about which I am not prepared to offer a running commentary.

'You won,' he says. 'Even with your sex scandal.'

It's not my sex scandal, I tell him. Mine was that other thing. Which wasn't even a scandal, anyway. Whatever my wife says.

'Anyway,' says the PM. 'No hard feelings. I just don't know how the hell you managed it.'

It's only thirty, I say. And I was single until I was thirty-three. So if you think about it, it's only two or three a year.

'The by-election,' says Dave.

'No idea,' I say.

GEORGE GALLOWAY
31 MARCH 2012

Another by-election. George Galloway, latterly best known as the cat impersonator from Celebrity Big Brother, *had won Bradford West (for Respect) after the sitting Labour MP resigned due to illness. The day after this article was published – astonishingly, and I swear this is true – he tweeted something about his victory in 'Blackburn'. Later, he claimed that his Twitter account had been hacked. Which is one possibility...*

MONDAY

I salute my own courage, strength and indefatigability. I really do. Would it be excessive to regard my impending victory to be the most remarkable thing that has happened on Earth since the extinction of the dinosaurs?

'It might be,' says my press guy.

'It was a rhetorical question,' I tell him. I'm at home in London, practising my campaigning rhetoric.

'And I am proud,' I continue, 'to have struck an early blow for the revolution, in the wonderful town I have long considered my second home, of Bedford!'

'Bradford,' says my press guy.

'What?' I say.

'Your second home,' he says. 'It's Bradford. Not Bedford.'

'Are you sure?' I say.

'Pretty sure,' he says.

'Oh,' I say.

TUESDAY

'The imperialistic misanthropy of the warmongers Bush
and Blair and the shameful acquiescence to their crimes
by their morally bankrupt successors are soon to reap
what they have sown!' I shout, although I tail off a bit at
the end because I'm short of breath.

'I'm not sure I grasp the relevance,' says the ticket
collector.

I'm on a train, heading up for some canvassing. This
flunky is refusing to accept my travel documents.

'Harassment,' I tell him. 'Your failure to validate my
Flexible Super Apex ticket to Bradford is the most brazen
political chicanery since Suez!'

'It's to Bedford,' he says.

'Bugger,' I say.

WEDNESDAY

'So,' says one of my new Bradford friends. 'It's a beautiful day. I think I know where you'll want to canvas first!'

'The beach?' I hazard.

'We're, uh, landlocked,' he says. 'I meant the university.'

'I knew that,' I tell him.

'Did you?' he says.

'Less of the Zionist backchat,' I say.

THURSDAY

'I reckon we're vulnerable on three fronts,' says my press
guy. 'The first being that you've not got much connection
to Bradford.'

'I know Bradford better than any man alive,' I say.
'That is the most grotesque calumny uttered since the
blood libel.'

'Mmm,' he says. 'And there's also your tendency towards
overstatement. It can make you look somewhat ridiculous.'

'But I'm the greatest orator since Cicero,' I say.

'Yeah,' he says. 'And finally, there's the sex cat thing. It still makes people squeamish.'

I don't say anything.

'No comeback?' he says.

'Not to that,' I sigh.

FRIDAY

I won! I am the victor in a by-election! This is the greatest thing mankind has done since walking on the Moon!

The hours fly by in a whirlwind of interviews, at which I excel.

'It's been a good day,' says my press guy, 'but I wish you hadn't said that thing about it being the Bradford Spring. People are sniggering a bit.'

'Oh dear,' I groan. 'I know why. Because I'm actually in Bedford?'

'No,' he says.

TONY BLAIR
31 OCTOBER 2009

Tony Blair, long out of office, is being touted as a possible President of Europe. Meanwhile, David Miliband is still not quite rebelling against Gordon Brown.

MONDAY

At the window in the Oval Office. Well, my oval office. It's not properly oval, but we've leaned some plywood boards against the corners to give it the right sort of feel. More of an octagon, really. I'm on the phone to Silvio Berlusconi.

'My beeahyootiful Tony!' he says. 'With the frog-faced wife! I think I know why you are calling, eh? Il Presidente? Eh? Eh?'

I would be not not unopposed to the possibility of allowing my name to be considered in candidacy for the presidency, I agree.

Silvio belches. 'You are in my final four,' he says. 'It's you, Monsieur Bologna, Herr Braunschweiger or Dr Knackwurst.'

But I have never heard of any of these people, I say.

Berlusconi is silent for a while. 'Maybe I have the wrong list,' he says. He's judging a pan-European sausage competition this afternoon, so there may have been some confusion.

Most people, I tell him, have me up against Herman Van Rompuy, Jean-Claude Juncker and Jan Peter Balkenende.

'Which is better with mustard?' asks Silvio, and belches again.

TUESDAY

Cherie comes barging in while I'm at my desk and asks what I'm doing. Solving the problems of the Middle East, I say, but it's a lie. Actually, I'm playing Risk online against George W. Bush. He's rubbish.

'Tony?' she says. 'Where will our palace be?'

Personally, I'd be content with a big house. A white one. How people choose to refer to it is up to them.

Cherie pouts. 'But I will have a crown?' she says.

Listen, I say. Cherie babes. You've got to stop talking like that. This isn't like being PM. In order to get this job, I've got to basically pretend I don't want it.

'Like when you pretended you didn't want to go to war?' says Cherie.

Sort of, I say.

WEDNESDAY

David Miliband sneaks round in the evening, under cover of darkness, and says that Gordon is thinking of backing me. Oh God, I say, and I think about what happened when Gordon started backing the England football team. Can't we stop him? David just shrugs.

'I wish he was backing me,' he says, miserably. 'They say I could be Europe's foreign secretary. I'd hate that.'

It's a sacrifice, I agree, and I gaze majestically across the room.

However, if one were to feel the hand of history upon one's shoulder, one could, feasibly, be not unkindly disposed towards the idea...

'No,' says David, wild-eyed. 'Listen to me. I don't want it.'

He's very good at this, I tell him.

'I don't want it!' David screams. 'I don't want it!'

Then he jumps up, kicks over his chair and runs out, shaking, into the street. Playing hard to get. Clever boy.

THURSDAY

George has beaten me in North Africa, which means he gets three extra armies at the beginning of his next turn. But worse, the whole president thing seems to be falling apart. It's Gordon's fault, I know it.

Basically I need the support of Nicolas Sarkozy and Angela Merkel, and suddenly I don't have either. I give Sarko a call.

'You've stabbed me in the back,' I snap. 'So which of these faceless nobodies do you want instead?'

Sarkozy is quiet for a while. Dr Siemens could be a compromise candidate, he says. And Herr Grundig has been a staunch supporter of the euro from the start.

'This is absurd,' I tell him. 'Even you can't remember what these people are called. You're plainly just staring around your living room, picking names at random.'

Bang and Olufsen are also both very promising, he says.

FRIDAY

Cherie bangs on the door and wants to know whether she'll have a horse-drawn carriage or a sedan chair. I drag one of the plywood boards from the corner and use my Fender Stratocaster to wedge it in front of the door. Then I go back to my computer. George has just lost control of the Ukraine. Looks like I might take Europe after all.

DAVID CAMERON
9 FEBRUARY 2013

*A more recent one, as David Cameron entered his own
'beleaguered' phase. Much British meat, meanwhile, had
been revealed to contain horse. Big fuss.*

MONDAY

A breakfast meeting with George.

'You're still in bed,' he says.

Yup, I say. And I'm staying here. This is going to be the
worst week ever. Gay marriage. The economy in freefall.
Govey reversing on education reform. And then I've got
to go to Europe. I can't face it.

'You have to get up,' says George. 'Half the party is
revolting.'

At least, I say.

'No,' says George. 'I mean, they're revolting. They're
in revolt.'

Oh, I say. Well, as long as there's no figurehead. Boris
isn't revolting, is he?

'No,' says George. 'Well, yes. But no.'

TUESDAY

Today's the day of the big gay marriage debate. George
arrives, close to tears.

'The IFS says Plan A isn't working,' he says. 'And our
party is in absolute disarray over a fight we've picked for

no reason at all. Now is no time to be catching up on your sleep!'

I'm mainly just lying here, I tell him. Staring at the ceiling. You should try it.

George says the gay marriage thing was supposed to be detoxifying our party's image, and instead it's doing the absolute opposite.

'You know how many gay marriages I've been invited to?' he says.

None, I say, glumly. Same as me.

'But you still ought to be out there, selling it,' says George.

But I really don't want to, I explain. I want to stay here, where everything is safe and in control, and I don't have to think about gays at all.

'Are you coming in?' I add.

'Yes,' says George.

WEDNESDAY

'Oi,' says Samantha. 'Dave. You gotta wake up, luv. It's PMQs, innit.'

I didn't want to. First I called Nick, but Nick hasn't been answering his phone since the AV referendum. Then I tried to call George, but it turned out that George was actually still sitting at the foot of our bed, covered in a blanket, and mumbling 'expansionary fiscal contraction' over and over again. God knows where Hague is. Not seen him in months.

It's good to be up. Except for the way it's apparently not just the Conservative Party which is broken, but also the NHS. And our plan for taxing spare bedrooms doesn't work. And Michael Gove is doing a U-turn over O-levels. And my party all hate me. And I need to go to Europe tomorrow, where they all hate me even more. But yeah. Apart from that.

THURSDAY

Off to Brussels, to find that François Hollande has skipped our pre-summit meeting, because he hates me.

'Zis is very amusing!' he says, when he finally turns up. 'Ze pain in your 'orse!'

'You mean Nick Clegg?' I say.

'Non,' he frowns. 'Cheval. 'Orse.'

Merkel leans in. 'Ve are tzinking you are not realising zat ze rest of Europe is ferry much liking 'orse,' she says.

'Zis is why we must defend ze CAP,' says Hollande. 'For ze 'orse.'

I think I might still be asleep.

FRIDAY

First I'm in bed all day, then I'm up all night. We struck a deal at 6.30 a.m. Sausages for breakfast. Didn't fancy them.

'Vous should know,' says Hollande, once it is all over. 'Je suis also having trouble over le gay marriage. Ze people are revolting.'

That doesn't mean they shouldn't be able to get married, I tell him, sternly.

'Non,' says Hollande. 'I meant zose opposed. Zey are revolting.'

I think of the horse thing.

'You're all revolting,' I say.

'Since 1789!' says Hollande, proudly.

'If you like,' I say.

And then I go home, and back to bed. George is still there, muttering something about the structural deficit.

'Get out,' I say.

SAMANTHA CAMERON
<u>20 MARCH 2010</u>

Sooner or later, male politicians with wives cooler than them (which is all male politicians) wheel them out, to show off. This was Samantha Cameron's week.

<u>MONDAY</u>

'All right mate,' I say, to the journalist. 'Welcome to my gaff. There's the Aga. Back in my youth, when I was pretty wild, maybe I knew some scary gangsters who would have used it to cook up crack. But today I'm baking organic scones. Innit.'

Dave is hovering at my elbow.

'She's very cool,' he says. 'Isn't she? Much cooler than me. Although, if my wife is that cool, I suppose it must mean that I'm not such an old fuddy-duddy after all. Eh?'

'That's the message,' he adds, keenly, 'that you ought to be getting from this.'

I'm seeing a lot of journalists this week. This is because I'm the Conservative Party's new secret weapon. I'm hip and cool, and I wear things like jeans.

'That's our problem,' George was saying, when he came around the other day for a pre-election crisis meeting. 'We're behind in the polls and we need to attract more people who wear jeans. Does anybody know anybody like that?'

Everybody went quiet. Including William Hague, and

he wasn't even at boarding school. Then I pointed out that I was wearing some, by James, which cost £200.

So, after everybody had gathered around for a look, they decided I was going to be integral to the election campaign. So that's why I went on telly and told Trevor McDonald about him not picking up his pants.

That was George's idea. He reckoned that, as vote winners go, it would be almost up there with a cut in VAT.

TUESDAY

On the radio today. I met Dave when I was a student, I'm saying. I was pretty wild back then. I'm not sure ... have I ever mentioned this before? I was in Bristol. Although I'd grown up in a stately home, I studied art and went clubbing with budding pop stars. Like all trendy art students on the Bristol scene in the early 1990s, what I really wanted to do was get married to a right-wing Young Conservative in a pinstripe suit who worked for Norman Lamont.

'Listen, geezer,' I'd say to the trip-hop druggie super-star Tricky, as we shot pool in a subterranean dive bar, 'the ERM wasn't intrinsically a bad idea, we just joined at the wrong point of the foreign exchange cycle. Know wot I mean?'

And then I met Dave, at a friend's villa in Tuscany. It's your typical indie fairytale.

WEDNESDAY

Wotcha. I'll tell you who inspires me. Gwen Stefani. You know the way that she has successfully combined the sex-laden iconography of 1980s-era Madonna with the urban ghetto credibility of R'n'B?

Well, that's exactly what I've tried to do with my luxury stationery brand, Smythson.

If I'm honest, if it hadn't been for the thrusting grime of 'Hollaback Girl', our black calf-skin travel wallet with riveted 14-carat gold corners (£340) would probably never have happened.

THURSDAY

Cor. Today I'm visiting an inner-city children's charity. It's the kind of thing that Sarah Brown often does, although she doesn't ever do it in jeans. This is why we are the future.

Along with the jeans, I'm in Converse trainers and a pashmina. Dave and George approve of the Converse, because they were only £29. But they aren't sure about the pashmina. George is worried it might be in gang colours.

'You've got to be careful with South London,' agrees Dave. 'Because maybe the kids on that particular estate wear a different colour of pashmina altogether.'

FRIDAY

'I'm not sure this is really working,' says Eric Pickles, surveying some of the press coverage of the past few days. 'In fact, I'm starting to suspect that some voters might be finding it all slightly patronising.'

'Nonsense,' says George. 'Sam is totally down with the kids on the street.'

'New Bond Street,' points out Eric.

'It's still a street,' insists George. 'And to be honest, some bits north of Claridge's are actually quite grotty.'

NICK CLEGG
24 APRIL 2010

I know it seems strange now, but there was a week during the 2010 election campaign when Nick Clegg was suddenly the sexiest, most appealing thing to have happened to British politics for decades, and people genuinely thought he might win the election. Remember? WTF?

MONDAY

'Buenos días, Nick!' says my wife, Miriam, as we sit down to our usual breakfast of black coffee, dry slices of meat, very small rolls and slices of anonymous yellow cheese, as is common in all civilised countries.

This morning, however, I frown. From now on, we must eat the sort of foul, greasy stodge that British people like. Because, now that I'm actually in with a chance of attracting new voters, I reckon it is important that I start to show everybody how totally fond of British culture I have always been.

'And I'll be saying as much,' I add, 'to our three children, Django, Xavier, and Fernández y Rasputin.'

Miriam thinks we should at least be allowed muesli and croissants.

'Out of the question!' I fret. 'Suddenly this election is mine to lose. Haven't you heard? I'm more popular than Churchill!'

'¿Quién es Churchill?' asks Miriam.

'I'm not sure,' I say as I tie my shiny golden tie. 'He might have been a Nazi.'

TUESDAY
Of course, on reflection, I know perfectly well who Churchill is. He's that nodding dog from the insurance adverts that you sometimes see in the back of cars. It just slipped my mind because I haven't had much to do with cars lately. I've been spending all of my time with senior Liberal Democrats, and, apart from Vince Cable, they all prefer adult tricycles.

Actually, Vince seems to be sulking. He used to be the Lib Dem that everybody wanted to know. But these days it's all, 'Nick, would you kiss my baby?' and 'Nick, might you sign this used tissue box with seashells glued on to it that I made for the Lib Dem jumble sale?' I'm trying to keep my feet on the ground. It's not easy.

WEDNESDAY
The polls are saying I'm more popular than Jesus, iPhones and Cheryl Cole combined. Which seems fair.

'See?' I say to Vince. 'At last the electorate has been won over by my plans to make the UK a bit like Belgium!'

He reckons it might be because the other two are increasingly reminiscent of Laurel and Hardy. He's probably just bitter. His ties are all old and dark.

THURSDAY
Today is the day of the leaders' debate.

Beforehand, I go to the green room at Sky News. 'Good evening,' I say, to Gordon Brown and David Cameron. 'I agree with you,' says Brown, and does his special smile. Cameron just stares at me, nastily. Eventually I catch the light with my golden tie to force him to look away.

To be honest, I'm feeling a bit nervous.

I just hope neither of them have read our manifesto. There's all manner of mad stuff in there. I suppose we'd have given it a little more thought if we'd realised anybody was going to read it.

FRIDAY

'Buenos días, Nick,' sighs Miriam, prodding miserably at a kipper. She's got spots now. We're giving the kids knives and have told them to spit at people and sniff glue. It's quite a sacrifice, but I think we all feel British as anything.

I'm glum, too. The other two weren't particularly rubbish last night, so I'm now only as popular as Barack Obama, or *Avatar*. Still, I suppose that's not too bad.

I have a vision for this country.

Electoral reform! The euro! High-speed trains, to get us to countries that are nicer! I'm more popular than Vince, and I didn't even have to dance.

Oh yes, life has certainly changed. I can't believe I had to tell *GQ* that I'd only slept with thirty people! Imagine if I was single now.

LORD JUSTICE LEVESON
1 DECEMBER 2012

This was the week that Lord Justice Leveson delivered his very, very long report into the Culture and Ethics of the British Press. There was much fuss about the difference between statutory regulation and statutory underpinned regulation, and the way he'd completely ignored the internet.

MONDAY

1. For the fourth time in under a month it is Monday again. Nobody could wish for a fifth.
2. In order to start the day, the judge requires somebody to fetch him a croissant.
3. Yet it would not be acceptable to demand a croissant by statutory decree.
4. The principle of the voluntary fetching of croissants by technical underlings (clerks, wives, Robert Jay QC) is a vital British tradition dating back centuries and I would be loath to jeopardise it.
5. But I suppose it might be viable to suggest a law which would force people to buy the judge croissants in the event that they failed to voluntarily do so.
6. Or is that just nonsense?
7. Hmmm.

TUESDAY

8. The delivery of the judge's croissant under the current system is still ongoing, and I am at pains not to jeopardise it.

8.1 Furthermore, I am hungry.

9. Yet it seems to me that there are certain parallels vis-à-vis croissant delivery and the future regulation of the press, on which I will be delivering an eagerly anticipated report in two days' time.

10. Which is really getting quite long now.

11. I'm particularly proud of the car chase, the bits with the Horcruxes and the sex scenes in the Red Room Of Pain.

12. Although I'm not sure they'll make the final edit.

WEDNESDAY

13. There have been many attacks on my report, which is outrageous, because nobody knows what is in it yet.

14. Ed Miliband has been in touch to say he'll endorse my report, which is very pleasing.

14.1 Although I suppose he doesn't know what is in it yet either.

15. Robert Jay QC calls, to ask if I've said anything about his beard.

15.1 'Some people seem to think it makes my head look upside down,' he says.

   'And I would be saddened if this was your judicial verdict.'

15.2. I tell him I haven't mentioned the beard at all.

15.3. I will send him a copy tomorrow, I continue, in a suitcase, in a taxi.

15.4. 'Or you could send it over the internet?' he says.

15.5 But I don't know what that is.

THURSDAY

16. Today is publication day.

17. My report remains very long, but I have been ruthless in my editing.

18. At the very least, I am now unlikely to win a Bad Sex Award.

19. The Prime Minister has rejected my call for statutory underpinning of press regulation.

20. The Leader of the Opposition called to remind me that there were already bronze impressions of Winston Churchill and Margaret Thatcher in the Houses of Parliament.

21. At first, I couldn't figure out what he was on about.

22. Then I realised he was confusing 'statutory' with 'statue of a Tory'.

23. This provided some levity.

FRIDAY

24. Amid a media storm, I am going on holiday to Australia.

25. In the continued absence of the necessary legislation, I have abandoned my quest for a breakfast croissant.

26. Instead, I shall fetch my own beans on toast.

27. But the airport café has run out of toast on which to put the beans.

27.1. 'Perhaps they could just be underpinned by toast?' I suggest.

28. But apparently that's basically the same thing.

KENNETH CLARKE
8 OCTOBER 2011

Conference again. Theresa May, the Home Secretary, makes a speech in which she says an illegal immigrant couldn't be deported because he owned a cat. Ken Clarke, the Justice Secretary, makes a speech in which he says this is nonsense. The rest of the Cabinet takes sides. Silly week, really.

MONDAY

Waking fairly late on the park bench I keep in our bedroom and sleep on fully clothed to get my suits to look just right, I leave the house via my customary route through our front garden hedgerow, backwards.

Then I pop into the car and nip up to Manchester, where the team of identical children who run my party are having their conference.

David and George want to see me.

'This is absolute nonsense,' I tell them. 'Childish drivel. I don't mean to be rude, but I've been in frontbench politics for forty years and this really is the greatest idiocy I've ever heard.'

'What is?' asks one of them.

I don't know. I wasn't listening. But it sounds like a safe bet.

'Now look here, Ken,' says the other one. 'You'll jolly well speak to George with a little more respect.'

'Aren't you George?' I say.

TUESDAY

Theresa May has made a speech about the Human Rights Act. There was a bit about a cat and it was sheer nonsense.

That afternoon, she calls.

'The cat is a myth,' I say.

'It's a myth that the cat is a myth,' she says.

'It's actually a myth that it's a myth that the cat is a myth,' I say.

'You've lost me,' she says.

'That's because you're an imbecile,' I say.

Later, I bump into Boris Johnson. The man talks a lot of rot, but I certainly admire his stylist.

WEDNESDAY

I'm walking down a corridor in the conference hotel when I'm spotted by that bald fellow from No. 10, who has cushions in his office instead of chairs. Sometimes I sneak in when he's out, for a nap and a Pot Noodle.

'Ken, old lad,' he says, putting an arm around my back. 'A word in your ear.'

'Take that arm off me right now, or I'll rip it out of its socket,' I tell him.

'Chillax,' he says, backing off. 'Let's do smoothies.'

I've been an MP since the First World War. I don't have to put up with this.

THURSDAY

Half of Fleet Street is trying to get hold of me on my mobile, which is, of course, an old Nokia held together with a rubber band, and with what looks like Cheddar seeping out from most of the keys.

I know what they want. I gave an interview in which I called Theresa's cat business 'nonsense' and 'child-like'.

Thank God they haven't spotted the one in which I called her 'a ragingly stupid representative of a government in which everybody except me is a total pillock'.

FRIDAY

Called in to Downing Street. There are three of them this time. One of them is almost certainly Nick Clegg. I quite like Nick Clegg.

'Now listen here, Ken,' he begins, and stops. 'Is it raining?' he says.

Only on me, I say, and then I tell him how much I agree with him about Europe and the Human Rights Act.

'I've been in government since the Great Reform Act,' I say, 'and it's great to meet somebody who isn't a nutter like David Cameron and these bloody Tories. Mind if I smoke in here?'

'I am David Cameron,' he says. 'And I do, actually.'

'Ah well,' I say, and I light up a big cigar.

ALISTAIR DARLING
25 APRIL 2009

God, but the end of the Brown government was depressing, wasn't it? With Britain in a fury about the MPs' expenses scandal, the Prime Minister had released a YouTube video, in which he smiled a lot and said he understood. Frankly he was going a bit weird by this point. There was also a Budget.

MONDAY

I'm sitting on a chair in Gordon's office. I don't like it in here. It's shuttered and cold, with none of the soothing beige tones of my own home. Gordon may be in here, although in the gloom it is hard to tell. There is a smell of old moss, and raisins.

Ed Balls is behind me, repeatedly firing a rubber band catapult at the back of my head.

'Gordon thinks you look too strange,' he says, and cocks his head to one side.

'Gordon thinks you should get a haircut.' I look around, nervously.

Gordon is in here?

'Gordon is everywhere,' says Ed Balls.

I gulp. Aside from Ed Balls, nobody has actually seen Gordon since the G20. Rumour has it that he spends all his time dressed only from the waist up, making strange videos to post on YouTube.

Occasionally the catering staff will open the ante-room to his office, and release a live chicken.

Nobody will ever see it again. Not even the beak.

He'll have to be there, I say, on Wednesday. 'He'll be there,' says Ed Balls. And washed, I add.

'If need be,' says Ed Balls, 'I'll wash him myself.'

TUESDAY

'Darling,' says my wife, as is our humorous custom. 'Your hair? I don't know what the hairdresser was thinking. It's far too short.'

I'm sitting up in our beige bed, working on my Budget speech. I sigh. She has a point.

'My hair has grown by minus 3.5 per cent,' I tell her. 'This is regrettable, but a global trend, which I expect to be reversed over the coming fortnight. By the first week of May it will be entirely back to normal.'

My wife looks sceptical. 'So soon?' she says.

Absolutely, I insist. This is entirely within the range of several independent predictions.

'Suit yourself,' yawns my wife, and turns over. 'But I think you're fooling yourself.'

WEDNESDAY

Budget day morning.

I'm back in the darkness of No. 10, speaking to Ed Balls and the faint smell of Gordon. Whenever I say something, Ed Balls repeats it back to me, in a squeaky baby voice. It's really annoying.

'I'm worried,' I tell them, 'about the maths.'

Once he's done repeating, Ed Balls tells me the maths will do what it is told. Ed Balls says that if the maths doesn't do what it is told, then maybe, entirely unconnected to him, word will get around on the internet that the maths has gone nuts and has started smoking crack. Ed Balls terrifies me.

I look around. 'Is Gordon...?' I begin.

'Is Gordon,' squeaks Ed Balls. Then he says that Gordon is fine. And washed. And ready. And listening. Always listening.

Good, I say, and then I hesitate. 'I saw his video,' I say. 'On YouTube. About expenses. With ... the smiling.'

Ed Balls sighs. Gordon recorded lots of videos, he says. In some, he was smiling. In some he was speaking in a voice like Dracula. Or Mickey Mouse. Or Ivana Trump. They knew one had been released but they didn't know which until they saw it on the news. Big relief.

'How did you think he came across?' says Ed Balls, looking hard into my eyes.

'Great!' I lie, looking into his.

After that we look at each other for a few moments more, with neither of us saying anything.

THURSDAY

Gordon was fine, actually. Aside from the feathers under his fingernails, I don't think anybody would have suspected a thing.

Between us, Budgets aren't that hard. You just say a bunch of stuff, and the next day they do all the tricky sums in the newspapers. Today they're saying we're missing £45 billion. Could have been worse.

I'll speak to Ed Balls. Maybe we can put it around that the £45 billion just had an affair with its secretary, and ran off to Acapulco.

FRIDAY

'I still think,' says my wife, 'that your hair looks really weird. Not just the length. It's just getting whiter and whiter. Maybe you could dye it.'

I sigh. She's overreacting. Honestly, I tell her. The green shoots of recovery are just around the corner.

'Black would be better,' yawns my wife. 'Or maybe beige. Still, suit yourself.'

GEORGE OSBORNE
<u>23 MARCH 2013</u>

Another Budget. This one turned up in the Evening Standard *shortly before the Chancellor had actually delivered it. Awkward.*

<u>MONDAY</u>

I think the main problem, I tell the Prime Minister, is the way that I have to do absolutely everything.

David says he doesn't think that's true at all. 'But anyway,' he adds, 'what's for supper?'

Casserole, I tell him. I just need to finalise growth predictions with the OBR, check in with Angela Merkel about the response to Cyprus, properly cost our childcare proposals, liaise with the 1922 Committee about their views on this press regulation stuff, decide what we're doing on public sector pay, and put out Oliver Letwin's clothes for tomorrow. Then I can get down to peeling the carrots.

The PM is standing in the middle of his office, knocking golf balls into a whisky tumbler.

'Surely there's somebody who can help you,' he says, 'with the carrots.'

I just can't think of anybody we could trust, I tell him. Not with a task as important as that.

'Ah well,' says Dave. 'All in it together, eh? Ooh! Look. Hole in one.'

TUESDAY

We've got a pre-Budget meeting with all the Cabinet heavyweights. It turns out that the Office for Budget Responsibility have downgraded growth prospects.

'This is an outrage!' says Ken Clarke.

It's only a setback, says Dave.

'Not that,' says Ken. 'Where are the damn scones?'

They're coming, I say, hurrying in. Careful. Still hot.

Nick Clegg and Danny Alexander are looking sombre. The Deputy PM says they want three things. First, an increase in the tax threshold. Second, some movement on housing. Third, strawberry jam.

'Blackberry?' I say. 'Raspberry?'

Vince Cable says he doesn't think this coalition is going to last.

WEDNESDAY

Budget day. Gosh, but what a morning. So far, I've done the maths, joined Twitter, finished my speech, briefed the Lib Dems, de-limescaled the loo, and written the front page of the *Evening Standard*. Now I'm in the chamber and about to speak. I just hope nobody notices Oliver Letwin isn't wearing a shirt or any shoes.

THURSDAY

Disaster! My budget is unravelling. Half the Cabinet has piled into No. 11 to shout at me.

'Everything is always unravelling with you,' says Theresa May, crossly.

'The man can't darn,' says William Hague. 'That's the problem. Have you seen poor Oliver's socks?'

I don't sleep, I say. I don't get the chance. I'm afraid to, in case I wake up and find out that you've all agreed to let Hugh Grant regulate the whole internet, or something.

'About that...' begins Oliver.

Just don't, I say. Then I say that I'm sorry about the housing announcement, and I appreciate there's a danger it might let people buy houses who already have houses.

'There are people without houses?' says IDS.

'But Chris Huhne has nine,' says Nick Clegg.

'This is why we need him,' says Dave. 'See? Who else knew that?'

FRIDAY

Dave, Oliver and Ken pop in, for a mid-morning cup of tea. Dave says I'm looking well.

Thanks, I say. I slept for two whole hours last night. Hence the way my skin is now pale white, rather than its customary greyish green.

The PM says we have two big problems, and the main one is the newspapers.

'All the stories are too hostile,' agrees Ken. 'You need to write them more nicely.'

I only write the *Evening Standard*, I tell them.

'Oh,' says Dave. 'Well, the other problem is growth.'

There's no easy solution, I say. People just need to work harder.

'That's rich coming from you,' says Oliver. 'When I'm not even wearing any trousers.'

I don't want to do this anymore, I say.

'Go on, then!' says Ken. 'Walk!'

'Wait!' says Dave. 'Does anybody else know how to use the kettle?'

Ken says that's a fair point. 'Two sugars, George,' he adds.

ED MILIBAND
2 APRIL 2011

Newly installed as the Leader of the Opposition, Ed Miliband gives a speech at a rally in Hyde Park against benefit cuts. He compares this fight to the American Civil Rights movement. It's kinda embarrassing. He also announces his wedding to his long-standing partner Justine.

MONDAY

'Oops,' says my press guy. 'I forgot to put sugar in your coffee. Sorry.'

Don't worry, I say. In keeping with the tradition established by Nelson Mandela coping with twenty-seven years in a brutal South African jail, I shall cope with unsweetened coffee. So help me God.

My press guy starts laughing, and then stops again very quickly.

'I think we need to have a talk,' he says, 'about your new habit of likening relatively small problems to the greatest civil rights outrages in history. Because it makes you sound kind of weird.'

But I stand upon their shoulders, I tell him. Just as Dreyfus and Martin Luther King faced persecution, so have I.

'In what way?' asks the press officer.

Some people say I look like the guy out of Wallace and Gromit, I tell him.

'It's not the same,' he says.

'I feel it is,' I say.

TUESDAY

'So anyway,' I say to Justine, with whom I biologically have two children, although legally only one, because I've been very busy. 'I've been thinking about the wedding.'

'The royal wedding?' she says.

'No,' I say. 'Our wedding.'

Justine says I didn't tell her that we were getting married.

'Not directly,' I concede, 'but I did tell the *Doncaster Free Press.*'

Justine agrees that this was very romantic of me.

'I want our wedding to stand on the shoulders of the most romantic weddings in history,' I tell her. 'Think big white dresses, wedding cakes, ushers, choirboys and a horse-drawn carriage!'

'Oh Ed!' says Justine, wiping away a tear. 'Is that what we're doing?'

'No,' I say. 'I was thinking of Camden register office. But still.'

WEDNESDAY

'Brave of you,' says Ed Balls, just after PMQs, 'to let go of that whole distant, unmarried, dweeby North London intelligentsia thing the voters are so keen on. Still, I shouldn't worry about it. Not when you're standing on the shoulders of the greatest civil rights heroes in history. You should say more stuff like that. Don't think you don't remind people of the Dalai Lama, because you totally do.'

'I agree,' I say. 'And thanks for the advice. It's a relief. Especially as the press guy was saying the total opposite!'

Ed says the press guy obviously doesn't have my best interests at heart.

'Now give me your lunch money,' he adds, 'or I'll give you a wedgie.'

THURSDAY

All my political heroes have had to make compromises. Emmeline Pankhurst suspended the suffragettes to fight the Germans. The Dalai Lama left Tibet. Joe Slovo entered in talks with the apartheid government. And I have agreed to ditch Camden register office in favour of a quite lovely country house near Nottingham. Nobody said this path was easy.

FRIDAY

On a bench at the top of Primrose Hill, I'm sitting with my brother David.

'I can see our house from here,' I say.

'Which one?' asks my brother.

'Almost all of them,' I say. He doesn't reply. It's not easy with David these days.

Eventually I tell him I want to talk about the wedding.

'I know you won't be my best man,' I say, 'but I still want you there. Even if you aren't, you know, next to me.'

David just stares into the distance.

'Oh God!' I sigh. 'What's happened to our family is awful! It's like when Gandhi and Jinnah fell out over civil disobedience, ultimately leading to the bloody and traumatic partition of India and Pakistan!'

'That's exactly what I was thinking,' says David.

LORD MANDELSON
17 JULY 2010

I can't believe I haven't done Lord Mandelson more often.
Here he is in the week of the publication of his memoirs,
which were called The Third Man *and I suppose I must*
have read.

MONDAY

The relationship between Tony Blair and Gordon Brown was a fascinating one, and I was right at the heart of it. Oh, you silly boy! Of course I was. Why, it's evident by the way neither of them ever quite told me what was going on, and I always had to find out by asking John Prescott! And by the way they sacked me, twice. And then sent me to live in another country.

Doubtless there will always be the naysayers who seek to sow dissent, but I'm perfectly confident that both Tony and Gordon are portrayed in my memoirs in a deeply flattering light. Don't you think Gordon actually benefits enormously from the revelation that we all thought he was a chubby weirdo who couldn't be trusted with scissors? And I happen to know that Tony couldn't be more thrilled to be shown as a flighty coward with a psycho wife and a crush on Mick Jagger.

My dear fellow, you simply mustn't set such store by gossip! What's not for them to like?

TUESDAY

Tony? Annoyed with moi? Good Lord, no! Why, you obviously haven't been paying attention. As it happens, I have a text from him right here, on my BlackBerry. Look, it says 'STILL FRNDS BUT PLS STOP BETRAYING STUFF I TELL YOU IN PRIVTE!!' Would you like to write it down? Shall I lend you a pen?

Of course, Tony has little time for such flippancies in this day and age. He's frightfully busy making peace in the Middle East, hadn't you heard? The relationship between Israel and Palestine is a fascinating one and obviously I'm right at the heart of it. Indeed you might even say it's not really about them. It's about me.

WEDNESDAY

Alastair Campbell calls. He says he thinks it's entirely unacceptable that I've disclosed so many private conversations in my memoirs. And he'll be saying as much, he adds, in his next memoir.

'Fine,' I shoot back. 'And I'll be saying what you said about your next memoir in my next memoir.'

'But I'll be saying what you said about your next memoir in my next memoir first,' spits Alastair. 'So it's going to be old news.'

I'm very fond of Alastair, having first worked with him when he was a fat, depressive alcoholic. I can't abide the way some people try to talk him down!

But the simple fact is, he's always been blindly jealous of my incredibly close friendship with Tony. Why, back in the early days, Tony and I would put a chair in front of the door so that Alastair and Cherie couldn't get in, and settle down on the Downing Street sofa to share a pot of Ben and Jerry's ice cream.

Tony had this game he'd play, where he'd pretend he wanted to get out. How we'd laugh!

THURSDAY

This evening we held my book launch. I can't pretend not to have been a little offended that Barack Obama didn't turn up. I'm close with Barack, having worked intimately with him from a distance on trips to America.

Tony didn't come either. 'I JST DON'T THNK I CN TRUST U,' he texted. 'EVRY CONVO OF PAST 15 YRS IS IN YR BOOK!!' Such an adorable sentiment from a lovely man! I put it in my speech.

FRIDAY

A quiet evening at the modest Georgian mansion I share with two adorable dogs and a person I'm curiously reluctant to ever acknowledge. Finally, Tony calls.

'Well,' I say. 'I suppose you'll want to say thank you.'

'Thank you?' says Tony. 'Thank you?'

Just the once would do, I tell him, graciously. Then I tell him I'm reclining on the sofa with a pot of Ben and Jerry's. Just like old times.

'As it happens,' I add, 'the relationship between Ben and Jerry was a fascinating one. And I was right at the heart of it.'

GILLIAN DUFFY
16 APRIL 2011

Gillian Duffy was the woman whom Gordon Brown called a 'bigot' during the election campaign after she asked where all these immigrants were flocking from. Remember that? A year later, the Labour Party wheeled her out to hassle Nick Clegg.

MONDAY

These Labour Party activists. Where are they flocking from? Haven't heard a thing from them for months, not since they bussed me down to the Labour Party conference, and we had that fight about them wanting me to pose for pictures with Ed Miliband, a whippet, and a Tunnocks Teacake.

Now they won't leave me alone. I had a couple at the door this morning. Very well spoken.

'Ey up, Gillian!' said one.

'Oooh,' I said. 'You're a Yorkshireman.'

'No,' he said, and they both looked at each other, confused. 'We're from Belsize Park. But I thought you all ... well, never mind. We've got that Nick Clegg coming to Rochdale this week. You know who I mean?'

'Nice boy,' I said. 'Pretty wife.'

'Um, no,' said the other one. 'He's Lib Dem. Nasty sort. Like a Tory. They probably want to close your mines.'

'Do we still have mines?' I said.

'Bound to,' he said. 'Place like this. But listen. We were

hoping you could, you know, ambush him. Say something bigoted, like you did with Gordon.'

'Bigoted?' I said.

'He didn't say bigoted,' said the first.

'I think he did,' I said.

'You misheard,' he said. 'Please don't tell anybody. Oh
God. Quick. Let's go.'

TUESDAY

Silly boys. They're back this morning, wearing flat caps.

'Ey up,' says one. 'Erm ... luv.'

'Look,' says the other. 'We didn't mean the bigot thing.
Slip of the tongue. But it would be great if you could
have a go at Clegg. Show how out of touch he is. And
don't do it for us. Do it for yourself. You're great at this
stuff. You should be on telly.'

'Really?' I say.

'Definitely,' he says. 'Even Ed Miliband said so. He
said you should interview everybody. Viewers would
come flocking!'

'No need to swear,' I say.

'Flocking is swearing?' says one.

'This explains a lot,' says the other.

WEDNESDAY

So today, I'm confronting Clegg outside a factory. I ask
him why he's teamed up with the Tories, and whether
everything is going wrong.

'I knew you'd come around,' says one of the Labour
activists. 'Good old Mrs Duffy! You know what side
your ciabatta is buttered on, eh?'

'They probably don't have ciabatta up here,' says the
other.

'Sorry Gillian,' says the first. 'It's a bit like fougasse.'

THURSDAY

Following my triumph with Nick Clegg, I have decided to pursue my media career more vigorously. So, I get Ed Miliband's number off the activists, and ask him to help me to secure an interview with Barack Obama.

'Brilliant!' he says. 'Who is this?'

'Gillian Duffy,' I say.

'You've got the voice just right,' he says. 'That impenetrable Northern accent! Bigoted woman! Hahaha!'

'I'm going to the press,' I say.

'Sorry,' he says. 'Didn't catch that.'

'I'm going to the press,' I say, again.

'Nope,' he says. 'Still not getting it. Send me a text.'

FRIDAY

The two activists have come round, with a basket of flowers from Ed Miliband. They say he'd have come himself, but he was worried that every TV camera in Britain might have suddenly appeared behind the door, like last time.

'He really is very sorry,' says one. 'Please don't go to the press. Especially not about the accent thing. His constituency is Doncaster, you know. Plus, it would really offend his gardener.'

'Tell him he's a flocking idiot,' I say. 'And flock off.'

MOTHER MILIBAND
<u>28 AUGUST 2010</u>

And another Miliband. This one is from the middle of the brothers' fierce battle for the Labour leadership.

<u>MONDAY</u>

'Now,' I say fondly to my boys at the family kitchen table in Primrose Hill. 'Who wants the last cup of tea?'

'Me,' both say, simultaneously.

Then they stare at each other, furiously. I sigh. It was always like this. David had a scientific calculator, so Ed had to have a scientific calculator, too. Ed had a poster of Arthur Scargill above his bed, so David had to get one immediately. You should have heard the screaming when the *Tribune* Gift Shop had only the one Nye Bevan pencil case!

'I should have the tea,' says David, 'for I am the eldest. I expressed interest in tea before he knew what it was.'

'But you drink tea so weirdly,' snarls Ed. 'The way you stick out that little finger. Everybody says so.'

Somehow, I get the feeling this isn't really about tea.

<u>TUESDAY</u>

Between us, part of the problem is that David has never rated Ed as his true equal. I remember when they were boys and Ed was in the garden arranging his stuffed animals into a rough simulacrum of the TUC conference.

David was scathing about every motion that Papa Bear brought to table.

'Boys!' I used to say, when they were a bit older. 'You don't need to build rival centre-left think-tanks out of Lego! You could build one big one, and play together!'

But they didn't. Not ever. Not once.

WEDNESDAY

Today, David has written a column in *The Times*, in which he effectively calls his brother well-meaning, but naive. Ed is furious.

'Why doesn't he realise?' he says, when he comes round. 'He's just too weird to be Prime Minister. He always has been. Remember on car journeys? When we used to pass the time by trying to list the constituencies of every Labour leader since Keir Hardie?'

'Happy days,' I sigh.

'He always got them all,' says Ed. 'Whereas I persistently forgot that John Robert Clynes represented Manchester Platting. Because I'm normal. And he's not.'

THURSDAY

Sometimes I wonder if we should have had more children. With twenty or so, the entire late-era New Labour Cabinet could have been comprehensively dominated by Milibands. With that kind of support, it's possible that David might actually have had the bottle to stand against Gordon Brown. Although I wouldn't have bet on it.

Today, Ed has hit back against David, accusing him of still being 'in New Labour's comfort zone'. My boys are used to the rough and tumble of British politics, but they've never faced anything like this.

Sure, some people have likened David to Mr Spock

from *Star Trek* and Ed to the chicken in *Chicken Run*, but those sorts of insults are easily borne. Particularly if you don't know enough about popular culture to have the first idea what they mean.

FRIDAY

I've called an emergency family conference to see if we can make this civil again. Already this is worse than the time Ed threw David's Fabian Society Action Man out the window because he felt it had displayed unsound views on the redistribution of capital. And believe me, that was awful.

'My boys,' I say, sadly. 'Look at you. You're both going grey.'

'I have been grey for years,' says David, sniffily. 'He never showed the remotest interest in being grey before. It's just not convincing.'

I offer them both a cup of tea and a biscuit.

'David would probably prefer a banana,' sneers Ed.

'Stop it!' I say.

They glower at each other, and suddenly I feel terribly sad. Sooner or later I'm going to have to tell them both I'm voting for Ed Balls.

DAVID MILIBAND
30 MARCH 2013

Last Miliband, I promise. Two years after losing the leadership election, and after a fun period during which his roles included the unpaid leadership of the Global Ocean Commission, David Miliband announced that he was moving to America, to head the International Rescue Committee.

MONDAY

It's annoying when people ask me why I don't have a big, impressive job. I've got loads. I'm the spokesman for fish, you know. All fish. But this week, I've decided to make a big change. So, I'm in Labour HQ, waiting to see Ed.

It feels a bit strange. He was always the one who waited to see me. I'd be out in the garden, perhaps arranging my action figures into an exciting re-enactment of a debate between the Fabian Society and the Co-op. And he'd stand there, patiently, until I was done.

'Ed will see you now,' the receptionist says, and I'm shown into the biggest office in the building. The Shadow Chancellor is standing there, holding a fruit bowl.

'What?' he says.

'I meant the other Ed,' I say.

'I always forget there's another Ed,' he says. 'Banana?'

TUESDAY

Some of the old Blairite gang are throwing me a leaving

dinner. It's funny, but I don't quite remember who any of them are.

'Hello,' I say to a middle-aged lady with a kind face. 'Were you the one who was strangely involved with Silvio Berlusconi? Or the other one, whose husband got caught watching porn.'

'That's what we'll miss about you,' says a balding man with grey hair. 'All that charm and tact.'

'John Reid?' I say.

'Charles Clarke,' he says.

'With the ears!' I say.

'Yes,' he says.

Then I spend a while asking them if they've all got big impressive jobs like mine, but they all go quiet and stare at their feet.

'Well,' I say, brightly. 'Never mind. Let's ask that waiter if our table is ready.'

'That's no waiter!' laughs Charles. 'That's Geoff Hoon!'

'Actually,' says Geoff, 'I'm a waiter too. Any drinks?'

WEDNESDAY

On the news, William Hague is in Congo with Angelina Jolie. I should be doing that kind of stuff. You just can't get Hollywood superstars interested in fish, though. It's weird.

Anyway, that's why I'm standing down as an MP and taking up a newer, bigger job at International Rescue. Actually, they've been calling me for ages. But because my nickname in Downing Street was 'Brains' I kept thinking they were Alastair Campbell doing a funny voice, and telling them to f*** off. Awkward.

THURSDAY

Peter Mandelson calls.

'You silly boy,' he says. 'Tony will be simply devastated.'

You were the last big hope, he says. The others have all gone. The guy with the ears, the guy with the sideburns, the guy with the suspicious tan. That religious lady with the funny voice and all the children. The other lady, who made everybody think of horses, and the other one everybody confused her with, who might have been Australian. The guy with the beard who took his dog everywhere, the Demon Headmaster, and whoever the hell Alan Milburn was. And that one with all the houses, who kept having to resign. All gone. All gone.

'I think that last one might have been you,' I say.

'I think you might be right,' he says.

FRIDAY

Finally, Ed has a window. He's sad.

'I don't want you to go,' he says.

I have to, I say. Otherwise people will just think I'm undermining you whenever I make a speech.

'They might not,' he says.

I'll never be able to do a funny voice, I continue, or else people will think I'm mocking your funny voice.

'Hold on,' he says.

I'll never be able to hold ridiculous reactionary policies that don't make any sense, I say. I'll never be able to make an announcement using the same lame catchphrase over and over again. I'll never even be able to walk around in a really stupid jerky fashion, or else people will think...

'Need a lift to the airport?' says Ed.

PART II

GLOBAL POLITICS

BARACK OBAMA
10 NOVEMBER 2012

A long and wearying US election is about to end. It has always seemed pretty unlikely that Mitt Romney would win, but Barack Obama doesn't seem to have been trying very hard. Meanwhile, Britain is enjoying one of those periodic 'who is a secret Establishment paedophile?' frenzies, after Phillip Schofield (a daytime TV presenter) handed David Cameron a list of names he found on the internet.

MONDAY

Today is a portentous day. For today is the day that may be the day before the day that America decides, on a fine autumn day, that there may be another day when the man who stands before you today as...

'Honey?' says Michelle. 'You're kinda raving again.'

I'm exhausted, I tell her. I literally have no interest in this job anymore. In fact, I was bored two years ago. Is it too late to hand over to Hillary?

'Now you stop that,' says my wife. 'America needs you to be President four more years. Sasha and Malia need you to be President four more years. Neither of them have even got a book deal, yet.'

I worry that we are losing ourselves, I tell her. The isolation. The constant scrutiny. The way the girls stole my BlackBerry and used it to call down a drone strike on Justin Bieber's girlfriend's house.

Michelle says all kids do that sort of thing.

'Do they?' I say.

'I don't remember,' says Michelle. 'Probably.'

TUESDAY

In our cities and our towns, in our factories and our farms. In our urban regeneration centres and our homesteads and our universities and our schools. In all these places I have stood, these past few weeks. And, my fellow Americans, I have struggled. To stay awake.

Today, I'm schlepping up to my home town of Chicago, to exercise my right at the ballot box.

'Might vote for the other guy,' I tell Michelle and the girls.

Malia wonders what are the GPS co-ordinates of the polling station. 'Out of interest,' she adds.

WEDNESDAY

Four more years. See my happy face. In the early hours, Mitt Romney calls to concede. 'Can't say I'm not disappointed,' he says.

'Tell me about it,' I say, and I ask if he's thought of mounting a legal challenge.

'Nope,' says Romney. 'Wouldn't help. In fact, by now, the only thing that would help would be if I could prove you'd been born in Kenya all along!'

'Hell,' I say. 'That's a good idea. Do you know anybody who can forge a birth certificate?'

'I'm confused,' says Romney. 'I thought you already had.'

THURSDAY

Today all the global leaders are calling to offer congratulations. First it's Putin.

'The election voz close and you are vizzibly ageing,' he says. 'In my country, neither of these things would be allowed.'

Then there's the guy from China, who is stepping down in a week and plainly doesn't give a damn.

'Fiscal criff!' he says. 'Velly funny!'

Next up it's the guy from Italy whose name I still don't know, but at least doesn't call me 'dusky' and talk about Michelle's ass, like the last one did. Then it's Angela Merkel from Germany, with whom I always have lots of long, awkward silences. Finally, it's David Cameron, from England. I put him on speakerphone.

'My good friends Barack and Michelle!' he says. 'I look forward to working together.'

Then he lowers his voice to a whisper, and tells me a man called Phillip Schofield has told him I'm a Muslim.

'Get his GPS co-ordinates,' hisses Michelle.

'Shhh,' I say.

FRIDAY
Mitt Romney calls again.

'Just bored, really,' he says. 'Whatcha doing?'

I just yawn. That's the thing about elections. You'll hear the determination in the voice of a young field organiser who's working his way through college. You'll hear the pride in the voice of a volunteer who's going door to door. You'll hear the deep patriotism in the voice of a military spouse.

And, after a while, you just want them all to shut the hell up.

'Four more years,' says Romney. Then he hangs up. Sorta laughing.

SILVIO BERLUSCONI
15 APRIL 2006

I miss Silvio Berlusconi. Is he back yet? It was always a happy feeling, getting to Friday and knowing I had an excuse to put him in a hot-tub, saying 'hubba'.

I think this was my first Berlusconi ever. Here he is after an election. In the UK, David Mills, the husband of Tessa Jowell (then the Culture Secretary) was facing allegations of being involved in shady Italian tax affairs.

LUNEDÌ

So! I am in my dressing room, trying on a new snakeskin three-piece victory suit, when my election agent knocks on the door.

'Come!' I shout, merrily. 'Your mother was a foul lactating haemorrhoid! Come on in!'

My election agent appears, cautiously.

'My mother was ... what?'

'Ha!' I say, and slap him on the back. 'A joke between friends! The grotesque old sow, eh? Ha! What news?'

'Not so great, Don Berlusconi,' he says. 'Romano Prodi's centre-left grouping looks a little ahead. Our best hope is to fashion some sort of collaborative coalition, much as Merkel has managed to in...'

'Backside!' I wisecrack. 'You dismal cretin! I'm not talking about the election. What do I care for formalities? I'm talking about my legacy. *Silvio: The Movie.* What news from Tom Cruise?'

'He doesn't seem keen. But Don Berlusconi, the election...'

'Election, election, election. As the Chinese whores used to say to your father, eh? Ha!'

My election agent leaves.

MARTEDÌ

I am at my villa in Sardinia, floating on a Lilo in the middle of my Italy-shaped pool. Also, I am on the telephone.

'You old son of a bitch on heat!' I say, pleasantly. 'Ha! Romano! I hope you don't mind that I give you this call?'

Romano is non-committal.

'My aides,' I continue, 'they say to me, don't call Romano Prodi. You cannot make a deal with this man. He is not like you. Hell, he probably doesn't even like women. You know?'

Romano remains non-committal.

'I tell them they are wrong! I say to them, Romano, he is a good guy. True, he is a dried-up old dullard with equipment, I am sure, like a prune, but he is no fool. He and I, we can sort something out. He has some votes, I have some votes. We are in the same boat.'

I belch.

'Although, of course, you don't have a boat.'

The line goes dead. Intolerable. I must buy another telecoms company.

MERCOLEDÌ

At lunchtime, I glance at a newspaper. MAFIA BOSS TOPPLED, says the headline.

'Oi! Testicle!' I shout, and my election agent comes running.

'Don Berlusconi?' he says, and I throw the newspaper at him.

'What is this?' I demand. 'How can they call me Mafia boss? I am a legitimate businessman!'

My election agent speaks soothingly. 'It's not you,' he says. 'It's Bernardo Provenzano, the Tractor of Corleone. The inspiration for the *Godfather* films, some say.'

'Hmm,' I muse. 'This reminds me. What news? Final decision from Tom Cruise?'

My election agent tells me he has firmly declined. 'But we have heard from another interested party,' he adds.

'Jude Law? Brad Pitt? Matt Damon? Ben Affleck?'

'Danny DeVito,' says my election agent.

GIOVEDÌ

In the morning, my new election agent brings me the telephone. Things grow desperate. I must consolidate my position internationally.

'Tony!' I say. 'My beautiful Tony! Too long, my friend! What is it that keeps you and your frog-faced wife from my side?'

Tony is speaking very quietly.

'Silvio,' he almost whispers. 'Great to hear from you! Sincerely, yeah? It's just, all this business with Tessa's husband? It's probably not a great idea that we speak.'

'Ha!' I roar. 'So you can buy your way into the House of Lords in Britain, but not out of the court?'

'Silvio!' breathes Tony. 'Please don't say things like that!'

'I joke! I joke! You English jockstrap! I joke! Listen, my Tony. Do I see you this summer? You and the toad, eh? Ha!'

'No,' says Tony. 'It's Cliff's year. Goodbye.'

I am starting to feel increasingly isolated.

VENERDÌ

I'm told Vin Diesel might do it. I suppose we can get him a wig.

Hardly any world leaders are returning my calls. How am I supposed to convince Italy to let me keep my job? I have a voicemail from President Ahmadinejad of Iran. Mother of God, help me to find another ally. I don't want him on my yacht. I have one more person to try. I pick up my special white telephone to the Vatican.

'So!' I roar. 'My old Nazi friend! Ha! How are those saucy nuns, eh?'

The Pope hangs up on me. Honestly. Some people have no sense of humour.

SILVIO BERLUSCONI
25 JULY 2009

This week, tapes had emerged of him supposedly hanging out with a prostitute in his villa in Rome, on the night of Barack Obama's first election victory in 2008. In them, he could be heard referring to a bed as 'Putin's bed'.

LUNEDÌ

'A tape?' I say to my private secretary. 'Impossible!'

My private secretary is loyal. Without my patronage, she would still be predicting cold fronts on Il Bazookas!, Italy's finest, nude, cable weather channel, which I own. Normally, she is a fine girl, firm-buttocked and unflappable. But today, standing there in her miniskirt, on the mirror that covers the floor surrounding my desk, she looks uncomfortable.

'It does not sound like a fake, Signor Berlusconi,' she says.

'But where could she have put the tape recorder?' I ask.

She says she doesn't know.

'The things we did,' I breathe. 'It is not possible. I shall draw you a diagram.'

My secretary says this won't be necessary.

'Anyway,' I continue. 'I have nothing to hide. What does this so-called tape have me say?'

My private secretary blushes and says something about a bed.

'A flower bed?' I suggest. 'Clearly I was considering making her Minister for Agriculture!'

'You called it the Putin bed,' she says. 'You said it had curtains.'

'And anyway,' she adds. 'You made me Minister for Agriculture. Remember? When I wore those heels.'

MARTEDÌ

I am hiding out in my office. In the morning, Putin calls. He's pretty angry.

'Now whole vorld is knowing that Putin bed is next to Silvio bed,' he says. 'I am looking nancy. Thees schleepover voz to be our secret. If you say I cry at scary ghost stories, I deny everything. Lasht varning. Or no more gas for Italy.'

'He is just bitter,' I say to my private secretary, once he has hung up. 'Because all his women look like potatoes! Ha!'

My private secretary says that I ought to stop making jokes like that.

'This is becoming a real issue,' she says. 'Especially for women voters. They're starting to think you might be a misogynist.'

'A misogynist?' I scoff. 'Even with so many hot pieces of ass in my Cabinet?'

'Even so,' says my private secretary.

Must be her time of the month.

MERCOLEDÌ

Still in the office. A Cabinet meeting. It's an unusually terse and uncomfortable affair, mainly because we're not having it in a hot-tub. Even so, I still allow all the women to wear tiny bikinis, and rub sun cream into each other as much as they like.

Misogynist indeed.

GIOVEDÌ

My God. Can it be true? Apparently there is another tape!

'Seriously,' I say to my private secretary, when she wakes me up on the sofa. 'How? The woman must work in a circus.'

My private secretary rubs her eyes. Perhaps, she says, it's time for a new strategy. One tape even suggests that I don't usually use condoms, for heaven's sake. It doesn't look good.

She thinks it's time to sound contrite. Release a statement. To all newspapers. Not just the ones I own.

'And no jokes,' she continues. 'OK?'

'Fine,' I sigh. 'Tell them I'm not a saint.' My private secretary writes this down.

'Although,' I add, 'a saint wouldn't use a condom either, eh? Eh?'

'Oops,' says my private secretary, grimly, 'broken pencil.'

VENERDÌ

Another night in the office. Where else can I go? I have many homes, but they are all full of young women in bikini bottoms and big sunglasses, who spend their time drinking champagne and calling me Papi. I'm suddenly worried that they might all have tape recorders. Somewhere.

All the same, I'm lonely.

Who can I invite over, without causing scandal? I pick up the phone, and dial Moscow.

'Vladimir,' I say. 'Fancy a sleepover? Scary ghost stories? I'm sleeping on the sofa, but there's another sofa for you.'

'Will it have curtains?' says Putin, sulkily.

'Sure,' I say. Putin says he'll be here in time for a midnight feast.

SILVIO BERLUSCONI
12 NOVEMBER 2011

Oh, OK then. One more Berlusconi. I know it's similar to the last one, but he's just the gift that keeps on giving. Here he is shortly before he resigned, after losing his parliamentary majority.

LUNEDÌ

Si, si. It is me. Silvio Berlusconi. And I am liking your ass. I am sorry! Did I say ass? So rude of me! I am an old man, and my mind wanders. I meant your boobies. Hubba hubba.

Perhaps you would like to be my new Minister of Finance? Certainly, you are raising my interest rates! Come, sit upon my knee. No, my sweet. Do not worry about that. It is only inflation. Eh? Eh? Woof!

What is that you say? You are already my Minister of Finance? But my darling, how rude of me. I did not recognise you with your clothes on. And what can I do for you? What can be so important that it cannot wait for Hot Tub Cabinet?

Eh? You are worried about our bonds? So tighten the bonds. Tighter! Now in my cupboard you will find a feather, and a ... hello? Pah. Time of the month.

MARTEDÌ

My Finance Minister has quit, to become a weather girl. They say Italy is suffering a terrible shortage of weather girls, since I appointed them all to my Hot Tub Cabinet. Fine politicians! They can blow my warm front any time. Eh? Hubba. Eh?

Today, a meeting with Nicolas Sarkozy.

'Vous needs to step down,' he says, coming close and eyeballing my chin.

'I'm not standing on anything!' I shout.

'As Prime Minister,' he adds.

'Oh,' I say.

MERCOLEDÌ

Come, my darling. Run your fingers through my hair, and let me tell you of my journey. Not that hair. It is fragile. My other hair. Si. Mmmm. You were a wise appointment.

Much I have survived. But I must push through this austerity vote, then I shall resign. Austerity, it is not my thing. Although I am worried. These euro votes are difficult. Just look at the troubles of David Cameron.

What is that, my little cupcake? He had to whip his entire party? Big deal. I have been to many parties like that. In fact, what are you doing later?

GIOVEDÌ

A conference call with global leaders to discuss the debt crisis. There is Merkel, Sarkozy and my dusky friend Barack Obama. And David Cameron. Him, I do not respect at all. His hair transplant is even less convincing than mine.

We are discussing relations between the inner and outer eurozones. Myself, I am of the view that once one starts in the outer zone, an intimate acquaintance with the inner is inevitable. At least if you want a promotion. Eh? Eh?

'You gotta go,' says Obama.

'Then what?' I ask him. 'Maybe I come to Washington, and see your wife? Eh? And her ass?'

'Call terminated,' says Obama.

'He's a pig,' says Sarkozy, later.

'I hate him,' says Obama.

'Silvio can still hear you!' I say.

'That's fine,' says Obama.

VENERDÌ

'Any other business?' says my party chair.

'Si,' I say. 'Somebody loofah Silvio's back. Harder. Hmmm.'

I am holding what may be my last Hot Tub Cabinet.

'Prime Minister?' says my new Minister of Finance. 'It's a bit cold in this hot tub.'

A problem with the bill, I say. Huddle close. Hubba.

A journalist calls, wanting to know what I plan to do once I step down.

'I'm not sure,' I say. 'Silvio may read the weather. I hear there are vacancies.'

'Not for long,' she says.

GENERAL STANLEY McCHRYSTAL
26 JUNE 2010

This fellow was the commander of international forces in Afghanistan. This week he had to resign, after an embedded reporter for Rolling Stone *magazine wrote a devastating account of how he and his staff conducted themselves, which included disparaging remarks about Barack Obama and all of America's allies. Oh, and there was a film called* Avatar *in the cinemas. Although you'd probably have got that bit by yourselves.*

MONDAY

I am the commander of ISAF forces in Afghanistan, and I am a dignified Special Forces warrior monk. My body is my temple, war is my holy creed. I am at my happiest in my tent, with my aides, where we all eat sand and hit each other in the faces with rifle butts, for fun.

But today I gotta go to the city, to speak with a politician from France. It's f***ing gay.

'Yo, sir,' says one of my aides. 'You wanna know more about this French bitch?'

Hell no. These civilians are all the same. Especially the Euros. They just don't understand the enemy we're facing out here. Fact is, these blue-skinned bastards put up a hell of a fight, and blowing up their holy tree just made 'em come at us all the harder. Some of 'em were riding dragons. I shit you not one bit.

'He's got issues,' sighs my aide.

'They all do. Reckon you're outta touch, gone loco, too fixated on your own myth, livin' like some general guy outta some Hollywood movie. It's BS.'

'Civilian assholes,' I snort. 'Wouldn't even know Unobtanium if they choked on it.'

'Um, what?' says my aide.

TUESDAY

Back in the tent. 'Yo, General?' says another aide. 'We got the President on the satellite phone. Sounds like he gotta hard-on 'bout somethin'. You wanna take it?'

'Tell him I'm out,' I say, idly scratching my crotch with a bayonet. 'The dumbass.'

The aide nods meaningfully towards a corner of the tent. There's some journalist dude sitting there, who we granted all kinda special access. Forgot all about him.

'And you can quote me on that,' I say.

'Where you from again?' *Grazia*, he says. It's a British gossip weekly. Apparently I've a good chance of getting on the cover. It's down to either me or Piers Morgan's wedding.

'Not bad,' I say. 'You gettin' much?'

'Not really,' says the journalist. Just me and my boys savagely ridiculing the US Ambassador, the Vice-President, the President, the British, the French, the Canadians, Hamid Karzai, Queen Elizabeth II, Pope Benedict XVI, Muslims, vegetarians, English football, ginger hair and anybody who wears spectacles.

'Huh,' I say. 'Well, sorry to waste your time.'

WEDNESDAY

Turns out I gotta go back to Earth to see the wimps in the White House. Apparently the Prez is peeved by some profile I did in a magazine. But which magazine? My aides aren't sure. Coulda been *National Enquirer*, coulda been *Oprah*.

'*Bridal Weekly* was pretty racy,' says one.

Hell. I just ain't ready to go. The people here are teaching me so much. Did you know that they have a tail coming out of their heads which they use to control their horses?

'Seriously?' says an aide. 'Under their ... like ... turbans?'

THURSDAY

Here I am, face to face with the Commander in Chief in the Oval Office. He's not happy.

'Godammitt General!' he shouts, leaning forward across his desk. 'This is unacceptable! Nobody doubts your abilities as a soldier, but high command requires other disciplines! Diplomacy! Tact! Respect for the civilian authorities! And right now I'm just not sure these are attributes you possess!'

This isn't going well. I ask if I might make a single point in my defence.

President Obama says it had better be good.

'With respect, sir,' I say, 'you're a retard.'

FRIDAY

So that's that. I'm finished. I'm being relieved in my command by General David Petraeus. He's a hell of a soldier, and the sort of guy you'd always want on your side. Provided he could get the stick out of his ass in time to hit people with it. And you can quote me on that.

We're debriefing, before he flies out.

'You gotta appreciate,' I'm saying. 'We're doing good stuff out there. Did you know we have enemy bodies, artificially grown in a lab, which our operators can control via a combination of computers and telekinetic psychic ability?'

General Petraeus says he didn't know that, no.

'Trust me,' I say. 'You do not want to go off base any other way. It's a jungle out there.'

The General is confused. Says he thought it was more kinda sandy.

NICOLAS SARKOZY
26 MARCH 2011

The French are always fun. This was the week that Britain and France went to war in Libya.

LUNDI

Je suis Skyping David Cameron, who is le grande rosbif and really looks like one. Je suis standing très close to the camera, so as to pretend je suis not tiny.

He thinks le war in Libya should be run by NATO. I think it should be run by moi.

'As long as you're still involved,' says le meaty PM. Then he sniggers slightly. 'Because we don't want to go into a war without the French on our side!'

What is with le sniggering?

'Joke,' says Cameron. 'About the way you guys always surrender. Sorry.'

'Slur!' je suis saying. 'Outrage!'

'But think about it,' says Cameron.

'Actually,' I say, 'on reflection, vous sort of have a point.'

'See?' he says.

MARDI

'Oh Nicolas!' says Carla, who is my totally hot Italian wife, albeit starting to look une bit like an android. 'Je suis finding you so very attractive now you have your own war.'

'Mais, this is not why I did it,' I lie. 'La France has always been on le side of le oppressed! Albeit sometimes feebly.'

Two things, says Carla, are important. The first is that I must not allow les grand rosbif to take ownership of my war.

And le second, she says, is that I must have a uniform. Peut-être like Mussolini.

Je suis not convinced I can get away with dressing like Mussolini. Napoleon?

'Alors,' says Carla, sniffily. 'I shall order un Napoleon costume from Amazon.fr. Ages 7–9, oui?'

Je think that Carla is miffed avec le Mussolini thing. She knows perfectly well je suis actuallement un 10–12.

MERCREDI

Aujourd'hui, je suis phoning Barack Obama in le White House.

'Who is this?' says Obama. 'Are you, like, Canadian?'

It is I, I say. Nicolas Sarkozy. From La France. In Europe. Le middle bit. Where Germany is?

'Oh right,' says le President. 'Sure. I remember. You guys have got a war on, right? With the guy who dresses like Elizabeth Taylor?'

C'est vrai, I say. And listen here, sonny Jim. We are appreciative of votre support thus far, such as the minor way vous have provided most of the bombs and planes and suchlike, but Nicolas Sarkozy must have ownership of this conflict. Standing proud comme un slightly taller Napoleon.

'Dude,' says Obama. 'Totally. Whatever. You own all the wars you like. Have Iraq, too, if you fancy it. But Jeez. How short was Napoleon?'

JEUDI

Catastrophe! Le grand stupid rosbif is insisting that our forces be run by Nato. Je suis furious. Mais not as furious as Carla. Even though je suis now wearing le Napoleon uniform, et looking très dapper, she is still dans le major huff.

'Les real men own wars!' she is shouting. 'Je should have shacked up with Tony Blair! Has his wife not said il est un very sensitive lover?'

Shhhh, I say. Mon cherie, it's not so bad. At le very least, le rosbif and I shall be standing shoulder to shoulder.

'Shoulder to elbow,' says Carla.

VENDREDI

Carla has convinced me. Alors, je suis Skyping David Cameron again. Je suis in my Napoleon uniform, mais je have removed le triangular hat so as to not look like le pillock.

'Jamais!' I am saying. 'Never, never, non, non, non. La France shall not back down! I shall not surrender command of the forces liberating Libya! I, Nicolas Sarkozy, must be in charge! This is final!'

'Please?' says le rosbif.

'Oh, OK then,' I say.

NICOLAS SARKOZY
22 OCTOBER 2011

And again. This was the week that a child was born to President Nicolas Sarkozy and his wife, Carla Bruni. At the time, the war in Libya was drawing to a close, and there was a euro crisis going on. I forget which one.

LUNDI

Alors. Notre enfant is being born this week and je suis terribly excited.

'Je suis looking forward to not being shorter than you anymore!' I say to my hot wife, Carla, whom I have been married to for ages, mais who allowed me to knock her up only quand je started bombing stuff.

'But Nicolas!' she says. 'Je suis always taller than you!'

'C'est vrai,' I agree, 'but not normally when vous are lying on votre back.'

We cannot decide upon le name. If it is a boy, I favour 'Louis'. Je suis unsure about a surname, but I would like it to start with an X. Or Napoleon. Napoleon is nice.

Having babies is always fun. I have had several, avec several women, for I am French.

This one, I have sworn not to exploit for le political capital. Although, for les purely personal reasons, je suis thinking of setting up le webcam.

MARDI

Normally, if I was to leave Paris to meet with another

woman, les Parisian magazines would buzz avec speculation of les extra-marital affairs. Pas this time. In part, this
is because la hot wife is avec le bun dans le oven, but also
it is because je suis visiting Angela Merkel.

With the greatest of respect, je ne would pas. Alors,
even Silvio Berlusconi ne would pas. J'assume.

'Nicolas,' says Angela, 'you must be sitting down.'

'But I am already sitting down,' I say, to which Angela
says she is sorry; it can be hard to tell. Then she says that
the eurozone is in crisis, and we must agree to write off
some debt.

'Je suis having a baby,' I say. 'C'est not a good time.'

'Euro is a nice name,' says Angela.

'No it isn't,' I say.

MERCREDI
Vous had better not be having affair avec that freakishly
tall doctor, I say to la hot wife when I call her in the
hospital.

'Je suis not particularly in le mood,' says Carla.
'Strangely. Also, il est five foot seven. Where are you? Je
suis about to pop.'

Je suis stuck in Frankfurt, I explain. Avec Angela.
Sounds a bit like I am going to miss it. Je suis sorry if
that gives vous le hump.

My hot wife is silent for a moment, and then says that
the doctor might be five foot nine, actuellement.

JEUDI
Back in Paris, where I get the news that my war has paid
off and Gaddafi is dead.

'Also,' says my driver, 'you have had a baby.'

Alors, back to le hospital, pour le brief visit avec la

hot wife and une baby. Malheureusement, I never did get round to setting up that webcam.

'Je presume vous at least tweeted?' I say.

Carla says non. Then I tell her I must rush off, for le politically vital campaigning visit to le provincial waste disposal centre.

'Shall I take her?' I say.

'Non!' says Carla, and reminds me that I promised not to exploit this birth for campaign purposes.

'Ce n'est pas that,' I say. 'She just makes me look taller.'

VENDREDI

Back in le hospital, I realise we have not yet decided upon a name. 'I have,' says Carla. 'I favour something Italian, as befits my dual heritage.'

Augustus has le nice ring to it, I say. Or Tiberius.

'Mais she is a girl,' says Carla, 'and I have called her Giulia.'

C'est bon, I say. Provided le middle name is Caesar.

CARLA BRUNI
13 MARCH 2010

Now here's his wife. This week, the French press was speculating as to their respective extra-marital affairs.

LUNDI

Je suis standing in le presidential bedchamber in the Élysée, reading of the latest internet rumours of our infidelity on le iPhone. Le husband, Nicolas, looks un peu nervous. He is terrified of le iPhone. Once, he was stuck underneath it for le whole weekend.

'There is no need to cower,' I tell him. 'For it is not as though I am about to fling le iPhone at your tiny, tiny head.'

Nicolas points out that he is not cowering. In fact, he is standing fully upright. 'You are deceived by le perspective,' he says, huffily.

'Gaaaah!' I shout. 'How dare you be spuriously linked to la karate-kicking ecology minister!'

You started it, he says, by being spuriously linked to le greasy, moonfaced French popstar nobody has ever heard of outside France, who is looking exactly like all zose other French popstars nobody has ever heard of outside France.

'How dare you!' I shout, again. 'Le French pop is le envy of the world!'

Then I start laughing, and so does he.

'No, but seriously,' I say after quite a while, wiping les eyes. 'Je suis genuinely quite cross.'

MARDI

'These rumours,' I say. 'They will not stand. We must do le press conference, to show that I am la demure little wife, and you are le powerful husband. So I shall wear le see-through chiffon shirt with no brassière, and you shall stand on le brick.'

Nicolas says non. He is not ashamed. He just has le hobby of standing slightly below les elbows of beautiful women.

I am jealous, he says, because all of my rumoured affairs have been so much lower-rent than his. He is not wrong. Je must find a mighty politician of my own, to have rumoured, untrue affair. Mais qui? Pas le Gordon Brown. Il smells kinda icky.

MERCREDI

Alors, je suis sitting at our dining table with le laptop. J'ai un plan to start beacoup de rumours about affairs on Twitter. J'ai un list of famous people, mainly politicians and rock stars, et je plan to get through them all by sundown. So to speak.

Nicolas clambers up into his highchair and scans the list.

'Silvio Berlusconi. Eric Clapton. The Dalai Lama. George Bush. Mick Jagger. The former French PM Laurent Fabius.'

He looks confused. 'Mais je suis pretty sure you have already bonked some of them,' he says.

I sigh. He may be right. But which?

JEUDI

Nicolas says le Twitter is le old hat.

'Tu wants to be speaking avec le British press,' he points out. 'Parce que en Angleterre, political glamour means dressing in green wellies et une shonky old dress from M&S. Ils sont gagging for it.'

C'est vrai. Le British press even kept suggesting that Nicolas fancied Rachida Dati. And she looks like le toothy fish without le chin.

VENDREDI

Aujourd'hui, Nicolas est in Londres avec le big old pongy Gordon Brown. Un journaliste asks about notre affairs. Je watch it on le telly.

'Do you think I have time for this?' he shouts. 'C'est un outrage! Je suis le President of la France! Je suis un terribly busy man!'

Later, je call him on the iPhone. 'You are right,' I tell him. 'I wouldn't really have time for an affair either.'

'I shall clear some space in our schedules,' promises Nicolas.

'Je t'aime,' I say.

SARAH PALIN
16 JANUARY 2010

Back to America. Whatever happened to Sarah Palin? Here she is post-election, having landed a pundit role with Fox TV.

MONDAY

'You wanna come and shoot some rocks off the wall?' says Todd. 'Me an' some of our many kids with made-up names are headin' out now.'

'Damnit Todd,' I snap. 'I ain't got time for shootin' no rocks. I'm starting a new job with Fox News. I gotta know all that fancy stuff. Pakistan, the bailout, healthcare, Beyoncé, Goldman Sachs suchlike and et cetera. Or else the commie liberal elite is going to tear me a new one.'

I'm holed up with my top advisers: a man called Derek who turned up yesterday sellin' encyclopaedias, and Billybob Jones, who won a rosette at the Wasilla Country Fair for identifying livestock.

'Razorback!' they'll shout at me, or 'Planet Earth!' Then they'll tell me the answers and I'll write them down on a white index card and put it in a pile. I wish I'd paid more attention to this sorta stuff before.

TUESDAY

'But Sarah,' says Todd, kicking his way into the room over a mountain of index cards. 'You ain't been out to shoot rocks in a week.'

I put my fingers in my ears. 'Fanny Mae ain't a person,' I say. 'The Bush Doctrine legitimises preventative war. The red wattle hog can reach 1,500lb.'

'You ain't eating,' he says. 'You ain't sleeping. And how come you're waving that gun around?'

'It's for Derek,' I say. 'So he don't leave.'

Derek looks towards the door. 'You can keep the encyclopaedias,' he says. 'Please. I got a wife.'

WEDNESDAY

Today I got to fly to New York, which is known as the Big Apple but apparently isn't one. There's so many index cards out in the hall that Todd, Track, Trig and Topper have to bring in the snowplough.

'Healthcare,' I tell them. 'Job creation. The capital of China is Beijing. Terrorists now come from Yemen.'

'What's a Tophead Tux?' shouts Billybob.

'Is it one of my kids?' I ask.

THURSDAY

That all went OK, even though they wouldn't let me take my cards on the show. I was surprised by the lack of livestock questions.

Afterwards, I got talking to Bill O'Reilly, the host. 'You were great,' I told him. 'Billybob can name a goat faster'n you can spit, but whoever does your briefing is smarter.'

'It's autocue,' said O'Reilly.

'That's a pretty name,' I say. 'Where's she from?'

FRIDAY

Back to Wasilla, where Todd and eight or nine of the kids snow-shoe to the airport. Derek escaped, they say. Tunnelled out under the index cards.

'I don't need him,' I tell them. 'I got this stuff licked. Chrysler! Basra! Hamid Karzai! Piece of cake.'

'Hell,' says Todd. 'You sound clever enough to be a liberal.'

So I guess I'd better stop there.

MICHELLE OBAMA
28 MAY 2011

Americans visiting Europe. It's always the same. This week there was a wardrobe malfunction outside Downing Street, and David Cameron got far too excited about a barbecue.

MONDAY

Barack whoops as Air Force One touches down on the runway, and says it feels like coming home.

'Ireland?' I say, looking up from my book. 'You're from Ireland now?'

Everywhere we go, my husband reckons he's from there. Someday soon, I reckon the Pentagon guys will wake up in the middle of the night to tell us they've found life on Mars. And it'll be the long-lost uncle of his third cousin, once removed.

'Honey,' says Barack. 'Don't talk like that. These people love the craic.'

'Sounds like Chicago,' I say.

'Different craic,' says Barack. 'And thus, I shall be drinking Guinness. Playing that weird hockey game. Potentially dancing. Electorally, it's vital. For thirty-five million Americans genuinely believe themselves to be residually Irish, in defiance of all evidence to the contrary.'

'Just like you,' I say.

'Oh,' says Barack. 'Wow.'

TUESDAY

We were meant to stay in Ireland last night, but we had to fly over to England early, because of some ash cloud from Iceland. Barack is in a filthy mood about it, because this meant he missed a night of craic.

'Does anything else come from Iceland?' he says, bitterly. 'Except for ash clouds?'

'You?' I suggest, but Barack isn't laughing. He spent the whole journey over in the Air Force One toilet, puking up his Guinness. Just as well he gave the craic a miss, in my view.

We're staying in Buckingham Palace tonight, which is the home of the Queen and a man called Philip, who my briefing notes say probably won't be allowed to talk to me. We've brought our own car because we don't trust British cars, and we've had the windows in the Palace replaced, because we don't trust British windows either.

'Shouldn't we have brought our own Queen?' I ask the nearest Secret Service guy. 'This one might have a bomb in it.'

His eye go wide and he runs off, muttering into his sleeve. I hate being American sometimes.

WEDNESDAY

We didn't have to defuse the Queen, because the Secret Service decided she wasn't big enough to keep a bomb in. Which was a relief.

And I was right about Prince Philip. He hardly said a word. Although when we stood on the doorstep and my dress blew up, I could tell he really wanted to.

THURSDAY

Bits of this country are really backward. Yesterday we

ate in Downing Street, where they still cook outside. Then Barack was addressing both houses of Parliament, and had to do it in this old draughty hall. They hadn't even painted it.

'So I'm confused,' I said to Barack afterwards. 'There's MPs and also Lords? So who was the most important person there?'

Barack said it was apparently somebody called John Bercow. Which was odd, as he wasn't even in the notes.

FRIDAY
Today I'm back in Washington.

'Where's Daddy?' asks Malia.

'France,' I tell her. 'He's probably from there.'

'Did you meet Princess Kate Middleton?' asks Sasha.

'Honey,' I say, firmly. 'She was a lovely girl, but she should not be your role model. She's only famous because of her husband.'

'Like you,' says Malia.

'Oh,' I say. 'Wow.'

MITT ROMNEY
28 JULY 2012

Although that trip was a triumph compared to this one. Just before the Olympic Games, Mitt Romney arrived in London. Michelle Obama was there too, generally being liked more.

MONDAY

This week I am embarking upon a tour of Yurp and I want to make a good impression.

And I'm planning on making this impression while wearing an air-tight bubble suit, so I don't need to touch anybody.

'Inadvisable, sir,' says my Yurpish etiquette aide, who is peering into a *Lonely Planet*. Apparently the Brits can be kinda prickly.

'Darn,' I say. 'I guess I can wear gloves. They're all just so very grubby. They still have leprosy in Yurp, right?'

Ann, my wife, is particularly concerned. She's taking over a horse to compete in the Olympic Games.

'But I'm worried,' she says, 'that a mob of malnourished, scrofulous London peasants might try to eat it.'

'Negative, ma'am,' says the aide. 'I mean, they might try, but hardly any of them can manage a decent bite. On account of their teeth.'

TUESDAY

'OK,' says the etiquette guide. 'I been reading up. You

wanna make friends? You gotta diss the Games. The cost, the chaos, the security. These Brits like a moan.'

This surprises me. I ran the Winter Olympics in Salt Lake City. If somebody had dissed them, I'd been mad enough to strap them to my car roof and drive them for twelve hours through the snow. Like I famously did with my dog.

But hell, these people scrape bits off pigs and eat them in pubs for fun. So whaddaya expect?

'This is the main guy you'll be meeting,' says the Yurp guy, bringing out some photos. 'David Cameron. He's the Prime Minister. Some folks don't like him, on account of the way he's rich.'

'As rich as me?' I say.

'Don't be ridiculous,' he says, and we all have a good old laugh.

'Hang on,' I say, leafing through the photos. 'Who's this clown?'

That's the Mayor of London, he says. A very educated fellow, by all accounts.

'Oh,' I say. 'That clownish exterior must be wholly misleading.'

'Apparently,' he says, 'not.'

WEDNESDAY

Darnit. This is a disaster. Seems the Brits don't like being told their Games might suck.

Even Cameron seems offended.

'Of course it's easier if you hold an Olympic Games in the middle of nowhere,' he told the press.

I guess he'll feel pretty damn stupid when he realises Salt Lake City isn't the middle of nowhere at all. Actually, it's off centre by a good few thousand miles.

Then I went to his house, and everybody got to sniggering because I was talking about 'looking out of the backside of Downing Street' and, apparently, 'backside' means 'ass'.

'I might as well have said fanny,' I shout at the Yurp guy, afterwards.

'Never say fanny,' he replies.

Then I met the new head of the Labour Party and had to call him 'Mr Leader' because I'd totally forgotten his name.

'What even is his name?' I asked Tony Blair, when I met him later.

'David Miliband,' said Blair. 'Or maybe Ed Miliband. Actually, I can't remember, either.'

THURSDAY

Barack Obama calls. This is unusual.

'Gather you're making a bit of a backside of things,' he says, sounding amused. 'In that country with which we share so much Anglo-Saxon heritage. Bumped into Michelle yet?'

'Screw you,' I say. 'Mr President, sir. Anyway, I got a plan to rescue my British reputation.'

'Oh yeah?' he says.

'Yeah,' I say. 'I'm going on CNN, to be interviewed by Piers Morgan.'

Obama says that should do the trick, given that the Brits watch CNN religiously, and love Morgan more than anyone else alive.

'That's what my Yurp guy says,' I tell him.

'I reckon you need a new Yurp guy,' he says.

FRIDAY

Last night, the clown mayor united 60,000 people in cheering how much of an idiot I was.

This trip has been such a mess that David Cameron calls, to say thanks.

'To be honest, I wasn't really sure whether Brits were going to get behind the Games,' he says, 'but you've really done the trick.'

Who needs England, anyway? I'm outta here.

Next stop Israel, where they're bound to love me. What could go wrong? I'm arriving on Saturday. Looking forward to some ribs.

VERONICA LARIO BERLUSCONI
9 MAY 2009

Back to Berlusconi. Well, Mrs Berlusconi. Well, the ex Mrs Berlusconi.

LUNEDÌ

It is important, as the wife of a world leader, to remain contained. Even when that world leader is very small, and un idiota.

'Ciao bella!' says my husband, who has called from his boat. 'Ha! So what do you think of the new gardener? Hot, eh?'

I look out of the window. The new gardener is showering under one of the sprinklers. She runs her hands over her black bikini and pouts at me.

'How is she with aphids?' I say, mildly.

Excellent, says Silvio. So good that he's thinking of making her Minister of Agriculture. Although not until she's older and can vote.

'But listen!' he continues. 'More importantly! Has she seen my statue?'

I grimace. 'The new statue?' I say. 'The one of Michelangelo's *David*, but with his face chiselled off and your face chiselled on?'

'Si!' smirks Silvio. 'Ha! Just tell her it isn't accurate from the waist down, eh?'

'Isn't it?' I say, and I slam the phone down.

MARTEDÌ

This morning, I learn that my husband has attended the birthday party of an 18-year-old actress. And worse, it turns out that I am expected to judge a wet T-shirt competition between his gardener, his chauffeur and his Finance Minister. No wife should stand for this! Normally I would merely write a letter of protest to the newspapers.

No longer. Ya basta! I call him and declare that I want a divorce.

'I warn you,' says Silvio. 'I have a very attractive lawyer.'

I don't care, I tell him. And nor will the judge.

'Seriously,' says Silvio. 'Great ass.' I sigh. He belches.

'What's your problem,' he says after a while, 'anyway?'

MERCOLEDÌ

Now the bishops are criticising his behaviour. There is a front page calling for 'sobriety' in their official newspaper. Grande sorpresa! A few years ago we had a very important Cardinal for tea.

Silvio came home late, approached him from behind, grabbed him on the backside and told him that all the best tarts wore red.

We had an argument about it later.

I was very angry. Silvio was very defensive.

'She was the ugliest bitch I ever saw!' he said. 'I was only trying to break the ice.'

GIOVEDÌ

He calls from his sunbed.

He says he wants more people to like him so he's trying to look more like Barack Obama.

'Nice,' I say.

'Amore!' sighs Silvio. 'Sweetheart!

'My leetle stella di pornografia! This is all so silly. My hot lawyer? She says we should patch things up. Me, I agree.

'You have been led astray! Would I be involved with a minor? Never! Not even a really sexy minor who was begging for it! You have been led astray by the left-wing media. And why? For they are jealous! For the women of the Left are disgusting!'

Have I, he asks, never seen women in the Cabinet of Gordon Brown? They all look like melting snowmen.

'You, my darling,' he adds, 'could never be of the Left. Even now, in your mature years, you could at worst be a Social Democrat!'

I hang up on him. He calls back to ask whether his lawyer can come and see the statue. I hang up on him again.

VENERDÌ

The new gardener is mashing up a flowerbed with a huge fork. Hair is everywhere, mascara is running down her cheeks and her bikini is streaked with mud.

'Arresto!' I shout. 'What are you doing?'

The gardener turns to me, crying.

He promised she could be an EU Commissioner, she says. Or at least an MEP. Even Minister for Agriculture would have done. But now he's changed his mind. She wants to know where the aphids are. He always asked about them. So now she's going to douse them in weedkiller.

'Aphids aren't flowers,' I tell her.

Then I tell her that, if she really wants to upset him, she should smash up his stupid statue.

'He wanted you to know that it wasn't accurate from the waist down,' I say.

'The brute.' The gardener goes storming off across the lawn.

Later, she comes back, brandishing a chisel.

'It is now,' she says.

VLADIMIR PUTIN
3 MARCH 2012

It's the run-up to the Russian elections. British media is dominated by the war in Syria and accusations that David Cameron rode a horse that the Metropolitan Police loaned to the former News International executive Rebekah Brooks.

MONDAY

Hallo, Eenglish. Da, I'm Putin. You vant shake hand? Is weak, your hand. Like hand of woman. And not Russian woman. Eenglish woman. In my country, ve are not even shaking hands as greeting. Ve are breaking cinderblocks, vith head. Dmitri! Fetch cinderblock for our friend. Nyet? Ladyman.

You vant vodka? Arm-wrestle? Sushi? You think I am joking? Of course I am joking. But tell me, Eenglish friend, why is the idea of me offering you sushi so funny? Spell it out for me, as though I am moron. You think I am moron? Huh? Dmitri! A glass of water for Eenglish, who is looking pale. You know, I am liking your country. Is good place. Although your Prime Minister is terrible ladyman, too. I call him, you know, when he arrive.

'David,' I say. 'You vant respect, you must wrestle bear.' He reply my suggestion quite amusing, because it sound like I suggest he do it naked. But I am not laughing. For who wears clothes to wrestle bear?

TUESDAY

Ah, Eenglish. You are still here? You vant cup of tea? Dmitri, fetch cup of tea. Dmitri is President, you know. Much respected. And biscuit, Dmitri! Move! I haff not much time, for I must go and relax, by fighting with hammers. But first, you are vishing to talk of election, yes? So many misunderstandings! Some are even believing that I, Putin, vould vish to round up those who do not vote for me, and conduct mafia-style hit, or put in gulag. But believe me, this is not something I vould ever consider. It vould take far too long.

WEDNESDAY

Syria, of course, ees big worry. Ve cannot keep supplying Assad vith endless stream of veapons used to slaughter his own population. For in time, ve may need them to slaughter our own population.

So, I am calling Obama. 'Listen,' I am saying, 'Ve must arrange conference. Me, you, the Chinamen. Perhaps the British and French. And then we can sit around big table, take off shirts, explain our positions, and create plan for ceasefire.'

'Sorry,' says the American. 'Take off our shirts, did you say?'

With photo-op, I tell him. Is one of two major preconditions. Other being that future of Assad Government must be guaranteed.

'No deal!' says Obama.

'In vests?' I suggest.

THURSDAY

You vill notice I haff no wrinkles. The face, it is smooth, like exposed shoulder bone of last judo partner. Often, many are wondering how this happens. In truth, there is not reason why man of early middle age should haff face like that of poisoned President of Ukraine. I am merely exercising face. I haff muscles in forehead can break rock. Test. Hit with rock.

Surgery? Nyet. Although I am not afraid of surgery. I would do it myself, with own fingernails. Without anaesthetic. For election literature. In snow.

FRIDAY

Three days till election. Ze future is not certain. Perhaps I will win, perhaps I will steal. Is 50-50. Two horse race. Da.

Today, David Cameron calls, to talk Syria. 'Obama has told you of plans for naked conference?' I tell him.

'I need a month,' says Cameron. 'I'm working out.'

Listen, I say. I hear you haff problem. Vith journalists, and horse. You vant advice? Kill horse. Chop head from horse, and leave in journalist bed.

Cameron says horse already dead. I haff new respect for this man. 'You vant arm wrestle?' I say.

REEM HADDAD
18 JUNE 2011

You might not remember this woman. She was the main spokesman at the Syrian ministry of information. She looked like Julianne Moore, she sounded like Miss Moneypenny, and everything she said was utterly mad. She lasted about three days. The same week, to much global fuss, a young lesbian blogger from Damascus who the world assumed had been abducted by the regime was revealed to actually be a male American student in Scotland.

MONDAY

Actually, it is not Monday. My God, where are you getting this from? I am a spokeswoman for the Syrian Ministry of Information, and I can tell you quite categorically that actually it is still last Thursday. So it is quite incorrect to state that my country has been racked with protest since Friday prayers, because Friday hasn't happened yet.

With respect, I am in Syria and you are not. How can you think you know better than me? But of course you are welcome to come to our country! What a suggestion! It is simply that if we find out you are a journalist, you might not leave again.

And if you were here, you would see that there are no protests. We would know. We have cameras everywhere. Literally, everywhere. Even in the toilets. So how can you say there are protests? That noise? There is no noise. Oh, that noise. That noise is just the wind. The screaming, shooting wind. Yes. And now I am hanging up.

TUESDAY

My country is beautiful and peaceful and these lies are hurting me. We have nail varnish here, you know. We have Dior. Look at my hair. Do we not have straighteners? How can you believe that a country with straighteners could be capable of doing these horrible things? In my country, people would not make these accusations. Certainly not twice.

No, I don't know if it is Tuesday yet. At the Ministry of Information we do not have that information. But I can tell you that you are quite wrong to suggest that protesters are being shot. Did I not mention that we have hair straighteners? In fact, it is perfectly simple. When you see your friends, you want to give them a present. Yes? So the soldiers in the army are seeing their friends, and doing that.

And yes, perhaps some of them are giving bullets. Quite quickly. But that is all. Goodbye.

WEDNESDAY

Of course this is not a video of a secret Syrian jail you are showing me! Good heavens, why would you think this? Because there is a picture of President Assad on the wall? In fact, that is not President Assad. It is a completely different northwest London optometrist.

Do you not realise that they all look the same? Even if it was, how can you make these terrible accusations? I see no evidence of torture. Clearly somebody has just dropped a bottle of ketchup. And that man is just having a bath.

A long, long facedown bath. Many Syrians are doing

this every day. In fact, it is a growing trend. But nothing more. Nightmares? Why would I be having nightmares? For God's sake! We have hair straighteners. I'm hanging up right now.

THURSDAY

Fired? For embarrassing the regime? Me? Actually that is a quite outrageous suggestion. In fact, I have been promoted to my new job, which is the highly prestigious position of person who sits in a darkened room in the basement of our state television station, not technically being allowed to speak to anybody.

No, actually the air-conditioning is perfect. My hair is not frizzy at all. Really, if you persist in telling these lies, I will have to hang up on you again. What sort of people are you?

FRIDAY

Goodness gracious, no. I am not a middle-aged man living in Edinburgh who is secretly pretending to be a Syrian woman. Between us, you've had me on the run some of the time this last week, but with this one you're totally barking up the wrong tree. My God. Wow.

MERKOZY
10 DECEMBER 2011

At the height of the euro crisis, the interests of France and Germany were so aligned that many started referring to Angela Merkel and Nicolas Sarkozy as a single entity.

MONDAY

We are THE MERKOZY. Hear us roar.

We are deeply efficient but also take long lunches. We dine upon sausage made out of snails. We have occasional disagreements about what you call dogs from the Alsace region, but that aside we speak with one voice. Neither of us has any objection to wearing heels.

This week, we must save the euro. Again. We have already saved Greece. We saved Italy, even though Italy kept humping our leg. Bleeugh.

'THERE MUST BE GREATER FISCAL INTEGRATION,' we have started saying. One of us thinks we could sell this better if we cloned ourselves into a more loveable mini-monster called MERKOZUKI. One of us finds this naff.

TUESDAY

Our disagreements never last long. One of us has a habit of surrendering to the other one. We think you know which one that is. Oui.

Today, we are speaking to President Obama. Sometimes, when negotiating with China, we team up to become THE OBAMERKOZY. We do not like it. Neither of us gets to be the head.

'Guys,' says President Obama. 'I know you've got your reasons. But do you really think you're going to get this Robin Hood Tax thing past the Brits?'

'WE ARE THE MERKOZY,' we tell him. 'WE STEAL FROM THE RICH TO GIVE TO THE POOR.'

'Whatever,' he says. 'You guys gotta week to save the euro.'

'WE HAVE SAVED IT BEFORE,' we say. 'EVEN WITH THE HUMPING.'

WEDNESDAY

We are speaking with Cameron.

'YOU MUST OBEY,' we say. 'OUR WRATH IS TO BE FEARED.'

It is not impossible that we are in a slightly bad mood. One of us fears our hot wife fancies us less since we became 50 per cent middle-aged German lady, and may shack up with a passing rock star.

'No can do,' says Cameron. 'Sorry.'

'SILENCE,' we shout. 'IF YOU PERSIST IN THIS BEHAVIOUR YOU WILL BE EXCLUDED FROM CORE EU DECISION-MAKING SUCH AS HOW YELLOW BANANAS MUST BE!'

'Oh no,' says Cameron. 'Oh boo-hoo. See my trembling lip.'

We do not understand his values.

THURSDAY

We are approaching crunch time. THE MERKOZY must save the euro again.

This time, there will be no humping. We have quite

lost track of what has happened to Silvio Berlusconi. We suspect he is in a hot tub somewhere.

'THE MERKOZY IS FEELING TENSE,' we keep shouting.

One of us is on a diet and one of us keeps eating sandwiches. Irritatingly, this is the same one of us.

FRIDAY

We are THE MERKOZY and we are feeling a bit knackered, frankly. British Cameron has taken his ball and gone home. We do not understand why our threats regarding British irrelevance in new laws over aubergine firmness, etc, have not worked.

'BUGGER,' we say. One thing is clear. Next time we have to morph into Camerkozy. It will be considerably harder to pull off.

'Am I bothered?' says Cameron. 'I'll just team up with the Hungarian guy.'

'WHAT WILL YOU BE CALLED?' we ask him, quite irritably.

'God knows,' says Cameron. 'Who is the Hungarian guy?'

'WE ARE THE MERKOZY,' we say. 'BUT WE DON'T KNOW EITHER.'

NELSON MANDELA
28 JUNE 2008

Nelson Mandela is in London. You can take the piss out of Nelson Mandela, right?

MONDAY
For twenty-seven years I was prisoner 46664 of the apartheid regime in South Africa. For eighteen of these years I lived in a small cell in Robben Island. My nights were spent sweating against rough woollen sheets. My days were spent working in the lime quarry. I received one letter every six months. This was a hard time. And yet, there was an upside. For I had no telephone. Bono never called.

Today I arrive in London, at the Dorchester Hotel. This, I enjoy. These are the trappings of wealth, denied to me for so many years. Fine curtains, which I may have made into a shirt. Luxurious carpets, which I may, who knows, have made into a shirt. How strange that, inside, I feel the same. Looking from my window, I come to accept that part of me may always be a prisoner. Because out there, somewhere, is Naomi Campbell.

TUESDAY
A man must make difficult choices. Everybody knows what I am talking about. When there is an individual who is loathed and despised by all, sometimes the honourable course is to hold back. To understand, not condemn.

So I will meet with Gordon Brown. But I will not go to his house. Instead, he comes to my hotel with Sarah, his wife.

'Nelson!' he says, sweating slightly. 'A real, uh, pleasure to see you. Great shirt.'

'Shakira says hi,' I tell him.

The Prime Minister has come to see me about Robert Mugabe. I tell him that this is a complex situation. Mugabe is my old comrade in arms, a fellow struggler for liberation. I am the old man of Africa. I must remain neutral. His shirts must remain drab. In private, I may disapprove of his actions. In public, I must bite my tongue.

I give Mr Brown a fatherly smile. 'As I notice,' I say, 'that you are so often biting your own.'

'It's a twitch,' explains Sarah.

WEDNESDAY

Tonight there is to be a dinner in my honour. Oprah Winfrey, Bob Geldof, Will Smith, Robert de Niro. True statesmen, every one. Naomi Campbell will be there, also. I am not concerned. Security is tight.

The news from Zimbabwe is most alarming. Opposition supporters are being beaten and killed. Morgan Tsvangirai has pulled out of the election. This has gone too far. In Harare, Mugabe's shirt is green, red, yellow and black. In Chitungwiza it is red, spotted with white. In Harare it is white, yellow, black and gold. A fetching shiny material. My heart is heavy. My arms are frail, but my fists still clench. Something must be done.

THURSDAY

Last night I condemned the tragic failure of leadership in Zimbabwe.

Afterwards the British Prime Minister approached to thank me.

'It had to be said,' I told him, sadly. 'But my friend, speak freely. I see that you are still biting your tongue.'

'It's a twitch,' said his wife. 'Remember?'

FRIDAY

Tonight a concert to celebrate my 90th birthday. Much money will be raised for 46664, my charity for HIV/Aids. I am particularly excited about seeing Leona Lewis, off *The X Factor*. Obviously.

Naomi Campbell has a ticket, but will not be allowed on stage. We are not expecting any trouble.

At lunchtime, a surprise. Robert Mugabe calls.

'Why have you sided with them?' he shouts. 'This is not about democracy! The homosexual imperialists will not be happy until Zimbabwe is a white man's country again! They will take everything! They will take the shirt from my back!'

I tell him I have first dibs.

CARLA BRUNI
18 JULY 2009

Back in France, on a similar theme, here's Carla Bruni again.

LUNDI

'Mais bien sûr!' I say to my husband, 'I must go to New York and sing one of my songs at the birthday concert for Nelson Mandela!'

My husband stops attempting to fit le adult toothbrush into his tiny, childlike mouth, and peers at me sideways. We are doing our morning ablutions at our twin sinks in the discreetly sloping bathroom in the Élysée Palace. Otherwise, alors, sideways would not be an option. And yet, little Nicolas adopts le uncertain face, and says he's not sure that this is une bon idée.

'Oh 'usband!' I laugh, nibbling coquettishly at my toothbrush. 'You are jealous? Because we were once lovers?'

'You and Nelson Mandela?' says Nicolas.

I shrug. Maybe not. It is so hard to keep le track.

But anyway, says Nicolas, it's not that. It's just the whole idea. What would I even sing?

'One of my big hits!' I tell him.

Nicolas starts choking.

'Sweetheart!' I say. 'Please! Less of this foolish pride! We must get you le enfant toothbrush!'

'Oui,' says Nicolas, quickly. 'Le toothbrush. That was it. Silly old moi.'

MARDI

I am decided. But it must be le duet. Also on the bill is Stevie Wonder.

Alors, I fetch le peculiar French telephone with le weird extra earpiece on the back, and give him a call.

'Stevie,' I say, affecting le premier sexy voice. 'I just called to say I love you.'

'Who is this?' says Stevie Wonder. 'And do you have laryngitis?'

I explain. It is I, le First Lady of France, the beautiful yet curiously accessible Carla Bruni. Perhaps we once were lovers. Who can say? This weekend, anyway, I suggest a duet. For Nelson.

'Oh yeah,' says Stevie Wonder. 'I heard you'd done a song. Wasn't it in French? Never realised you'd made a career out of it.'

I sigh. There have been many songs, and many albums. And all in French. Poor Stevie Wonder! It must be so hard keeping up with things that everybody else knows, when one is blind!

'Not usually,' says Stevie Wonder.

MERCREDI

Aretha Franklin isn't returning my calls. And no luck with Cyndi Lauper, either. She agrees that les girls just wanna have le fun, but says that she'd rather have fun on stage with Lil' Kim.

'Although I quite liked that French song,' she said. Le slag.

Soon, I may start throwing things. Je suis in a right mood.

'Ha!' I say to le husband, bitterly. 'You are ashamed of my music! I hate you! It is no wonder that you are cowering behind le sofa!'

'I am merely standing behind le sofa,' says Nicolas.

'Sorry,' I say.

JEUDI

I cannot begin to understand this reluctance. It is almost as though these other artists feel I am not a performer of their calibre, but merely famous for removing le clothes and marrying le shortarse.

'Or something,' agrees Nicolas. 'So. Best call le whole thing off, eh?'

Non! For there is still Dave Stewart, of Eurythmics! For he has agreed to a duet, and we were never even lovers. I think. New York here we come!

Nicolas still feels it is a bad idea.

'Oh 'usband,' I tease. 'You are just worried that Barack Obama will be ostentatiously peering at le bottom again!'

If he does, I add, he must simply take revenge by ostentatiously peering at le bottom of Michelle.

'But I'll be doing that anyway,' Nicolas reminds me. 'For I am French.'

VENDREDI

An argument while we pack, when Nicolas says we shouldn't bother packing my guitar.

'Fine!' I shout. 'And we shouldn't pack your brick, either!'

Nicolas hates to travel without his brick. At a podium, without it, he must stand on books. For a President, this is undignified. He hangs his head.

'OK,' he sighs. 'You win. Take le guitar. Oui, you belong on stage with Aretha Franklin, Gloria Gaynor and the like. Oui, I did worry you would look foolish. I am now prepared to admit every one of your songs is le timeless classic. Just let me have the brick.'

'Merci,' I say, primly. 'And of my many songs, tell me, which is your favourite?'

'Oh, le French one,' says my husband. 'Definitely.'

MAHMOUD AHMADINEJAD
20 JUNE 2009

Iran is in turmoil, after a blatantly rigged election. The Green Revolution grows.

DO SHANBEH

The post-election lull. I wind down by further loosening my already quite loose collar and inviting a couple of young Basiji militiamen to my home for an evening of board games. We start with Scrabble. The first Basiji scores eleven and the second scores thirty-two. Then I score 11,073.

'Seriously?' says one Basiji.

Then the other one hits him with an iron bar. Hurriedly, the first Basiji insists that he's not accusing me of cheating.

'It's just an unexpectedly large number of points,' he explains. 'If you'd said fifty, I'd probably have let it go. But 11,073? It's just not plausible.'

The other one hits him with the iron bar again.

'Brother,' I say, gently. 'Why this dissent? Am I not an honourable man? Was it not a triple-word score? And is it not clear that 95 per cent of the people in this room consider me to be the clear winner?'

The first Basiji spits out a tooth.

'But ... there ... are only three of us here,' he mumbles. 'And even if you'd had the Q and the X...'

His friend hits him a third time and he slumps onto the table.

'Now,' I say, clapping my hands. 'Monopoly?'

SE SHANBEH

A splendid game, in the end, during which the first Basiji had no houses, his friend achieved four or five hotels, and I managed to have everywhere from Piccadilly to Mayfair covered in little plastic models of the Empire State Building and the Forbidden Palace.

And then, to the airport. Today I am at a very important regional conference in Russia. President Medvedev is wearing a very expensive suit.

'Nice of you to wear a tie,' he says, archly, and offers to lend me a razor.

'I am a humble man,' I tell him.

Medvedev sighs. They're all on my side, he says. Obviously. Him, Chávez, the Chinese. All the famously sensible world leaders. But when I appear with them, looking like the American detective Columbo after a night on a park bench, it just lowers the tone. Don't I know that Tehran is burning?

'I blame the Zionists,' I tell him.

'They stole your washbag?' he asks.

CHAAR SHANBEH

Actually, it's kind of awkward. Between you and me, I don't even know how to tie a tie. I do have a clip-on one, for emergencies, but it's bright green. Probably best not.

Still in Russia. Protests continue. A crisis phone call from the Supreme Ruler of all Iran, Ayatollah Khamenei. 'Kh-aye-main-ah-ee,' he corrects me, and then sighs.

We have a problem, he says. It's not just that I faked the election results. It's that I faked them so incredibly badly. It's made the whole Islamic revolution look really slapdash.

'And who has to hold it all together?' he says. 'Muggins here, that's who. I'll have to make a speech to the nation on Friday.'

If anybody can do it, I tell him, he can. After all, he's the Ayatollah Khamenei.

'Kh-ahman-ayeye,' he says.

'I'm sure that's not what you said last time,' I say.

The Supreme Leader gives a guilty chuckle. Then he admits he keeps changing it, to confuse the BBC.

PANJ SHANBEH

Back in Iran. Medvedev keeps calling. Really annoying. Before I left yesterday, we all went out for lunch. When the bill came, I just chucked some coins on the table.

'That should pay my share,' I said, loudly, 'which I calculate to be 2 per cent!'

President Medvedev frowned. 'There are only five of us here,' he said. 'And we all ate the same.'

If I'd said 10 per cent, added Hugo Chávez, they'd have let it go. But 2 per cent? That's just rude. It's like I think they're all morons.

That was when I legged it to the airport. Didn't have an iron bar.

JOME

'Well,' says the Supreme Leader, after addressing the nation at Friday prayers. 'That should have fixed it. Or my name's not Ayatollah Kh-ah-mee-nay-aye!'

'And is it?' I ask.

The Ayatollah shrugs. 'Roughly,' he says. 'Now. What was the other cock-up?'

'Restaurant bill,' I say, meekly.

'Ah yes,' he sighs, and I hand him the phone.

MUAMMAR GADDAFI
2 JUNE 2007

Tony Blair is in Tripoli, on a mission to bring Colonel Gaddafi in from the cold. Whoops.

MONDAY

I am in my communications tent. My personal translator wears red lipstick, a tight camouflage uniform and a revolver in a shoulder holster.

'Tell this Mr Blair,' I instruct her, 'that this is a very brave decision.'

My translator translates.

'Tell this Mr Blair,' I add, 'that there will be photographs taken, comparisons drawn and conclusions made.'

My translator translates again.

'Tell this Mr Blair,' I continue, thoughtfully, 'that he must appreciate the inherent danger for a respected international statesman to associate himself with the pariah despot of a so-called rogue state.'

My translator continues to translate.

'But tell this Mr Blair,' I conclude, 'that, for him, I am prepared to risk it.'

Once again, my translator translates.

TUESDAY

I am in my wardrobe tent. My personal stylist wears red lipstick, a tight camouflage uniform and a revolver in a shoulder holster.

'So, my Colonel,' she says. 'What is it to be, for your meeting with this Mr Blair? The olive green, with the golden epaulettes? The desert beige? Or some kind of matching hat and kaftan set?'

I muse awhile.

'Brown,' I say, finally. 'Brown robes. They will be flattering, and attractively hug my curves. And black beret. With sunglasses.'

My personal stylist nods, and rifles through the sunglasses box.

'What sort of sunglasses?' she says. 'Idi Amin sunglasses? *Top Gun* sunglasses? Elvis Presley sunglasses?'

'Elvis Presley sunglasses,' I reply, surprising myself.

WEDNESDAY

So. I sit in my diplomatic tent with this despot Blair. I have the beginnings of a beard, and a fly whisk. My beret is black, my robes are brown, flattering, and attractively hug my curves. My sunglasses do, indeed, look quite a lot like Elvis Presley's.

Blair, despite having been offered the services of my personal stylist, wears a pinstripe suit and a tie.

'What does he think this is?' I ask my personal translator. 'Fancy dress?'

THURSDAY

I am in my radio tent, watching television. I would be in the television tent, but there was a problem with the plumbing. Tents are lousy for plumbing.

The tyrant Blair is now in Sierra Leone. And there, to my shock and horror, he is dressed in the ceremonial garb of a paramount chief. I roar, and my personal anger management therapist comes running. She wears red lipstick, a tight camouflage uniform and a revolver in a shoulder holster.

'What is this?' I rage. 'He wears their clothes, and he wouldn't wear mine? Are my clothes not more flattering than those of a paramount chief? Do they not attractively hug my curves?'

My personal anger management therapist agrees that this is a gross insult.

'If he wears one of Nelson Mandela's horrible shirts,' I warn, 'there will be trouble.'

FRIDAY

And now I am back in my television tent, watching a report about the pariah Blair in South Africa. My personal plumber wears red lipstick, a tight camouflage uniform and a revolver in a shoulder holster. My personal telephone rings. I answer.

'Hullo?' says a bright, English voice. 'Tony here! Nelson Mandela says hi. Look mate, I just wanted to say thanks for the meet and greet, yeah? Totally appreciated. Hope we can do it again sometime.'

I feel my knuckles tighten. 'Next time,' I say, in halting English, 'you will wear red lipstick, a tight camouflage uniform, and a revolver in a shoulder holster.'

'Um ... what?' says Tony Blair, after a while.

I don my Elvis Presley sunglasses, and very slowly put the telephone down.

NORTH KOREA STATE FOOTBALL PUNDIT
19 JUNE 2010

Much to everybody's surprise, apparently except for theirs, North Korea qualified for the 2010 World Cup in South Africa. First they lost 2-1 to Brazil, then 7-0 to Portugal, then 3-0 to Cote D'Ivoire. Then they went home. According to ABC News, the coach later claimed to receive 'regular tactical advice during matches' from Kim Jong-il, 'using mobile phones that are not visible to the naked eye'.

MONDAY

And it is lovely evening here in Africa, tiny island three thousand mile off coast of the Democratic People Republic of Korea continent. I am here for covering World Cup Football, sport invented by DEAR LEADER and exported, recently, to rest of world. It is game requiring eleven players.

All hail KIM JONG 11! This very funny pun in English. Apparently.

Vzzzzzz. Enjoy my capitalist VUVUZELA. Tomorrow we are to playing Brazil, international minnow nation who must be bricking it. Match will not be broadcast live but with 24-hour delay, for reasons despite CAPITALIST RUMOURS entirely uninvolving time required to Photoshop head of DEAR LEADER on to body of KIM JONG 11 goal-scoring striker.

Of course, DEMOCRATIC PEOPLE REPUBLIC is

not only Korea in contest. Also team from oppressed capitalist lackey sister state of South Korea. In gesture of magnanimity, DEAR LEADER has decreed that cheering, thereof, is acceptable. For, in facing down rest of barbarian world, two Koreas are in same boat. And, if same boat should sink owing to missile from mysterious SUBMARINE, we never done it. Honest. Vzzzz.

TUESDAY

So! Welcome to brief written match report of historic DEMOCRATIC PEOPLE heroism at Ellis Park in Johannesburg! (Redacted in part for reasons of national security.) FIRST QUARTER: Kick-off! And Korea has the ball!

SECOND QUARTER: Defence impenetrable! Vzzzzzz! All hail the Kim Jong 11!

HALF-TIME. THIRD QUARTER: And it is starting well! A long pass ... XXXXX XXXX XXXXX XXXX XXX XX XXXXX Vzzzzz! XXX XXXX, FOURTH QUARTER: XXXX XX XXXX XXX XXXXXXXX XXX XXXXXX GOAL!!!!!!!

FINAL SCORE: XX-XX Vzzzzz. ENDS

WEDNESDAY

Hurrah! Come, gather around recently installed municipal television and witness glorious DEMOCRATIC PEOPLE REPUBLIC slightly-delayed football match! Witness DEAR LEADER hand-picked team display effortless superiority of rice and dust-based diet and whip-and-execution-based training to rest of world!

See the inferior Brazil crumble under the might of the KIM JONG 11! Marvel at Democratic People footwork! Be awestruck by DEMOCRATIC PEOPLE style and exuberance! FYI, we're the ones in yellow.

THURSDAY

Vzzzzzz! Greetings once more from South Africa, tiny, impoverished nation where we happy, well-fed DEMOCRATIC PEOPLE are slumming it, frankly. Floor in South Africa so dirty that people must eat and sleep on raised platforms. Poverty so great that many cannot even afford bicycle and must travel by car. Koreans envy of world.

Hence unpleasant rumours today of defections. For record, DEAR LEADER hand-picked team has ALWAYS been known by nickname KIM JONG VII. Football game requiring SEVEN PLAYERS. Suggestions otherwise due to FALSE MEMORY.

Last great DEMOCRATIC PEOPLE REPUBLIC football victory in 1966 in land of Siminutive Satan of England, back under earlier DEAR LEADER. Same spectacles as current DEAR LEADER, but less backcombing.

Some capitalist nations feel this long time ago, and of little relevance. England itself not so bothered, strangely.

FRIDAY

Next match not until Monday, against capitalist client state of Portugal. For now, witness footage of cheering DEMOCRATIC PEOPLE crowds!

Similarity to bit-part actors you may remember from Chinese soap operas entirely mistaken! Further absurd rumours of glorious team defections most displeasing. To reassure fretful DEMOCRATIC REPUBLIC PEOPLE, witness glorious team of KIM JONG II taking well-earned rest. See? Both of them still present.

Remember, football is game requiring TWO PLAYERS. Capitalist teams invariably cheating.

CARDINAL SOMETHING
16 MARCH 2013

This was the week of the Papal Conclave. While it was going on, you may remember, the Labour MP David Lammy criticised the BBC for their racist innuendo in tweeting speculation as to whether the eventual smoke would be black or white.

I haven't made a joke about that. I just wanted to remind you.

MONDAY

Here we all are! Again. Cardinals on tour! Whoop! Whoop! Hey, how's it going? Not seen you since the last one. Loving the red hat. You will notice that I am also wearing a red hat. How embarrassing.

So who've we got? Any funny names this time? Remember Cardinal Sin from Manila? That just never stopped being funny. Apparently we've got a Cardinal Man from Vietnam, which is mildly amusing, and a Cardinal Sarah from Guinea. Bet he's wearing a frock! Yeah, we all are. So what? Shh. And no, I have no jokes to make about Cardinal Koch, from Switzerland. Come on. We're above that. Where's that Scottish guy from last time? He was fun. Oh. Seriously? Missed that.

Anyway, what are we after this time? Humility, obviously. We're here in the richest city-state in the world, after all, where even the gold things have gold leaf on them. So humility should be a given. But what else?

Because we're a diverse bunch, we cardinals. Different nationalities, different backgrounds. And, of course, wildly different takes on the major social issues of the day, such as gay marriage and contraception! Will the next Pope be against them, or really, really against them? Nobody knows!

TUESDAY

Well, batten down the hatches Conclave! Into the Sistine Chapel, lads! No women! Girls smell! No, I'm only kidding. I've literally no idea if they smell or not. Doors all sealed? Wicked.

Who's got the cigars? No, I won't blow it up the chimney. Every time, you make that joke. Hey, are we allowed to tweet in here? Oh, OK. But I can keep my iPhone? Come on, this could last for days. What am I to do without Angry Birds? Seriously? There's a Wii? And a PS3? Bless you, brother. Best conclave ever.

Time for black smoke? Already? Hey, guys! Wouldn't it be funny if we had a conclave at Christmas and tried to put smoke up the chimney while Santa was coming down it! Huh? What do you mean, there's no Santa? What the Hell are we even doing here, if there's no Santa? Oh, wait. Santa. Right.

WEDNESDAY

Bored. Bored, bored, bored. There's nothing to do here. This morning, I spent forty-five minutes lying on my back on the floor, looking at the roof. It's kinda like *ET* isn't it? Totally never realised that.

This morning we sent up some more black smoke. All the usual marshmallow jokes. It's lunchtime now. Hey, guys? Shall we order a pizza? Oh. Seriously? They won't?

Even though we're in Italy? Oh, man! No, not you. NOT YOU! Jeez.

Anyone speak Vietnamese? Anyway, better knuckle under. This stuff really matters. The new Pope will face grave challenges at this difficult time. Strong leadership is required! I mean, that whole clerical abuse scandal isn't just going to piously ignore itself, is it?

THURSDAY

Puff of white smoke! It happened last night, and the crowds outside went wild. Hey, it's not like they were going to boo if we got it wrong, is it? To be honest, me and the lads weren't even sure if we could get it wrong. Apparently it's kinda contentious.

Anyway, today, we gathered for our new Pope's first Mass. He's a humble man; everybody says. Not for him the jaunty red shoes of his predecessor. His robes shall be plain; his cross unadorned. He shall not wear a funny hat. Great news for the Church! But, for the purveyors of aphoristic truisms, perhaps confusing.

FRIDAY

So. Might as well go home.

'I felt less pressure this time, Brother,' I told another Cardinal, as we walked in the sunshine of St Peter's Square. 'Back in the day, you chose a Pope and that was that until he died, or turned out to be a secret woman!'

'*Omnia mutantur*,' he agreed, gravely.

Whereas these days, I mused, it's more like getting married. Get it wrong, and you can just get divorced!

'Brother?' he said.

'What?' I said.

HANK PAULSON
20 SEPTEMBER 2008

This was the week of the collapse of Lehman Brothers, and this guy was the US Treasury Secretary when the banking crisis hit. The idea for this was born when a journalist friend in New York called up in hysterics after waiting outside the big US banking summit, and seeing all the limos backing up down the street.

MONDAY

I'm in the vault. I work here. I live here. When you're the US Treasury Secretary, you need to know exactly how much money you have. All the time. It's not much fun, living in a vault. Cash all over the place. No room to breathe. No room to swing a cat. Just me, my whiz-kid staff and a whole lot of dollars.

'Get me a coffee and a pretzel,' I say to the nearest whiz-kid, because I'm exhausted.

The kid looks cunning. He says: 'How about you give me the money for a coffee and a pretzel? And then tomorrow, if market conditions are right, I'll bring you two?'

I don't have time for these coffee and pretzel mind games. I was up all weekend, trying to do something about Lehman Brothers and trying to sort out Merrill Lynch. I've had every damn banker in Wall Street crammed in here, all refusing to do anything. They all turned up in their limos. Whole damn street full of limos.

Traffic jam of limos. Bastards. I haven't got a limo. I'm just a public servant. I've just got a vault.

TUESDAY
Haven't slept yet. Kinda seeing things. And I still can't persuade any of these damn whiz-kids to get me a coffee and a pretzel. They all reckon there are now so many people selling coffee and pretzels that coffee and pretzels aren't worth anything, and that the only sensible way to get hold of either is for me to nationalise a coffee and pretzel shop.

'No,' I say, although I can't see how a coffee and pretzel shop is going to make much difference. Last night we nationalised AIG for $85 billion. First time anybody has nationalised anything financial since Roosevelt. This is a blow. On the upside, the whiz-kids now have enough room to play Twister.

In the afternoon, I call the old chief executive of AIG and fire him.

'But I'll lose my limo,' he wails. 'What kind of banker will I be without a limo?'

I sigh. 'Can you make coffee? Or pretzels?'

'No,' he says.

'Bummer,' I say.

WEDNESDAY
Met with the President last night. Had to explain the global economy, the intricacies of short-selling and the nature of toxic debts bundled into complex packages in the derivatives market. For Chrissakes, the guy wears Velcro shoes.

THURSDAY
I'm so tired. And I'm starving. I used to be the chief

executive of Goldman Sachs. Those were the days. My own limo, and everything. An office you could move about in, and coffee and pretzels coming out my ears. I'd love to have that again when this job ends. Just got to make sure there's still some banks.

For now I'd settle for some more room in the vault. So basically I've got to find a way to save some banks, and simultaneously unload a few hundred billion dollars more. Maybe even a trillion. Then this place could have a squash court.

FRIDAY

Got it! I have hatched a plan to buy up billions of dollars' worth of bad mortgages. Had to tell the President. He was on a swing in the White House garden, holding a coffee and a pretzel. He asked me to explain everything in terms he would understand, so I told him to imagine that the pretzel was a sub-prime mortgage, the coffee was the weak dollar and that I was the Federal Reserve. Then I drank the coffee and ate the pretzel.

'I don't get it,' he said.

'Get me another coffee and another pretzel,' I told him, 'and we'll try again.'

PART III

CELEBRITY, SPORT AND ARTS

BEYONCÉ
26 JANUARY 2013

Barack Obama is sworn in as President again. Beyoncé sings at the inauguration. Midway through, she pulls out her earpiece and the world cheers. Then it emerged she'd been miming. Apparently this isn't unusual and, the time before, somebody had actually mimed playing a cello. Things you learn, eh?

Michelle has new hair.

MONDAY

Yesterday, my husband Jay-Z and I were in the White House. 'Honey,' said Michelle. 'We are so pleased you're going to sing for us tomorrow.'

I told her it was an honour, and that I thought her new hair was awesome.

'Oh good,' said Michelle. 'Barack says it looks like Darth Vader's helmet.'

But that's what I meant, I said. I love Darth Vader. Particularly his sexy voice.

'You know that's not really his voice?' said Michelle. 'He's just pretending.'

'That's interesting,' I said.

TUESDAY

The inauguration went well. And afterwards, Barack called. 'In their homes and their workplaces,' he said, 'Americans heard you sing our anthem.'

'Sort of,' I said, wondering if I should tell him.

'In their fields and their farmsteads,' he said, 'their brownfields and their greenfields. Their citylands and their croplands. In their high up places and their low down places. In their buildings with slates on the roof and with other things on the roof. In their American-made cars and their foreign-made cars, provided they had radios. In their...'

'Sorry,' I interrupted. 'Is your basic point here that lots of people were listening?'

'Yes,' said the President.

'Took a while,' I said.

WEDNESDAY

There's a bit of fuss about the way I lip-synced. I didn't think it would be a problem. Jay-Z and I had talked it over the night before. Or rather, I had. He just kept looking out the window and stealing my french fries.

'Gotta mime,' he had said. 'Gotta mime to dance in time.'

I'm not going to dance, I told him. He yawned. 'Gotta dance,' he said. 'Gotta dance if you wanna advance.'

Jay-Z raps a lot. Sometimes it doesn't really make sense. Sometimes I also think he only married me so he could rhyme 'fiancée' with 'Beyoncé'. He also always takes my last french fry, which I find infuriating.

'If you liked it,' said Jay-Z, 'then you shoulda put an onion ring on it.'

THURSDAY

The lip-sync thing has really taken off! So many reporters are calling that I've put my cellphone on silent. It's not even like I was trying to keep it a secret!

'Yeah,' says Jay-Z. 'Except for the way you were

moving your lips,' he adds, helpfully. 'Oh God,' I say. 'I wonder if the Obamas have called.'

'How to tell? Where's your cell?' raps Jay-Z.

I don't know, I say. It could be anywhere. It's on silent.

'If you liked it then you should have put a ringtone on it,' says Jay-Z.

FRIDAY

Today, Jay-Z and I go back to the White House, to see Barack. He's behind his desk, in the Oval Office.

'I'm so sorry,' I say. 'I know how sensitive you are about accusations of fakery. Especially with the birth certificate thing. I can't apologise enough.'

Barack stares at me for a few moments. Then he puts his fingertips together.

'In our schools and our universities,' he begins. 'Our shops and our parks. In our eating-spaces and our drink-ing-spaces. Our sheep farms and our horse farms and our turkey farms. Our airports and our heliports. In our supermarkets and our fishmarkets. On our mountains and in our streams. In our retail outlets for jeans and for sweaters and even for crockery. In our proud open valleys and smaller, less proud valleys. In our...'

After a while, I let myself out.

USAIN BOLT
11 AUGUST 2012

At the 2012 Olympics, Usain Bolt wins everything he tries to win. Then he goes home.

MONDAY

I'm fast, man. The things you do, I do quicker. You get up, get dressed, have a shower, maybe go to the toilet. Probably that's half your morning gone. Me, it's all done in a little under three minutes. It's a bummer. I got time to kill.

'Take up a hobby,' people say. But I do hobbies fast, too. You want to play me at Connect Four? I will beat your ass in fifty-seven seconds. See my pointy hands. You want to build boats out of matchsticks? Dude, you blinked and I built the *Potemkin*.

I try all sorts to fill the hours. Last night I tweeted a picture of me and the Swedish handball team partying at 3 a.m. Coach was furious.

'Usain,' he said, 'you got a heat this morning! How much did you sleep?'

Nobody gets this. I sleep faster than you, too. I get your eight hours' sleep in forty-two minutes. What am I gonna do the rest of the time? I'm bored, man. I'm so totally bored.

TUESDAY

'You want breakfast?' says Coach.

I had it, I tell him. I had it before you even finished saying that sentence. Are these Olympics still going on? I feel like I've been here for thirty years.

Coach says I need to train. So I go out and I run the 100 metres, and I've still got twenty-three hours, fifty-nine minutes and fifty seconds to kill. You want me to do that all day, again and again?

Coach says I could maybe take up reading books or something. But I already read most of them, too. The other day, he gave me that *Fifty Shades Of Grey*. There's eight minutes and fifty-three seconds I could have put to better use. Jeez.

WEDNESDAY

No way is it still Wednesday. I am totally twiddling my thumbs. And I twiddle thumbs fast. Fires start.

Coach says all these British dignitaries want to meet me.

'Prince Harry?' I say. We met in Jamaica. That royal dude has talents I can understand. You want to see how fast he can roll a spliff.

'David Cameron,' says Coach. 'The PM. I think he wants to be able to say, "Yesterday I met a black man who is the fastest sprinter in the world".'

It takes me 0.07 seconds to realise I'm utterly not up for this.

'I'm surprised it took you so long,' says Coach.

THURSDAY

I've probably got some race on today. Oh yeah, the 200 metres. I should go do that. Oh look. I just did. Now what?

I am the greatest.

There has never been anybody greater than me.

All the same, I wish I was great at something that took a bit longer. Did you hear about this rover that took eight months to get to Mars? There are opportunities here, for all of mankind. I simply would not have taken that long.

But probably I should stick with sport. Sir Alex Ferguson says I can have a trial at Manchester United. At least, I think he does. He called this afternoon.

'I've never had to say this before,' I said to him, 'but could you speak a bit more slowly?'

FRIDAY

Chances are I'll win another gold medal tomorrow. I've lost track of how many that is. I could count them, faster than you'd believe, but I can't really be bothered.

Prince Harry calls.

'Dude!' I say. 'What took you so long? You gotta come on down to the Olympic village. Muchos global totty. You would not believe how quickly I got those Swedish chicks into my room.'

'Let's make it a race,' says the Prince.

'Nice try,' I say. 'But I know my limits.'

JUSTIN BIEBER
9 MARCH 2013

Justin Bieber is visiting Britain. A London concert starts a few hours late and Fleet Street erupts in outrage. Probably because most of it was there, under protest, with its kids.

MONDAY

'Justin, baby,' says my manager. 'What's up with you these days?'

'Do not mess with me,' I say. 'Or I will unleash the Beliebers.'

'Please don't unleash the Beliebers,' says my manager, going quite pale. Then he recovers and says he's just worried about me. The late nights, the wild behaviour.

'Although it could be a good new image,' he says. 'If you're entering a Robbie Williams phase.'

'I don't know who that is,' I tell him. I've been touring since I was fourteen and I kinda missed a lot.

'Not the Mork guy,' he says.

'I don't know who that is either.'

'Robbie Williams?' he says. 'Went wild? Got kicked out of Take That?'

I just shrug, because I'm not into classical music.

'You're unbelievable sometimes,' he tells me.

'Unbeliebable,' I murmur.

'And quite irritating,' he says.

TUESDAY

We don't know how many Beliebers there are, but it's a lot. If they all screamed at once, I reckon the moon might crack. Mess with me and they will make your Twitter column a living hell. You better belieb it.

Today, though, half the English ones are really upset because I came on stage late last night and they all had to leave a few minutes in.

'But people are normally happy to wait for me,' I say.

'They had to catch a train,' says my manager.

'Not following,' I say.

'A train?' he says, a bit after that. 'Like … a train?'

'I don't think we have those in America,' I say.

My manager says he sometimes wonders what they've done to me.

'All that fame so early,' he says. 'I think we left you a bit naive.'

'Naibe,' I mutter.

'And there's that thing,' he says.

'What thing?' I say.

WEDNESDAY

'Annoying,' says my manager.

He was hoping that the late thing would boost my new bad-boy image, and that I might even get condemned by some guy called the Prime Minister. Apparently he'll condemn almost anything. Novelists, comedians, TV shows. Anything.

'Is he a rapper?' I ask.

'No,' says my manager. 'But he's not playing ball. Too scared of the Beliebers.'

Everything goes wrong here. This is almost as bad as that time I came over a few years ago, and got wet after midnight, and these things called Jedward burst out of my back.

THURSDAY

First I spend a while on Twitter, calling down the wrath of the Beliebers on Domino's Pizza because they pretend not to understand when I ask them to delieber a ham and olibe. Then I get to my dressing room and there's some old guy there, in a suit and a purple tie.

'My name's Ed Miliband,' he says. He says he wants to talk to me about the whole Beliebers thing. He thinks a similar grassroots online militia would help him to overthrow the Conservative-led coalition.

'The Belabours!' he says.

'I don't understand a word you just said,' I say. 'And I really don't think that's my fault.'

Ed looks sad. 'But I'm like you,' he says. 'We're the New Generation.'

I think he was in the Beatles.

FRIDAY

Today I almost got into a fight with a paparazzo and yesterday I got short of breath in front of thousands of my fans.

'Justin, baby,' says my manager. 'I like the fighting thing. Very cool. But dude. *They* should faint when they see *you*.'

I'm just exhausted, I tell him. And angry. I just don't get treated like this anywhere else, I say. Not Geneba. Not even Tel Abib.

One more gig, he says.

'Yeah,' I say. 'And then we can make like a tree, and leab.'

JUSTIN BIEBER'S MONKEY
27 APRIL 2013

I couldn't do Justin Bieber again, could I? This week he was touring around Europe. Arriving in Germany, his young capuchin monkey was confiscated, because it didn't have the correct papers. And then things began to unravel...

MONDAY

Really, if you think about it, it's incredibly cruel to take a simple creature from its mother, when it's still far too young to defend itself or understand what might be going on, and drag it around the globe on a world tour. But that's what these promoters have done with Justin Bieber. It must be very frightening for him.

At least he's got the correct health documentation, though. Unlike me. I'm his pet baby capuchin monkey, and I was seized at customs in Munich almost a month ago. I've basically missed the whole tour. Sometimes, though, the German border guards give me updates.

'Hey monkey!' they'll say. 'You vill not be guessing vot your Chustin Bieber has done now! He is punching ze photographer and leaping around Copenhagen in a vunzie!'

'Huh!' I'll say, and then I'll feel a little bit sad. And they all know why. Without his monkey, he's out there going ape.

TUESDAY

I won't lie. This isn't how I'd envisaged life as a celebrity pet. I thought it would be all glamour. The White House dog, George Clooney's pigs, Tom Cruise's wives; those guys look like they have it good.

'Hey monkey!' says one of the border guards. 'I am actually never hearing of your Chustin Bieber until last week, venn he is making ze scene off himself mit de Anne Frank museum in Amsterdam. Can you be singing vunn of his songs?' I think for a while, and hum a line.

'But this vas vorse than Vunn Direction!' says the border guard.

I shrug.

'Also,' says the border guard, 'Vhy vere you grabbing ze crotch unt jumping up unt down?' I just shrug again. Monkey see, monkey do.

WEDNESDAY

Apparently Justin's management have been in touch. They have demanded that I be given freedom to travel, a temporary passport, petrol money and a hire car.

'I am zinking,' says the border guard. 'Zees people are idiots, yah?' No kidding. You should see them trying to have a tea party. 'Anyvay,' says the border guard. 'Today's news is that your Chustin Bieber has caused a fuss in Copenhagen by throwing a tantrum at a photo-shoot. Vot is vith this guy? It is like he is surrounded by total knuckle-draggers!' I just stare at him.

'No offence,' he says.

THURSDAY

'Hey monkey!' says the border guard. 'Ve haff bad news!' At first I think he's talking about JLS splitting up, and I'm pretty sanguine about that. But no.

'Your Chustin Bieber is not coming back,' says the border guard. 'He is saying ze monkey must be staying here. So. You are becoming property of Federal Republic of Germany.'

This is a real blow. One of my uncles was the monkey in *Friends*, you know. And I've a very close relative who used to be the singer in Oasis.

Showbusiness is in my blood. And we had plans! Eventually, there were going to be three monkeys, all on stage. I was going to be Speak No Evil, and one of the others was going to be See No Evil. We hadn't decided what to call the third monkey. Hear No Evil obviously wouldn't work.

FRIDAY

At lunchtime, the border guard gives me a mobile telephone. I put it to my ear.

'Yo, monkey?' says Justin Bieber. 'How is it, like, hanging?' I don't say anything. 'Totally feel bad for ditching you, dude,' he says. 'No hard feelings?' I still don't say anything. I'm just wondering who is going to look after him now.

Justin says he's in Stockholm now. He's also having a bad few days, because the police raided the tour bus, because they thought he was getting high.

'And I was, like, "dude!"' he says. '"Not cool! I have never been high in my life!"'

I suck my teeth.

'Then I told them I had to go and telephone my monkey,' says Justin.

I just sigh.

MY SPEECH: KATE WINSLET
27 JANUARY 2009

This one isn't strictly speaking a My Week *but it's the same sort of thing. Having been lost for words winning a Screen Actors Guild Award, one cherished British actress prepares for the Baftas and Oscars.*

IF SHE WINS...
(Arise from seat, hands over mouth. Push belly out/pull in depending on whether officially Thin 'Kate Winslet' or Fat 'Kate Winslet' this particular week. Approach stage)

'Ladies and gentlemen. Gosh! Blimey!'

(Gauge reaction. If extreme Britishness goes down well, repeat. If extremely confident, risk a 'lawks')

'This time, I am absolutely not lost for words. I have lots of words. I've practised them. I'd like to start by thanking my director and my husband, who may or may not, in this film, have been the same person.'

(Point, wink, DO NOT wave)

'I'd like to thank everybody who worked with me on this particular film, whichever film it was. If it's the one with Leonardo DiCaprio, I'd like to apologise for turfing him off that door into the sea in *Titanic* without even bothering to check he was dead.'

(Pause for laughter. Wait for camera to cut to Leo)

'If it's for the Holocaust one, of course, all humour would be misplaced.'

(Look grave)

'But I'd like to thank Ricky Gervais for giving me that cameo in *Extras* in which my character noted that a sure way to get awards was to do a Holocaust film.

Because I'd be lying if I said it didn't get me thinking. Bloody hell. This bit won't get on the news, will it?'

(Pause for Bafta audience laughter. If Oscar audience does not laugh, say 'blimey' again. That should do it)

'I'd also like to thank my fellow nominees.'

(Earnest face. At Baftas say...)

'Angelina, you're so beautiful, you've been so great in all those totally disposable action films, and I'm really sorry I forgot your name at the Golden Globes! Kristin, you really did blaze a trail for an actually-quite-a-lot-older generation of British actresses! And Meryl, my mum is such a fan!'

(At Oscars skip Kristin but add...)

'Melissa, I'm really sorry I still don't know who you are but I bet you're wonderful! Anne, it's not true what people say about your weak chin!'

(And then ...)

'You're all so deserving! Everybody should get a prize. It shouldn't just be me.'

(Hand on chest, allow tear to roll down cheek)

'Because I'm just a mum. I'm just a girl who's sometimes fat and sometimes thin, and likes pints and pies and long walks that leave me all ruddy cheeked and saying "crikey!" So if I can do it, anyone can. Even you, Kristin and Meryl, despite being so very much older than me. Even you, the other one, best known for *Tomb Raider*. This room is too full of heroes.

We are the best people in the world.'

(Full-on sobbing now)

'I love you. I love you all. Lor' luv a duck, chim-chim-cheroo. Gather. Gather. Thank you.'

AND IF SHE LOSES...

(Smile. Do not stop smiling. Not even if it's Angelina. Under no circumstances stand up. If you feel yourself starting to cry, ham it up. Throw back your head. Howl. If the cameras are still on you after twenty seconds, look straight at them and, very clearly, mouth the word 'f***'. British audiences will love this. American audiences will swiftly cut away to somebody else)

NOTE: She won. Didn't use the speech, though.

JEREMY CLARKSON
3 DECEMBER 2011

Public sector trade unions go on strike, over cuts. Appearing on The One Show *(BBC1) the host of* Top Gear *says that they should all be shot. They mind.*

MONDAY

'I think they should all be shot,' I say. 'All of them. Every last one.'

I'm sipping at a glass of fizzy piss made by some onion-munching, war-losing Frog. We're having an informal drinks party with the Chipping Norton set. Everybody wants to be in the Chipping Norton set. Richard Hammond and the other one are doing the coats.

'I shot a baboon once,' says A. A. Gill, who is staying over.

'Who should be shot, darling?' says Lady something or other, who lives next door, makes jam, and runs a music festival.

All of them, I say. The French, the Mexicans, the Japanese, social workers, the Labour Party, people with electric cars, Spanish fishermen, the European Union, basket weavers, the bulk of lesbians, bus drivers, people who go on caravanning holidays, pacifists, the Health and Safety Executive, footballers' wives, people who eat pasta and farmers I don't specifically know. And the BBC. Especially the BBC. All of it. Except for me. And Piers Morgan. Although I'm coming round to him.

'You are joking?' says the bass player from Blur.

'Of course I am,' I say. 'But that doesn't mean I don't mean it.'

'I shot a baboon once,' says A. A. Gill.

'Yes,' says the Prime Minister, sounding tired. 'Yes, you said.'

TUESDAY

A meeting today with some dolly bird from the BBC. I've got a book coming out, or a DVD, or something, and they're keen to cross-promote.

'We thought you could go on *The One Show*,' she says, 'and say something controversial about the strikers. What do you think of them?'

I think they should be guillotined, I tell her. I think that their heads should be chopped off, and put on spikes, and used to decorate the houses of ordinary decent taxpayers until their skulls fall down and are kicked around in the streets in a game of football by their own...

'That could be funny,' she says.

'I didn't realise you wanted me to be funny,' I say.

WEDNESDAY

A day in the *Top Gear* studio with Hammond and the other one, brainstorming new ways to be rude about the Germans.

Some people reckon it's easy coming up with all this stuff about efficiency, Nazis and lederhosen. But they never stop to consider just how many bloody cars the Krauts bring out each year. It's exhausting.

'Ve haf vays of making your car door close quietly,' muses Hammond. 'Or there's always sausages. Good vein of gags in sausages.'

'Sausages,' I say. 'Fine. Hammond's cracked it.'

'But I'm Hammond,' says the other one.

'Astonishing,' I say. 'All these years.'

THURSDAY

Spot of bother. The trade unions are upset with my comments on *The One Show* about how their members should all be shot.

'You said they should be shot in front of their families,' says the BBC dolly bird. 'You went too far.'

'Fine,' I say. 'I'll apologise. I'll say that they should be shot privately. By themselves in cells. Or grouped together, in some sort of stadium.'

'Jeremy!' she says. 'No, you will not. We are the BBC. This sort of thing is simply not acceptable.'

'Oh for God's sake,' I say. 'This is ridiculous. It's not like I actually shot one. A. A. Gill shot a baboon!'

'I know,' says the producer. 'He told me.'

FRIDAY

I'm in China now to do some filming.

The Prime Minister calls, just as I'm meeting a chap from the Chinese Government.

'Dave!' I say. 'You forgot your Barbour. Hammond and the other one can't have been concentrating. Are we seeing you next weekend?'

The PM says he doesn't want to be in the Chipping Norton set anymore. If people think we're friends, he says, my views could tarnish his government's reputation.

'It was a bloody joke!' I shout, but he's hung up.

'Problem, Mr Jeremy?' says the Chinese official.

I said something on telly, I sigh. About shooting trade unionists if they went on strike.

'That really works,' agrees my host. 'We do it all the time.'

'That's hilarious!' I say.

'Sort of,' he says.

JAMES CAAN
8 JUNE 2013

James Caan, of Dragons' Den *fame, has been appointed as the government's social mobility tsar, and has hit out over nepotism. Then it emerges that he employs both of his own daughters.*

MONDAY

I'm in Downing Street for a meeting with Nick Clegg and a couple of his civil servants.

They're sitting down and I'm sitting down. This isn't how my meetings normally start.

'Don't you hate it,' I say, 'when there are four people at a meeting, and four scones, and the first person into the room takes two? Don't you think that's just totally unacceptable?'

The Deputy Prime Minister looks confused. 'But that's, uh, what you just did,' he says.

It's different for me, I explain. Because I was really hungry. Now, what can I do for him?

Clegg says they have a proposal for me.

'Don't tell me,' I say. 'It's a toaster for pasta. Wait! A lamp in the shape of a cereal packet? A jacket for dogs? A cigarette lighter-cum-flick-knife? Hell, I'm in. Pleasure doing business with you. How much do you want?'

Clegg says it's nothing like that. They want me to be the government's new social mobility tsar, speaking up for talent and against inherited privilege.

'Love to,' I say. 'I'm dead against that. In fact, it annoys me almost as much as people who answer their mobile phones in meetings!

'Oh, wait,' I add. 'I've got a call. Talk among yourselves.'

TUESDAY

So this morning I go on the *Today* programme, and tell John Humphrys we'd have a much fairer society if people didn't hand out jobs to their families and friends, but always picked the best people.

'Anyway,' I say to Sarah Montague, afterwards. 'What's it like being on the radio with your dad?'

'No, no,' says Humphrys. 'She's just a colleague.'

'Bit weird,' I say.

WEDNESDAY

Nick Clegg calls at 4 a.m. 'I want a word with you!' he roars.

A frisbee ashtray, I yawn? An underwater laptop? Couldn't this have waited?

'You employ both your daughters?' shouts Clegg. 'Both of them? Don't you realise how stupid this makes us look?'

'Oh come on,' I say. 'They were the best people for their jobs.' Honestly. None of my other relatives can even type.

'Here's my proposal,' says Clegg. 'You go back on the *Today* programme this morning and get us out of this hole. And then we never speak again.'

'I admire your passion but it's hard to see the money angle,' I tell him.

Clegg hangs up.

THURSDAY

This morning I blag a meeting with David Cameron

to see if I can keep my job as the social mobility tsar anyway.

The Prime Minister says that he doesn't really understand what has been going on.

'What is social mobility anyway?' he asks. 'Is it something to do with buses?'

No, I explain. It's about how wrong it is to hand out jobs to your friends and family. Apparently.

'Oh,' says Cameron. 'Yes. I can see how we'd have to get somebody else in to handle that.'

I just didn't realise employing my daughters was so bad, I tell him. I mean, he would give jobs to his daughters, wouldn't he?

'No,' says Cameron, firmly. 'Never. Absolutely not. That would be inexcusable.'

'Oh,' I say.

'Because they're aged nine and two,' he explains.

FRIDAY

I can feel that my fledgling political career is somehow slipping away. And I was really looking forward to having one. It's so much more rewarding than handing out tens of thousands of pounds to people who want to make teapots that glow in the dark.

So I go and wait outside Ed Miliband's office.

'I hate it when people wait outside my office,' I tell him, when he arrives for work. 'I think it's inexcusable.'

'You're confusing me,' he says.

I'm James Caan, I tell him. I'm a social mobility guru. He might have seen me on *Dragons' Den*. Miliband says he only watches BBC Four. But he thinks he heard about me on the radio.

He's my last hope for political influence, I say. I was working with the government, but I became a public laughing stock because I gave jobs to my family.

'I have the opposite problem,' says Miliband. 'You'd better come in.'

HEATHER MILLS
16 FEBRUARY 2008

We've all forgotten about Heather Mills now, but for a while she was in the papers all the time. Here she is, during her divorce battle with Sir Paul McCartney. I seem to remember her going on daytime TV this week, and it being ASTONISHING.

MONDAY

So I've sacked my lawyer. Why not? Anyone can be a lawyer. In fact, I was a lawyer. I ran away from home when I was eleven and set up one of the most successful legal firms in the history of the North East of England. A child! I was a child!

People call me a fantasist but they never saw me when I was getting murderers and paedophiles jailed when I was ten, basically like Ally McBeal. In fact they wanted me to be in *Ally McBeal* instead of that skinny bitch, but I said no. I was too busy promoting vegetarianism, which I invented.

I don't care about the money. I don't even need money. If I didn't have any money I could make anything I wanted: clothes, food, probably even a boat.

I've had death threats! Don't forget about Marilyn Monroe. They killed Gandhi, they killed JFK, where is it going to end? I'd be happy with hardly any money. Fifty million, maybe a hundred. And I want a house.

TUESDAY

I've got rid of my plumber too. If he can be a plumber, I can be a plumber. You think I can't plumb? I left home when I was seven. I'm only thinking of my daughter. I'm thirsty and my carpets are wet. Maybe I should just jump off a cliff so she could be with Paul and everybody would be happy. Actually, somebody once threw me off a cliff. Yes! The highest cliff in the world. I was fine. Although not emotionally. But does anybody care about that?

I don't have a lawyer but I do have a personal trainer, a hairdresser, a bodyguard, a make-up artist, my sister, my driver, my manicurist and my stylist. They all come with me to court. The papers think I'm just showing off. They're on Paul's side.

Nobody knows the truth. When I'm not here anymore, you'll all be sorry.

WEDNESDAY

I'm in front of a mirror at home, practising how to shout and pout at the same time.

Look what we are doing to Kate McCann, for God's sake! Look at Princess Diana! Do you know what it is like to be a veal calf? I'm in a prison! A prison! Three years of lies! What's £60 million to him? I left home when I was six years old!

'Perhaps,' suggests my chiropodist, 'the judge would prefer you to stick to the point?'

So I've sacked my chiropodist too. At Christmas, they chop off the turkeys' beaks. Are you OK with that? Because I'm not.

THURSDAY

I'm just trying to protect Paul. If I wanted money, I'd just go and work in a bank. You think I haven't had offers? I love him but it's time to go it alone. Does he have cameras in his face all day? Would we treat a battery hen like this?

The things I have been accused of! I didn't kill my neighbours' dog! And don't think I don't know what it is like to be a photographer. I probably used to be one. I probably won awards.

FRIDAY

People are dying! So I've sacked the paparazzi and I'm doing that myself too. I've sacked everybody. You think it's easy to wave a camera in your own face?

When I'm my own driver, and my own bodyguard, and my own make-up artist and my own sister too? Would a murderer have to do that? Would a paedophile? I've had enough! I'm going to sack Paul and divorce myself. I'm only thinking of my daughter. Ninety per cent of global warming comes from cows! I left home before I was born. You people make me sick.

MR JUSTICE BENNETT
22 MARCH 2008

The actual divorce dragged on through the courts for ages. At the end of it, Heather Mills threw a glass of water over McCartney's big-haired lawyer, Fiona Shackleton. The judge's verdict was released to the public and reported everywhere. It was a bit like this:

MONDAY

1. I am giving judgment in the family courts of the High Court of Justice Family Division in the case of James Paul McCartney ('the husband') and Heather Anne Mills McCartney ('the wife').

2. I have found the husband to be a reliable witness, although I am mildly irritated by the thing with the thumbs.

3. I have found the wife to be a less than reliable witness.

4. I have also found that the bears s**t in the woods.

5. The likelihood of the Pope wearing a funny hat is not, in my judgment, of any relevance to this case.

TUESDAY

6. I have no doubt that the husband found the wife very attractive. The hair of the wife is a sleek, glossy, blonde affair, much like that of footballers' wives, models and television actresses the world over.

7. The hair of the husband's lawyer cannot be so easily summarised. In such a case, one must seek recourse to Rod Stewart, and Madge from *Neighbours*, and a theoretical circus act involving the delicate cranial balancing of a badly blow-dried golden retriever.

8. Vis-a-vis its suspension above the head, the laws of physics as I find them do not appear to support it.

9. It is, however, considerably smaller when wet.

10. It is not without significance that a carafe of water, placed next to the wife while my judgment was read out, did thereafter appear to have been discharged.

11. The wife is an explosive and volatile character.

12. Accordingly, I am prepared to accept that these two facts are connected.

13. But who knows?

WEDNESDAY

14. With the case of husband and wife now settled, I am no longer needed in court.

15. Unless I decide to hold the wife in contempt over that water thing.

16. Hmmm.

17. Nah.

THURSDAY

18. I have found, over breakfast, that I am twiddling my thumbs.

19. The consistency of my orange juice was, in my judgment, balanced. It was accurate and honest.

20. But I cannot say the same about the cornflakes. Having smelt and tasted them, having applied the milk and given every allowance for my enormous

appetite I can only conclude that their reputation as the king of cereals is not just inconsistent and inaccurate but also less than candid. Overall they were a less than impressive breakfast.

FRIDAY

21.   I have found my old Beatles records in the attic. I have found that she has a ticket to ride, and I do not care. I have found that here comes the sun, do do do do.

22.   It is my learned judgment that I am the walrus, goo goo g'joob.

23.   In conclusion, I have found that I may now be a little bit bored.

CHERYL COLE
<u>14 MAY 2011</u>

Cheryl Cole flies out to America to be a judge on one of Simon Cowell's shows. Her clothes are entirely baffling. Close your eyes. You can still see them, right?

<u>MONDAY</u>

'Arreet, pet,' I say to the runner who has come to meet me at Los Angeles airport.

He's been sent by the producers of the American *X Factor*, and he looks confused.

'You brought a pet?' he says. 'Is it on your head?'

'What?' I say.

'Like, ohmigod,' says the runner, and he puts a hand to his mouth. 'Simon didn't say anything about a pet. He said collect the girl with the big hair and the speech impediment and give her anything she wants.'

'Speeyatch impediment!' I say, furiously.

The runner says he could probably get some spinach, but not immediately.

'Gorran have wurds with that Simon fuh shoohah,' I say.

The runner puts a hand on my arm. 'Ohmigod,' he says. 'What did they do to you?'

<u>TUESDAY</u>

First thing in the morning, Simon Cowell collects me from my hotel and takes me to meet the executive producer.

'Nice tits,' he says.

'Don't worry,' says Simon. 'He's talking to me. They love my tits out here.'

'Of course we do, baby,' says the producer. 'What a line-up we got on this show! Random record-industry guy nobody ever heard of, Paula Abdul and the man with the best tits in the world! And now we got the beautiful English girl with the disease of the tongue!'

'I beg your pardon?' I say.

'Is she choking?' says the producer.

Simon says I'm fine, and leads me quickly away. Once we're out of earshot, he explains that Americans would never have bought the idea that lots of people in Britain speak in a way they simply cannot understand.

So, for the sake of my image, he's been telling people there's something wrong with me. I tell him this is really offensive, and I'm truly shocked.

'In fairness,' says Simon, 'I didn't actually catch that myself.'

WEDNESDAY

Today, we're doing the first auditions for the new show.

'Wait,' I say, to Paula, who is staring at Simon's chest. 'Isn't David Hasselhoff on this one?'

Paula holds up her hand and tells one of the runners that she thinks I've got a hairball. Then she turns to me and tells me that my bravery makes her cry.

'It's heart-breaking,' she says, tearfully. 'So beautiful, yet cursed with that terrible affliction! And colour-blind, too!'

'She's not actually colour-blind,' says Simon.

'Then what the hell is she wearing?' says Paula.

THURSDAY

Today the other judge, who nobody has ever heard of,

and nobody really speaks to, quietly told me that he's really pleased I've come to America.

'We love the Brits,' he says. 'Piers Martin, Derek and Veronica Beckham, the Princess of York. You guys are great.'

'That's really nice to hear,' I say.

'Oh wait,' he says. 'You're Dutch?'

FRIDAY

It's like Ant and Dec once said to me, when I was just starting out. 'Ding a de'el gonna say whit yan patties neesh gorran, pet.' And I think we can all relate to that.

There's no tea here. Not even any kettles. And I can't communicate with anybody, not even my stylists. If this goes on, there's a chance that one day I might step out looking really stupid.

'I'm sick of it already,' I say to Simon. 'I thought I was going to be emerging as a propah American stah, like.'

'You are, darling,' says Simon. 'Just a silent one. Like Charlie Chaplin.'

'No,' I say. 'It won't do. It makes me feel like they only hired me as something beautiful for people to stare at.'

'Imagine how much worse it would be,' says Simon, 'if you had my tits.'

PIERS MORGAN
6 AUGUST 2011

In America, Piers Morgan has just taken over Larry King's old show on CNN. In Britain, phone hacking is the big story following the closure of the News of the World, *and Morgan (who edited both the* NOTW *and the* Daily Mirror*) has just appeared in front of the Leveson Inquiry, where he was asked about stories based upon voicemails left by Sir Paul McCartney. Heather Mills, the Beatle's former wife, denies involvement.*

MONDAY

From America, where I am now a hugely successful TV star – maybe you've heard about this? – I telephone a British MP who has been making allegations about my role in phone hacking at the *Daily Mirror*.

'Hello, Bagshawe,' I say. 'Stop the lies.'

'Mensch,' she says. 'My name is Louise Mensch.'

She totally fancies me. 'I suppose you're wondering how I got this number,' I say.

'My office number?' says Bagshawe.

'You probably wouldn't want to know,' I say, airily.

'My hunch would be the switchboard,' she says.

'Dark arts,' I say.

'Not that dark,' she says.

TUESDAY

A meeting with the bosses at CNN. Two men and a

woman are sitting behind a desk. For the most part, all three are thrilled with the way I've totally reinvigorated Larry King's tired old show, mainly by shrugging off the dead wood of millions of viewers that were really weighing it down.

'Piers, baby,' says one. 'We love you. You know that. But we gotta know that these damaging allegations coming outta England are totally false.'

Entirely false, I say. Completely without foundation.

The woman leans forward. 'So there's no truth at all,' she says, 'in these rumours that you used to edit tabloid newspapers?'

'Oh,' I say. 'Wait. Sorry. That one's true.'

WEDNESDAY

Simon Cowell calls. 'I suppose you're wondering how I got your number,' I say.

'But I called you,' said Simon, and then we fall into some good-natured matey banter for a while about which one of us has the most money and the bigger penis.

He totally fancies me.

'Listen, mate,' he says, after a while. 'You never hacked my phone, did you?'

I never hacked anybody's phones, I tell him. All this stuff is utterly fabricated in a manner so glaring that only an absolute fool could fail to notice.

'A bit like those troop abuse photos which got you sacked from the *Mirror*?' he says.

'My house is bigger and I have a marginally more attractive wife,' I tell him, angrily. 'And anyway, that's never been conclusively established.'

THURSDAY

Heather Mills calls to tell me she feels like a veal calf

in a box being force-fed a tissue of lies and she knows how Jackie Kennedy must have felt and that she didn't murder her neighbours' dog and the chickens are coming home to roost and have I heard what they do to chickens and it's outrageous and I'm going to get what's coming to me and that's fine by her and now everybody knows that my newspaper hacked her phone.

'Why would we do that?' I say. 'You called every paper every day, anyway.'

'I suppose you're wondering how I got your number,' says Heather.

'Damn right,' I say.

FRIDAY

Some people are saying I should go back to Britain and face the music.

Another meeting with the bosses from CNN.

'OK, Piers,' says the woman. 'We've looked into these allegations in more depth and we've decided we're going to stand by you, utterly.'

'Well, thank you,' I say, and I wonder if this is the moment to talk about a pay rise.

'So you edited tabloid newspapers?' says one of the men. 'Big deal! It's not like one of them was actually the *News of the World*!'

'Oh, for heaven's sake,' I say. 'Can't you guys Google this stuff?'

PIERS MORGAN
13 FEBRUARY 2010

Here's another Piers Morgan, from when he was still in Britain. This week he did an hour-long, prime-time interview with the Prime Minister. Moving, probing and heartbreaking as it undeniably was, many cynics (hello) also noted that there was an election on the way. Morgan, as you will remember, left the Daily Mirror *after photographs of British soldiers abusing Iraqi detainees, which he put on the front page, were shown to be fake.*

MONDAY

When my phone rings it could be anyone. Barack Obama, Neil Armstrong, Naomi Campbell, Elton John, Bob Dylan, Nelson Mandela, any one of the people I call my best mates, albeit often quite loudly when they're walking quite fast the opposite way. This time it's only the Prime Minister.

'Hello mate, you fat f***ing tosser!!' I say, because he's a mate, and if mates aren't the people who call you a fat f***ing tosser every time they hear your voice, then I don't have any mates at all. 'What can I do you for?' Gordon's upset. Says he wants to know how our private intimate conversation, recorded in front of a live audience for broadcast on ITV, ended up yesterday on the front page of the *Mail on Sunday*.

Gordon says he's been speaking to Alastair, and Alastair reckoned I might have had something to do with it. On account of the way I write a column for the *Mail on Sunday*, too.

'Campbell?' I say. 'Didn't you see him on telly the other day, trying to get people to like him by being all weepy? Different for you, mate,' I tell him. 'Natural all the way!'

'Oh,' says Gordon. 'Good.'

Then he hangs up. Then he calls back again, to say 'mate'.

TUESDAY

Can't pretend I'm all that happy with the Brown interview, to be honest. People sometimes assume I'm all about the showbiz, but I'm actually a pretty savvy political operator, too. Well, I did edit the *Daily Mirror*!!

'Look Gordon,' I said to him, beforehand. 'We don't want any of that sit-down Paxman rubbish. We want a three-way thing with me, Simon Cowell and Amanda Holden. Bit of a warm-up with Ant and Dec. You on the stage in something spangly, then a musical number with a key change.'

Gordon just wasn't up for it. Got to say, I'm pretty disappointed. Has he forgotten how much good I did for Nick Clegg?

WEDNESDAY

Still lots of stories about our interview. Gordon wants me to pop around to No. 10 tomorrow for a quiet chat, but I convince him it would be actually far more discreet if we lunched at the Ivy with Dannii Minogue and the fat guy out of *Gavin and Stacey*.

THURSDAY

In the end, Gordon just pulls up outside and makes me come out to the car. Says all the coverage was the wrong tone, and that he wished he hadn't done the interview in the first place. Wonders if we could get ITV to pull it.

'No chance, mate,' I tell him, fondly punching him in the goolies. 'And don't go blaming me! You vetoed all the good questions! Favourite celebrity breasts, what Sarah wears in bed, amusing tales of flatulence, all the real statesman stuff.' Gordon wonders if we should record a follow-up. 'Deffo, mate!' I say, thinking that this is going to be real *Frost/Nixon* stuff. Then I tell him I've got to get back inside, because I reckon Billie Piper was giving me the eye.

FRIDAY

Gordon calls again. Says he doesn't want to do another interview after all. Says he'd rather cut his losses.

'Don't be so hasty,' I snarl. 'I have photos. You and Ed Balls in a shipping container. Doing unspeakable things to the Miliband brothers.'

Gordon goes quiet for a minute. But they can't be real photos, he says, eventually.

'So?' I say.

SALLY BERCOW
5 FEBRUARY 2011

Sally Bercow is the wife of John Bercow, the Speaker of the House of Commons. This was written the week she posed in ES *Magazine wearing only a sheet, with the House of Commons in the background. Later that year she did* Celebrity Big Brother.

<u>MONDAY</u>

'Darling?' says my husband. 'Would you mind fetching me the biscuit tin off the shelf?'

'Righto,' I say, because as the Speaker of the House of Commons he's terribly important and shouldn't have to stand on his dignity. Or a chair.

'You seem a bit glum,' he says, as we sit facing each other on the new sofa suite, which is just one of the perks of his job as the person cleaning up Parliament after the expenses scandal.

'I was on Twitter earlier,' I sigh, 'and lots of beastly people were saying I was freeloading off your position for publicity.'

John says they're just jealous of the way we're both so happy and sexy and totally not amusing in silhouette when we walk hand in hand.

'If it really bothers you,' he adds, 'you should probably exploit your position to do lots of interviews in which you vehemently protest that you aren't exploiting your position.'

'That hasn't worked yet,' I muse.

'Give it time,' he says.

TUESDAY

It really annoys me the way some people on Twitter think John's a Tory. Actually, he's above politics. Like God.

'He's neutral!' I tweet. 'Even the thought of being a dirty f***ing Tory makes him want to vomit!'

This is what neutral means, right?

WEDNESDAY

I'm a Labour activist. It's a great thing to be, because it gives them something to put under my name when I go on Sky News, but I don't actually have to do anything about it.

I do worry, though, that some people try to use this to undermine John. The truth of the matter is, lots of Tory MPs don't like John because he's not a racist anymore.

So now, when he makes loads of totally reasonable and traditional requests about how MPs should behave towards the Speaker in the House – 'get out my way'; 'buy me a coffee'; 'walk backwards chanting my name with your forehead touching the carpet' – they simply refuse.

It's just so petty.

THURSDAY

In a way, I'm the Carla Bruni of British politics. And not just because my husband wears heels. Also because neither of us is afraid of posing nude.

'John?' I say. 'This is, of course, terribly embarrassing, but remember all those interviews I was doing? In particular, remember the one where I posed for the *Evening Standard* magazine draped in a sheet, and went on and on about how much I loved doing it to the sound of Big Ben?'

My husband says lots of things like 'grr' and 'woof' at the thought. That's just the way we are. We're totally into sex. With each other. Deal with it.

'No,' I say. 'But listen. They've syndicated the photos. They'll be everywhere, probably alongside a really out-of-context list of stuff I've said on Twitter.'

'To be honest,' says John, 'I still don't really know what Twitter is. But as long as it isn't an online forum on which you unhesitatingly broadcast your innermost thoughts as soon as you have them, I reckon we'll be fine.'

FRIDAY

Today we've both decided that I should get out there and do loads of interviews about how unwise I was to do interviews.

'On the plus side,' I say to John, as we study my nearly naked form in every newspaper in the country, 'at least nobody can say I'm not finally getting some publicity in my own right!'

'Only because you can't see I'm under there, too,' says John.

VICTORIA BECKHAM
8 JANUARY 2011

Victoria Beckham was all over the papers this week. Since when did she need an actual reason?

MONDAY

In the kitchen of our enormous desirable home in fashionable Los Angeles – where coincidentally we're actually very good friends with Tom Cruise and his fashionable wife from *Dawson's Creek* – my son Romeo is eating a small bowl of corn flakes in his Dolce & Gabbana pyjamas.

I kiss him on the top of the head, and tell him he's made me very proud.

'But you could eat a small bowl of corn flakes, too,' he says. 'If you really tried.'

No, darling, I say, and I tell him it's actually because he's been named as one of the best dressed men in the world by *GQ* magazine.

'I had better be on there, too,' says David, my fashionable husband. Then he sits splayed in his armchair, looking stricken.

Probably best not to do that in your sarong, darling, I tell him.

David crosses his legs, mumbling something about being old and past it.

'It's not so bad,' I whisper in his ear. 'After all, it's not like he chooses his own clothes.'

'But I don't get to choose my own clothes either,' says David.

TUESDAY

Breakfast again. Can't believe the dent I've made in my January grapefruit already. Am turning into a right pig. Romeo's triumph is all over the papers. David is stomping around, eyeing all the boys resentfully.

'How come they're all allowed pyjamas?' he says. 'You know I wanted some for Christmas. I'm sick of this thing. I never liked it.'

'I wanted a toy tractor,' says Romeo.

'You didn't,' I say.

'I think I did,' says Romeo. 'I wrote to Santa.'

'Yes dear,' I say. 'And you asked him for a tailor-made Savile Row suit, inside leg eighteen inches.'

'I never did,' says Romeo.

'Go to your room,' I say.

WEDNESDAY

'David!' I shout, when I see him standing very far away at the other end of our fashionable corridor. 'Come and have a look at this!'

Unfortunately it's not David standing very far away, but in fact our youngest son standing quite close. Such are the perils of having an identical family, all of whom you have personally designed, as though they were dolls.

'Oops,' I say, and I quickly hide the newspaper I'm waving, in which the world has finally learnt about my secret boob job.

'Come off it, Mum,' says Cruz, who is five. 'Everybody knew about that already.'

THURSDAY

Today it's David's turn to be in the paper, amid furious speculation that he is about to move back to Britain to play for Tottenham Hotspur.

On the downside, this would mean we'd have to leave behind our great friends Tom and Thingy Cruise. On the plus side, though, we'd be bound to be in some really fantastic photos as we all arrive in London.

'What would you like to wear for the airport?' I ask Romeo.

'Why aren't you asking me?' wails David.

'Spider-Man costume,' says Romeo.

'Spider-Man blue and red?' I ask. 'Or Spider-Man in Karl Lagerfeld's spring/summer 2011 collection with fur waistcoat and harem pants?'

'Spider-Man never wore that,' says Romeo.

'Don't answer back,' I say.

FRIDAY

The boob thing is still all over the papers.

'Actually,' says David, 'I'm quite proud of you.'

'Did she eat a small bowl of cereal?' says Cruz.

'No,' says David.

'Did she finish the grapefruit?' says Brooklyn.

No, I say. I told the truth about having had my unfashionable fake breasts removed.

'Aren't fake breasts fashionable anymore?' says Romeo.

No, I say.

'And that's probably why you haven't all got them,' says David.

NAOMI CAMPBELL
7 AUGUST 2010

This week, the supermodel Naomi Campbell gave evidence to the trial of Charles Taylor of Liberia at the Hague. If this sounds like an incredibly weird thing to have happened, that's probably because it was an incredibly weird thing to have happened.

MONDAY

My lawyer comes in, wearing one of the crash helmets I keep for guests by the front door.

'Bad news, Naomi,' he says. 'I'm afraid you've been called to appear before a war crimes tribunal, because of the events of thirteen years ago.'

'But it was only a BlackBerry,' I say. 'And I wasn't even aiming at her.'

'No,' says my lawyer. 'I'm talking about that time that a group of mysterious men appeared at your door after a fancy dinner with international celebrities, and gave you a bag of priceless diamonds.'

'Narrow it down?' I say, because this sort of thing happens quite a lot.

My lawyer sighs and says it's something to do with a dinner I once went to, where I sat next to a man called Charles from a place called Liberia. Apparently I've got to appear in court in Holland, because my testimony could link him to the trade in blood diamonds and war crimes in Sierra Leone.

'That's horrific,' I say. It'll be OK, says my lawyer. Nobody thinks I knew.

'But Holland?' I say. 'I had plans.'

TUESDAY

Honestly, how am I supposed to remember anything about this? It was thirteen years ago! I don't even remember what my phone was thirteen years ago. Although I'd imagine I probably broke it.

'Darling,' I explain to my lawyer, 'people come up and give me stuff all the time. It's just part of being an internationally famous supermodel. Like that man in the waistcoat, who just brought me that bowl of bread.'

'We're in a restaurant,' says my lawyer.

'Exactly,' I say. 'Even here.'

WEDNESDAY

Today, we're flying to Holland. I've never really heard of Holland before, but I suppose there's every chance I once sat next to the person who owns it at a dinner. That can happen if you're friends with Nelson Mandela. He knows all the most interesting people.

Thinking about it, I suppose I do dimly remember something about some dirty little stones. It never occurred to me they might be diamonds. Not that long ago, somebody tried to pay me off after a modelling job with a bag full of dirty little bits of paper. Next he'll be telling me they were valuable, too!

'Not unless they had the Queen's head on them,' says my lawyer, who sounds exhausted.

Jeez. What am I, an expert?

THURSDAY

Today's the day. Thankfully, the war crimes tribunal is

making a special case of me, and is protecting me from the photographers outside. After all, I've got an international modelling career to protect. The last thing I want is people knowing what I look like.

'Got to go, Naomi,' says my lawyer, as I try on various dresses and do astonishing, yet demure, things with my hair.

'Seriously,' he says, a while later. 'They need you now. They've sent a car.'

'That's very sweet,' I say, 'but I've already got a car.'

FRIDAY

At last, this nightmare is behind me. My lawyer and I are flying home. Complete strangers keep coming up and giving me things. Tiny drinks, usually.

'Oh my God,' I say, nudging my lawyer awake. 'That man just gave me this small packet of mysterious brown things! More blood diamonds!'

'Or peanuts,' says my lawyer, yawning. 'But you never know.'

STEVEN SPIELBERG
11 AUGUST 2007

You may have forgotten this, but Steven Spielberg was due to direct the opening ceremony of the Beijing Olympics. A few months after this, he pulled out. Maybe he read it?

MONDAY

A Chinese general has flown over to see me in Hollywood. 'What we want,' he says, 'is arien. Cute rittle thing. Face rike jobby.'

Ages ago, I agreed to help to organise the opening ceremony for the Chinese Olympics in 2008. Seemed a good idea at the time. Then I forgot about it.

'Maybe,' I say. 'Aliens are cool. Only, I'm more into high concept these days. Save the world. Peace. Nazis. Yeah?'

'Shark?' suggests the Chinese general. 'Dinosoah?'

I sigh. 'I'm thinking of a third of the world's population, in an emerging democracy,' I suggest. 'Sound and light. I'm thinking of a huge crowd, all taking part in a giant high-kicking synchronised dance of life, love and freedom. Maybe they could rebuild a mini version of the Great Wall?'

'Yes!' says the Chinese general, clapping his hands. 'We use death row prisoners. They velly cheap labour!'

TUESDAY

Am perturbed. Mia Farrow calls.

'Who are you, again?' I say.

'God knows,' says Mia Farrow. 'Some actress. I may once have had something to do with Woody Allen. But look, never mind that. You need to do something about Darfur. There's a really nasty genocide going on there.'

'I love it,' I say. 'Brilliant. Do we have a script? I'll call Tom Hanks.'

Mia gets quite shrill. Turns out she isn't calling about a film. Seems China is involved in Darfur.

'I'm talking about the Olympics,' she says. 'Don't you know what happens? The Janjaweed militias attack villages on horseback, while the Sudanese Air Force attacks from above! And China doesn't care. You have to do something about it!'

'I dunno,' I muse. 'Seems a bit tactless. I'll stick with the big dance.'

WEDNESDAY

I call Tom Hanks anyway. We play squash. I hate playing squash with Tom. He's rubbish at it, but ever since *Saving Private Ryan* he's had this special look of quiet forlorn dignity. He does it whenever I win a point.

'So anyway,' I pant, as we swing, 'whaddaya think about China?'

'China?' says Tom. 'Definite Oscar material. Ancient civilisation, Cultural Revolution, executions, human rights abuses, crackdowns on religious minorities, support of African dictators, I love it. China is even better than the Nazis. Who would be in it?'

'High-kicking death row slaves rebuilding the Great Wall as part of a huge dancing sound and light show to publicise the 2008 Olympic Games,' I say, slamming the ball into the top left corner.

Tom does his look of quiet forlorn dignity. Then he says he'd need to straighten his hair.

THURSDAY

Another meeting with that Chinese general. There have been problems. The new Great Wall idea is fine, but apparently the high kicks of the death row prisoners just aren't high enough to symbolise the wondrous, soaring, optimistic freedom of the new China.

'Tomollow,' he suggests, 'perhaps we lemove reg irons.'

FRIDAY

OK, so I'm a bit worried about China. Why the hell did I ever agree to this? Maybe I had them confused with Taiwan. I call Tom Hanks.

'Tom,' I say. 'I'm sorry. You were right. The Chinese regime is awful. Even Mia Farrow thinks so.'

'Remind me,' says Tom, 'which one is Mia Farrow?'

'I dunno,' I say. 'I think she had something to do with Woody Allen.'

Now. Time for a couple of e-mails...

From: Rifkind, Hugo
To: Private Eye
Subject: erm

Top of Pseuds Corner in May eleventh issue
– Geri Halliwell quote from 'My Week' in *The
Times* – 'muesli is a bit like a rebirth'. My
Week is my Saturday parody column. I know a
fine parody can be hard to spot, but I sort of
thought that you lot, of all people, might be
up to it.

From: Private Eye
To: Rifkind, Hugo
Subject: Re: erm

Did we? God. Can we publish this as a letter
to the editor?

From: Private Eye
To: Rifkind, Hugo
Subject: Re: erm

You'll be pleased to know news of our mistake
was just greeted by the editor with the words
'bastard, bastard, bastard'.

GERI HALLIWELL
14 APRIL 2007

God, I was proud. This week, the former Spice Girl published a children's book.

MONDAY

For me, eating a bowl of muesli is a bit like a rebirth. It's just so holistic, don't you think?

Well, I do. I'm a very spiritual person, you see. I find myself using words like 'rebirth' and 'holistic' even when I'm talking about things that are actually rather mundane. Like muesli.

I used to be so selfish. All I cared about was my celebrity friends, and what they thought of me. But then George Michael told me to stop all that and pull myself together. So I have. I've decided I'm going to be an author. I'm going to write children's books.

One minute I'm a pop star, and a UN Goodwill Ambassador, the next I'm a children's author. That's me all over. I'm an enigma. Like Madonna. But nicer. Although she's great.

TUESDAY

Into London today to see my publishers. 'Writing this children's book,' I tell them, brightly, 'is a bit like a rebirth.'

Everybody smiles and nods. They are all making a real effort to be polite, because of a slightly embarrassing incident downstairs.

Not that I was embarrassed. Some people would really mind if they turned up at their publishers and their publishers didn't recognise them because the last time they came in they were really fat and the time before that they were really thin, and the idiot stupid publishers, who were never into pop even though it was Girl Power and really important, didn't realise that the really fat person and the really thin person and now this totally normal-sized person were actually the same person who was totally ****ing famous and a UN Goodwill ****ing Ambassador.

Like I said, some people would be upset by that. Me, I'm cool. I don't get upset.

That's just who I am.

WEDNESDAY

'You're upset,' yawns my friend George Michael, who is dozing on my sofa. He's come around to read the newspapers. George won't have newspapers in the house. Of course, he's forgotten that I won't have newspapers in the house either. So later, we're going round to our friend Elton John's place, to read the papers there.

Elton won't have them in the house either, but he has a very big garage.

'Shhh,' I tell George, pacing around with a notebook. 'I'm thinking. I need some characters for my book. I'm thinking that the heroine is going to be this feisty young girl with ginger hair. There's going to be a Princess Posh who has all the best things, and grumpy Gordon the chef.'

'They sound, uh, familiar,' says George.

'How so?' I ask, but he's fallen asleep.

Oooh. I've just thought of another. Big Gay Sleepy George. I'm so creative. It's probably holistic.

THURSDAY

I call my publishers, to tell them about the new characters. I do love speaking to my publishers. I suppose it's like a rebirth. In a way.

'Geri Halliwell speaking,' I say to the switchboard.

'Which one?' says the receptionist.

Some people would find this kind of impertinent, slack-jawed ****ing idiocy really ****ing annoying. But not me. I don't get angry. I do yoga.

FRIDAY

Everybody is very excited about the books. Apparently, it's in all the papers.

George and I head to Elton's to read them, but Elton has decided he hates the press so much that he doesn't even want them in his garage anymore. So all three of us go round to Gordon Ramsay's.

While we're there, Wayne Rooney's girlfriend calls. She's heard that I'm planning to write about a spend-thrift character called Chav Queen Coleen.

'And what,' I ask her, 'has that got to do with you?'

PART IV
LITERATURE

HILARY MANTEL
23 FEBRUARY 2013

This section ('LITERATURE' he says, grandly) is actually pretty different from the rest of this book. There are some great newspaper satirists – notably Craig Brown and John Crace – who are basically parodists. I'm not really clever enough for that. Sometimes I'll mock speaking styles, when I think they'll be recognised, but usually I get my jokes out of soul and public image. Actually grappling with text and twisting it is much harder, partly because you need to be confident that your reader has read the thing you're taking the piss out of. Normally, I'm not.

Anyway, here's a few in which I try. This first week, Hilary Mantel, the author of Wolf Hall, *faces tabloid crucifixion for writing disobliging things about the Duchess of Cambridge. Technically, she was discussing the media portrayal of our Kate, rather than Kate herself, but nobody really cared about that.*

MONDAY
'So now get up.'

Felled, dazed silent, I am lying; stretched full length on the sheets of my bed. My head turns sideways; my eyes turned outwards towards the wall. It is blue, blue. Or maybe green; greenish blue. Cyan. It could be cyan; I must Google it.

The noise rings; I rise; I fall. A semi-colon; a semi-colon; a semi-colon; too many; far too many; I must stop using them; but it's so hard to; once you start; it's hard to stop; so hard; so very hard. Phew.

'Seriously,' says my husband. 'At least let me turn the alarm off.'

'Yeah, OK,' I say. 'Put it on snooze.'

TUESDAY

My agent calls. 'We need to talk.'

I'm sorry, I say. I'm sorry that everybody thinks you're stupid.

'What?' she says.

Sorry; so sorry. It's not you. It's your face; your stupid face. Or rather, it looks stupid. To us. The dim eyes, too close together. Not really too close; never really, portrayed as too close. By this cruel society of ours. By the media. So stupid. As painfully stupid as anyone could wish.

'Right,' she says. 'OK. But more importantly...' And fat, I say. Fat; so fat. Not your fault. Nor even the fault of whales; whales which are the shape of you. Also, ugly. Why should it be that face like a bulldog; like a scaly bulldog, really, should be so perceived? Your poor face. Your poor, stupid, fat, ugly, whale-sized, bulldog face.

'I'm hanging up now,' says my agent. 'Because I'm quite offended.'

'But why?' I say, genuinely bemused.

WEDNESDAY

I call my agent back. 'OK,' I say. 'I see what you wanted to talk about, now. All this from a fuss from an essay in the *London Review of Books*?' 'I'm sorry,' says my agent. 'But I'm too fat, stupid and ugly to comprehend what you are saying. Apparently.'

'No!' I say. 'You aren't! I was talking about the objectifying shallow media in which...' 'Yes, yes,' says my agent.

I'm genuinely shocked, I tell her. How could anybody think my article was an attack on Kate Middleton? Even the Prime Minister! When clearly it was an attack on the media? 'Because it's just not like you to write something that nobody quite understands,' says my agent. 'Is it?' It's almost like they read the first bit so they could show off about it, and then didn't bother to read any more, I say.

'Imagine,' says my agent.

THURSDAY

David Cameron calls, the Prime Minister. He says he's sorry. I say he should be. He says yes, yes. You can say that again. Yes, yes. You said it, no you said it. Yes, no, I did, you, I did, I did. Who, me, you, yes. Quite.

Then he says he's lost track of who is saying what, actually, because of my weird habit of not using paragraph breaks.

'Although to be fair,' he continues, 'I reckon we're pretty much equal. Because I told everybody *Wolf Hall* was great, and I hadn't read that either.'

FRIDAY

Fuming, still, this Friday of now. Up in bed. Sitting. Is what I am doing; sitting. Cyan walls. Cyan, I think to myself, cyan.

I call Downing Street.

I'm also sorry, I say. 'You're sorry?' says the Prime Minister. I'm sorry everybody thinks you have a face like a bum, I say. A face, a face; a bum. And a bald spot. And a stupid voice, not that you do, just a perception; an unfair perception. Due to eyes. Also, ears.

'Apology accepted,' says Cameron.

'Dimwit,' I say.

DAN BROWN
19 SEPTEMBER 2009

The novelist Dan Brown (who wrote The Da Vinci Code*) had a new book out. He's actually even harder to parody as a writer than most, because he's just so very, very, inimitably bad.*

MONDAY

I could feel a nose that was about to sneeze, and I knew it was my own.

I'm going to sneeze.

'Have a tissue,' said my 47-year-old literary agent who was wearing a red and green striped tie and a brown corduroy jacket with patches on the elbows and other stuff that I'll mysteriously not mention despite being so incredibly specific thus far.

'Thank you,' I said, and I sneezed like I did the first time we met over a decade ago when I had no idea that I would one day be the incredibly famous bestselling 45-year-old author Dan Brown who wrote *The Da Vinci Code.*

Today we were meeting to discuss my next novel which will be a bestselling story about where all the odd socks go.

'That's a rubbish idea,' said my agent. And even when I told him that the mystery would be solved by an intelligent and beautiful Harvard sockologist who looks like Angelina Jolie he did not change his mind.

'The famous author is disappointed,' I told him.

'You don't need to tell me that,' said my agent. 'I can infer it from the look on your face and the general circumstances of the situation.'

'I don't understand,' I said.

'I know,' said my agent.

TUESDAY

I am very disappointed with my 47-year-old agent's reaction to the socks idea.

He didn't like it. I'll have to think of another one.

It isn't easy thinking up new ideas for bestselling conspiracy novels.

Particularly if they have to be fresh and original like mine always are.

Suddenly my 56-year-old wife and alleged art historian Blythe stands silhouetted in the doorway with her brown eyes flashing like small bits of wood.

My wife and I collaborate on much of my work although she isn't always sure that my similes work. We also disagree on what 'silhouette' means.

'Honey?' she says. 'If you're stuck, why not just write another book about the renowned Harvard symbologist Robert Langdon?'

Hmmm. Maybe.

If I'm honest I'm trying to phase him out. I've never actually met a Harvard symbologist. I'm worried that a real one will come along and tell me I'm getting things wrong.

WEDNESDAY

There was a bestselling author who was still trying to think of a plot for his next novel and that bestselling author was the famous 45-year-old Dan Brown who was me.

'I have a terrible cold,' he said aloud to nobody in

particular but mainly because he couldn't think of any other way to get the information on to the page.

'Honey,' says the silhouette of my 56-year-old wife. 'You're getting weird.'

THURSDAY

In desperation I call Tom Hanks. He's a 53-year-old actor who looks like an old Tom Hanks.

'Tom,' I say. 'I need a new conspiracy. I've just done Freemasons and the US Government. I can't think where else to go.'

Tom, who might be wearing a polo shirt and slacks but might not be because how would I know, asks me what my options are.

'Not sure,' I say. 'Obviously there will be an albino monk hitman, but other than that I'm sort of stumped. Any ideas? You're bound to end up starring in it.'

Tom Hanks starts crying and says something about how he won Oscars back in the 1990s and people used to think he might be president.

'Your acting lights up the world,' I tell him. 'Like a fabulous trumpet.'

'Leave me alone,' says Tom Hanks.

FRIDAY

Back in to see my 48-year-old agent who has had a birthday.

'How is your nose?' he asks.

'It burns,' I tell him. 'Like sandpaper.'

My agent closes his eyes and asks if I've had a better idea yet.

'Nope,' I say. 'Still keen on the sock one.'

'Oh, what the hell,' says my agent. 'Let's go for a first print run of seventeen million copies.'

E. L. JAMES
14 JULY 2012

Fifty Shades of Grey *is a global bestseller. Nobody knows why.*

MONDAY

The chair is upholstered in expensive leather and reclined at an awkward angle. I lie back, so flushed with anticipation that I am afraid to breathe.

Derek leans over me, intimately close. 'I warn you, Ms James,' he growls, 'this could be a little painful.'

His deft fingers skim my skin, brushing my hair from my face. His touch weakens me. I can imagine his strong hands piloting an expensive private jet.

Staring deep into my eyes, he covers the lower part of his face with a mask and looms over me, clutching gleaming tools. I am consumed with anticipation for something I dare not name.

'Steady,' he warns. 'The more you move, the more this will hurt.'

'Yes!' I cry, wild with want. 'Hurt me!'

'You're freaking me out,' says Derek, standing up. 'I hereby resign as your dentist.'

TUESDAY

Since writing the bestselling sado-masochistic erotic fiction *Fifty Shades of Grey*, my life has changed enormously. The reviews have all been terrible. I find this deeply arousing.

People keep asking me how I first developed an interest in BDSM. Between us, it was all the result of a typo, when I was Googling for driving lessons.

'OK,' says my instructor. 'Ease off the gas. Do you want to crash?'

His hands are clad in driving gloves which might be made of expensive calf's leather, but might come from Halfords.

'Do you want me to?' I ask, my voice thick with forbidden longing.

'Um, no?' he says, so I drive into the back of a van.

'No means no!' he shouts.

'Oh, come off it,' I say.

WEDNESDAY

I have a meeting with a producer who wants to make my novel into a movie.

'Baby,' he says. 'Awesome sales figures. What a coup. This is totally going to happen. You must be really excited.'

To be honest, I tell him, I'm a bit conflicted. On the one hand, I'm really thrilled. On the other, the submissive in me would be a lot more happy if he was actually standing there telling me he thought it was total crap.

'Oh don't worry,' he says. 'I do totally think that. Everybody does.'

'Thank you,' I swoon.

THURSDAY

All these sudden riches have allowed my husband and I to put our old flat on the market and move into somewhere much bigger.

We're having a bit of a disagreement, though, over what to do with all the space. I want a Red Room Of Pain And Humiliation. He wants a shed.

'I'm finding this really difficult,' he says. 'I don't know whether you want me to give in or not.'

In the end, we go for a red shed. We're going to share the pliers.

FRIDAY

I can hear nothing, just the pounding thud of my heart.

'Please,' I moan at the man in black, 'loosen the clamp.' I'm writhing. His sheer erotic mastery of the situation is making me tingle all over. His voice is slow and deliberate. 'I think we both know I can't do that,' he says.

Holy cow! From his pocket, he pulls a small book bound in tight black leather. His eyes pierce into mine. I'm trembling all over. His tongue caresses my vehicle registration number.

'Hold on!' shouts the man from BSM. 'Sorry! Just nipped into the shop.'

'Lucky escape,' says the traffic warden. 'But don't do it again.'

JULIE MYERSON
14 MARCH 2009

Some explanation probably required here. Julie Myerson was the anonymous author of a detailed and confessional column entitled Living With Teenagers, but denied it to her own teenagers three times. The truth came out in 2009, when she published an equally detailed and confessional book called The Lost Child. *This detailed her estrangement from her eldest teenage son, kicked out of home because of his cannabis habit. The son wished she hadn't.*

This provoked a national debate about parenthood and the ethics of the writer. In the midst of all this, she gave interviews, he gave interviews, her partner gave interviews; there was quite the media circus. Even on Newsnight. *Even in* The Sun. *Then it all went away.*

MONDAY

Our beautiful boy, the other one, who had virtually no pubic hair until really quite recently, is eating Coco Pops at the kitchen table.

Again? My partner and I exchange glances over the top of his head.

'God!' shouts our boy, this son, who used to wet the bed and told us confidentially the other day that he fancies a girl in his class called Lucy.

'Aaargh! It's cereal! Everybody eats cereal! You guys are so naive!'

I don't think we are naive. We live in South London and we both work in the media. And we're vegetarians. So actually, I think we're pretty switched on. I tried cereal myself, when I was a student.

But cereal was different then. It was so much less sugary. This stuff is so chocolatey it even turns the milk brown. It's terrifying.

Clearly our boy is an addict. My partner thinks we should kick him out. I think we should wait a while.

There's just no money in short stories these days.

TUESDAY

Our wonderful girl, who you would never guess used to have such terrible skin, has lost a shoe.

'Did you sell it?' shouts my partner. 'For amphetamines? Get out!'

Is that with an F, I ask, or a PH?

'PH,' says my partner, peering over my shoulder into my notebook. 'God, that's really good, actually. Especially that phrase, just there. You've totally captured the way she went all pale when I started shouting.'

I am pleased. But doesn't he think I've overdone all the stuff about always loving her, and how amazing she was as a small child?

'Not at all,' says my partner. 'And you were right to mention her bad skin. That was a really upsetting time for us, wasn't it?'

My girl stamps her foot and wants to know whether she's being kicked out or not.

'Shhh, darling,' says my partner. 'Mummy's working.'

WEDNESDAY

It's so hard! These Coco Pops are tearing our perfect family apart! My partner and I have decided that, if we aren't to kick our boy out, we should at least write a series of newspaper articles all about the time he soiled himself on a swing when he was a toddler, and about his first wet dream.

'That doesn't follow at all!' he shouted, in that furious way he sometimes has, that makes me wonder how somebody I love more than life itself can seem to hate me so much.

You wouldn't understand I told him, as I touched him on his beautiful cheek. Because you are not a writer.

THURSDAY

Our other boy comes round. He's the one who brought shame on our family by selling his story to the *Daily Mail*, rather than to a publisher or a left-leaning broadsheet, like he was brought up to do. He said he knew we'd had a bad week, but he thought we could put it behind us.

'Please,' he said. 'Just stop writing everything down, and selling it, and then pretending you haven't. I'm begging you.'

Actually, the way he said it was even more heart-rending than that. But I went off to get my Dictaphone, and he just wouldn't say it again.

He was such a sweet boy. When did he become so selfish?

FRIDAY

A family meeting over breakfast. The older boy doesn't come. He's angry because there was an anonymous column in the newspapers this morning about a mother whose son begs her to stop writing anonymous columns in the newspapers. I denied everything, but he doesn't believe me. I feel so guilty about lying to him. I suppose I'll have to write an anonymous column about it.

'Listen,' says my partner. 'Family announcement.'

He tells the kids that I've decided to turn our battle against Coco Pops and amphetamines into a Hollywood script. 'But obviously,' he adds, 'she won't do it unless you guys say it's OK. So?'

Absolutely not, says our darling boy.

Please God, no, says our beautiful girl.

'So we're agreed!' says my partner, clapping his hands. 'Full steam ahead! Now. Anybody fancy a vegetarian omelette?'

IAN McEWAN
8 SEPTEMBER 2007

Ian McEwan is nominated for a Booker Prize, while the adaptation of Atonement *is at the cinema. The previous year, he had been accused of plagiarism, after a passage in* Atonement *closely resembled another in a memoir he cited in the footnotes.*

MONDAY

Some hours after dawn, really at quite a normal time of the morning, I find myself at the top of the stairs in my Oxford home, lowering one foot into the deep pile of my carpet with a springy crunch.

The foot is in a brogue of deep brown, and that brown reminds me of the steak I ate for dinner last night, with chips and ketchup.

The ketchup was in a plastic bottle, smooth, sensuous and contoured, like the hull of a pedalo I once took on Lake Como, a lake which always makes me think of other lakes, which makes me think of bathtubs and childhood and loss.

I am startled from my reverie by the impact of my second foot upon the second step. A not entirely unpleasurable sensation.

This foot, too, is in a brown brogue. There are holes picked out on it, like the pockmarks of an old man's skin. I don't feel old.

Nor do I feel young. I am neither tired nor untired,

not sad nor unsad. In fact, I feel neutral, a state of being which has left these last sentences quite entirely uncalled for. I prepare myself to lower my first foot, once more.

'Ian?' calls my wife, from the kitchen.

'Are you ever going to get down those bloody stairs?'

TUESDAY

It is Tuesday. Tuesday always reminds me of other days, including Sundays. Sundays remind me of bad sex. And childhood. And loss.

My novel *Atonement* has been made into a film, which reminds me of another novel, *Enduring Love*, which was also made into a film. This is what it is to be a writer.

One thing reminds you of another.

Atonement stars the actress Keira Knightley. She reminds me of other actresses.

WEDNESDAY

After a long journey which I won't go into but may describe in eye-watering detail over thirty pages of my next novel, I meet my agent in London.

He is very excited. Apparently, I may be on the Booker shortlist for *On Chesil Beach*.

This, I tell him, reminds me of 1997, 1998, 2001 and 2005, when we also thought I was going to be on the Booker shortlist and, sometimes, I wasn't.

My agent asks me if I have started a new book yet. I tell him I haven't. I can't think what to write about.

'Do what you always do when you get stuck,' suggests my agent. 'Pick the most interesting story out of the newspapers, turn it into a novel, and work in some themes of childhood and loss. And bad sex. Then, if you have any space left over, fill it with descriptions of people looking at things.'

THURSDAY

I have started work on a new novel. It is about a novelist who wrote a book that has been made into a film starring Keira Knightley. In chapter one he wakes up and walks down a flight of stairs looking at his shoes. Brogues, I think.

FRIDAY

My agent calls. It seems *On Chesil Beach* is on the Booker shortlist after all.

'I have started a new novel,' I tell him. 'It is about the most interesting story in the newspapers. I was worried it might be a bit thin, like *Amsterdam*, but I've had this great idea to pad it out with descriptions of people looking at things.

'Was that your idea?' says my agent, 'I thought it was my idea.'

'It was inspired by your idea,' I correct him.

'Oh,' says my agent.

SIR SALMAN RUSHDIE
23 JUNE 2007

*Salman Rushdie receives a knighthood. There is a predict-
able barrage of effigies, riots and threats against his life
from predictable parts of the world. This one, I fear, may
have been a touch too faithful to the source text. In that,
looking at it now, I can't really figure out what I was
on about.*

MONDAY

It was Monday, in the city of New York. No, that won't
do, there is no getting away from the date: it was the
Monday after the world learnt of my knighthood. O yes!
Quite a very important Monday indeed!

'Ho ji! Ho ji!' I cried, as I awoke, tumbling from
the heavens. Twenty-nine thousand and two feet from the
ground, or thereabouts, high above Manhattan. Who am
I? Not just Salman Rushdie, but also the angel Gibreel and
the devil Chamcha, the three of us again, falling as one.

'Ta-taa! Taka-thun!' Plummeting towards every race
and creed, all looking up once more at our descent.
Look! A yellow car-thing! And look! A statue-thing with
a torch-thing! And look! A bird-thing and a...'

'Come off it,' interrupts my wife, peering over my
shoulder. 'This plainly isn't what actually happened on
Monday.'

'Is it not?' I say, raising my eyebrows enigmatically.

'No,' she says. 'It really isn't.'

TUESDAY

My wife is the goddess Padma Lakshmi, almost as famous as me, for reasons neither one of us can quite discern. I remember when I first saw her, in the swimwear section of a catalogue.

O yes! You will not be surprised to learn that, looking deep into her eyes, I knew at once that this was my intellectual soul mate.

It is evening. This morning, I gave her my redrafted version of Monday. Her thoughts?

'Oh,' she says. 'Yeah. I started it, and I really wanted to get to the end. But then it got a bit odd, and I sort of lost interest. Sorry.'

WEDNESDAY

I have written a long letter to the Pakistani Ambassador. I am hoping we can meet.

I think I have a very clever idea to make this all die down.

Last night Padma and I ate out at a restaurant. My protection officers are jumpy.

They want to review everywhere we went, everything we saw and everybody we spoke to, just in case.

'Just to be clear,' says one of the policemen. 'This waiter – you don't know for a fact that he was a direct descendant of Christopher Columbus, yet possessed by the spirit of Genghis Khan's dog. Or do you?'

Oh, this is vexing! I must be two entirely separate Salman Rushdies. Conjoined twins, caught in the global theopolitic web! One of whom must ignore the magic in the world, and another who cannot see anything else.

Note to self: idea for next novel? Perhaps make one of the Salman Rushdies gay / disabled / the reincarnation of Marco Polo?

THURSDAY

O Salman, can this truly be beginning again? A riot thing in Malaysia? An effigy-thing in Karachi?

Yes, Salman, it can. But fear not! The Pakistani Ambassador must have my letter by now. My solution to the furore over my knighthood is truly most clever indeed!

Do I doubt it, Salman? O! At any moment, must not the telephone ring?

Well done, Salman!

Thank you, Salman!

I'm getting quite into this.

FRIDAY

I am pacing around the apartment. The protection officers won't let me go out. I spend a while working on my new novel. One of the Salman twins is going to accept his knighthood, and the other is going to turn it down. But which?

Speaking of this matter, I still haven't heard from the Pakistani Ambassador about my letter. I call his office.

'He started it,' says the secretary, 'and he really wanted to get to the end. But then it got a bit odd, and he sort of lost interest. Sorry.'

HOLDEN CAULFIELD
<u>30 JANUARY 2010</u>

J. D. Salinger died this week, after spending the bulk of his adult life as an enigmatic recluse. So there wasn't really any other option.

<u>MONDAY</u>

If you really want to hear about it, the first thing you'll probably want to know is what I've been up to for the past sixty years, and what my lousy adulthood was like, and what the hell J. D. Salinger has been doing, and all that David Copperfield kind of crap, but I don't feel like going into it, if you want to know the truth. In the first place that stuff bores me, and in the second place he was touchy as hell about that sort of thing, hence him locking me in the cellar.

I'll just tell you about this madman stuff that's going on this week. All these academic phonies have realised he's about to die, so they're calling the place trying to find out about other novels I might be in.

I'm not kidding. They really are.

'Holden,' they'll say, 'we want to know whether you're in any sequels.' Sure I'm in goddam sequels, I'll say. You bet. My favourite is the one where I go to Harvard and become a renowned symbologist and uncover a conspiracy by the Roman Catholic Church to keep it secret that Jesus had a wife.

'Oh no,' they'll say. 'Please God, no.'

Then they'll hang up. They really will. It makes me so goddam mad I don't even like to talk about it.

TUESDAY

It's ironical, to tell the truth. I don't even much like novels. My favourite writer is my brother D.B. He's in Hollywood these days, being ninety-eight and mainly asking strangers if they are his nephew. That's another thing all those phonies from universities want to know. How's the family? How's Phoebe? And did we ever find out how my brother Allie died, who had the baseball glove?

Sure, I told them. That was one of the prequels that Salinger put in the safe. Turned out in actual fact that he was still alive, but had just turned to the Dark Side and all. He started breathing funny and wearing a big goddam black helmet. I'm not kidding. That was the best story in the world.

The phonies were basically sobbing at that. I swear to God they were. It damn near made me sick.

WEDNESDAY

The old man died today so the academic phonies were calling dawn till dusk, and plenty of journalist phonies, too. That's exactly the kind of guys they are. Going on about how he was their favourite author ever, even though they only really knew one of his books and it didn't even have a single goddam alien or car chase in it.

THURSDAY

Some agent phoney was out the house today, and some phoney publisher broads, too. Said they appreciated I must be feeling sad and all, what with the death of my creator, but that it was also an opportunity for people finally to see what J. D. Salinger had been doing all these years and whether he really was a genius or something.

'Fact is,' said the agent, who was this really crummy-looking guy, 'people all over the world want to know what happened to you. Did you ever get into another school?'

Sure I did, I said, and I winked at one of the publishing broads, mainly because I felt sorry for her, on account of her squinty eyes and falsies that were pointing all over the place.

I went to Wizard School, I told them. There were loads of books about that. I thought they might have noticed my broom in the hall, for chrissake, but some people never notice anything.

FRIDAY

So they came into the house and they got the books out of the safe and they looked at them and then they all shouted at each other, put them back in the safe, and they went away.

Maybe they were disappointed or something. Who the hell knows? Not me. Turns out they didn't want all the new books after all. If you want to know the truth, I'm sorry I told so many people about them. It goes to show that you shouldn't ever tell anybody anything, like I always said.

PART V

ROYALTY AND ESTABLISHMENT

PRINCE HARRY
25 AUGUST 2012

On any given week, I'd rather write one of these about Prince Harry than almost anybody else alive. This was after he was photographed naked in Las Vegas. Prince William, meanwhile, was working as a helicopter rescue pilot in Wales.

MONDAY

'Dude,' I croak at one of my bodyguards, 'you got a light?' My bodyguard yawns, and scratches his crotch with his semi-automatic pistol.

'Why not just stick your face into the blazing fireplace?' he suggests.

'Awesome,' I say, and I crawl across the floor.

We're in Las Vegas. Last night is a blur. I remember a swimming pool, and Michael Phelps. Possibly, I remember Jennifer Lopez. After that, it gets totes hazy. Definitely, there was a game of snooker, although I don't think I was playing very well. The worse I played, though, the happier I felt. Weird.

'Where are my clothes?' I say.

'Where are my eyebrows?' says the bodyguard.

Dim hunch we might have overdone it last night, actually. Sexy bender. Gone properly Fergie. There's a blonde chick asleep on the couch. Think she might be wearing my Union Jack boxer shorts.

'Need a beer,' I say. 'Anybody got a bottle opener?'

'Hold still,' says my bodyguard. 'I'll shoot it open.'
I love these guys. They keep me safe.

TUESDAY

Still in Vegas. Skyping Wills and Kate.

'Bro,' he says. 'You look naked from this angle.'

'Bro,' I tell him. 'Say hello to the little prince.'

Kate leaves the room. Wills waits until she's gone and says he's sick to death of Anglesey, and jealous as anything of me partying in Vegas.

'It's been totes amazeballs,' I tell him.

Yesterday we woke up with Mike Tyson's tiger in the toilet. Then we lost one of the bodyguards on the roof, and then some Chinese guy jumped out of the boot of the car and beat us up with a stick.

'That sounds like a film,' says Wills, doubtfully.

I think it was also a film, I tell him.

WEDNESDAY

Heading back to Blighty today. But there's bad news. An American website has published pictures of me naked, showing some naked blonde totty how to play billiards.

'Oh my God,' I say. 'I can't believe this.'

'Me neither,' says my bodyguard. 'We played billiards?'

This is going to be embarrassing. I mean, hell, it could be worse. I could be dressed like a Nazi. Or worse, I could be married. Hold on.

'Dude,' I say to the bodyguard. 'Are we totally sure I didn't get married?'

He shrugs. Suddenly I'm sweating. The bodyguard says he'll open a window.

'Stop!' I shout.

'Why?' he says.

'Because we're in an aeroplane,' I say.

'Are we?' he says.

THURSDAY

They've given me a new bodyguard. This one doesn't say much. He takes me into Clarence House, to face the music with Dad and Camilla. Dad puts an arm around my shoulders and says he thinks we should be spending a bit more time together.

'Funny,' I say. 'Uncle Andy called this morning, and said exactly the same.'

'I don't mean in Las Vegas,' clarifies my dad.

'Oh,' I say.

Camilla tells me she's shocked, saddened and deeply disappointed.

'Really?' I say.

'You were completely naked!' she says.

'Darling, I'm surprised at you,' says Dad. 'It's not the end of the world.'

'But just think how bad he must be at billiards,' she says.

FRIDAY

Up to Balmoral to see Gran and Gramps. They're always good about this sort of thing.

'Go on, son,' says Gramps, sitting up in bed. 'Bluddy good week, what? Why, if I hadn't been saddled with this old ball and chain for most of the past century...'

'You aren't cross?' I say.

Gran says not to be silly and it's all a load of intrusive nonsense. Especially all this drivel about press freedom, just so they can put her naked grandson in the newspaper.

'I suppose even you've seen them now,' I say, glumly.

'Oh, we'd seen them already,' says Gran. 'Philly has an iPhone.'

PRINCE WILLIAM
<u>23 JANUARY 2010</u>

Here's his brother, on a visit down under.

<u>MONDAY</u>

It's obvious, says Kate, who won't get off the phone despite it being 3 a.m. here, why I've come to Australasia. It's to meet women, she says. Just like my father.

'My father and I,' I tell her, 'have very different tastes.'

Except for Camilla, points out Kate.

'Well obviously,' I say. 'Everybody fancies her.'

Kate makes a screeching noise. That was tactless of me. It's tough for her, always having to compete with Camilla. The clothes, the skin, the figure. Forever in her shadow.

'You're out there to meet hot sheilas in string bikinis,' she says, furiously. 'You want them to throw themselves at you on the beach. Everybody says so. Even Harry. And don't try telling me he's just stoned again. We both know he doesn't do that anymore.'

Her mother, she says, reckons she should fly out to Australia immediately and put on a bikini herself. She's even offered her some Air Miles. Apparently she still has loads.

'But darling,' I say, reasonably. 'What if they find a photo of Camilla in a string bikini, and put it next to you in the paper? You'll just look a frumpy mess.'

Kate stifles a sob, and hangs up.

TUESDAY

Jet-lagged. Lying awake in the Auckland royal residence at 2.47 a.m., and the phone rings.

'Oh hullo,' I yawn. 'You again.'

'I saw you in the paper!' hisses Kate. 'Smooching with some Australian girl!'

This is a surprise. I mean, obviously Kate is right. I am only here to meet hot girls in string bikinis. There haven't been any. It's damn annoying.

'She was called Marie,' wails Kate. 'Or maybe Moira. You were all over her.'

Maori, I say. It's not a name. It was a traditional greeting. And it was an old man. Plus, I'm in New Zealand, which is sort of a different country. Like Wales.

'But aren't you a prince of Wales?' she says.

I'm prince of all sorts of places, I tell her. Apparently even here.

WEDNESDAY

Off to Australia proper today.

'Sir?' says a flunky, once we get to Sydney. 'Our next visitor will only be wearing a loincloth and some body paint. Just a warning, sir. To avoid any embarrassment.'

Woof! Harry will be jealous! What's her name? 'Uncle Max Van Eulo,' says the flunky, studying the card. 'An aboriginal elder, sir.'

'Not Sheila, then?' I say.

'No sir,' he says.

THURSDAY

I'm getting a bit bloody sick of this, to be honest. Harry said it would be wall-to-wall totty. Dad said I'd probably even get groped. But so far, nothing.

Today I meet Kevin Rudd, the Australian Prime Minister. Nice chap.

'I'm told you're a Republican,' I say, shaking his hand. 'That must be fascinating.'

He blushes. And no wonder, frankly, because that George W. Bush is a right tosser.

'So,' he says, after a while. 'How are you enjoying life down under? Met any nice sheilas?' I really wanted to, I tell him. But they've all turned out to be men.

'Yeah,' he says. 'There's a lot of that. Priscilla was a big hit. But there's plenty of regular sheilas too.'

Oh don't worry, I say. I'm not prejudiced. After all, I've got an aunt called Michael.

FRIDAY

Finally! Totty! There's sheilas everywhere today, lining the streets, waving banners, doing wolf-whistles and everything. I must have been kissed by hundreds. Harry is sick as a pike.

I kept texting him and sending him photos. Eventually he turned off his phone, and went to Boujis. And then, late at night, I get a call from Kate.

'My mum brought round all the papers,' she says. 'So don't think I don't know what's been going on. And this time they're definitely women. Beautiful women. What have you got to say for yourself?'

Sweetheart, I say. Shhh. You're the one for me. You're more beautiful than any of them.

'Am I more beautiful than Camilla?' says Kate, in a small voice.

Let's not get carried away, I say.

A ROYAL REPORTER FOR TV NEWS
20 NOVEMBER 2010

Some journalists, of course, have to cover these people all the time. Poor sods. This was the week when Prince William and (as she then was) Kate Middleton announced their engagement.

MONDAY

(ring ring) Hello? What? Yes, of course I'm here. I'm always bloody here.

Standing outside Buckingham Palace or Clarence House, rain or shine, waiting for something to happen. God, I'm cold. Look, what do you want? I was about to have a kip on a bench.

What's that? Big story brewing? Hold on, I think Nicholas Witchell can hear me. Let me move down the road. He's so ghastly, he really is. Now look, are you sure? I'd have heard. Harry hasn't dressed up as one of the Khmer Rouge, has he? Fergie shacked up with one of Jedward? Prince Philip headbutted a bongo dancer? None of those? Well, what then? You don't know? Yes, of course I'll be here tomorrow. Where else would I bloody be? Oh God, it's raining now. Look, nothing interesting has happened here for months. Can't you send me to Kabul or something? Hello? Hello?

TUESDAY

...and of course, those of us in the inner circle have known that this has been brewing for some time. And, if you're just joining us, Prince William and Kate Middleton have just announced their engagement! The long wait is over!

And, well, what a lot you have missed this morning! Her Majesty the Queen has told us that she is 'pleased', the Prince of Wales thinks it is 'good'. And stop me if I sound too excited, but I'm hearing that there are further monosyllabic platitudes to come.

Now, for the latest pictures from the Newscopter. As you will see, Buckingham Palace is still there! And isn't that a joyful sight on this most joyful of days? One can only wonder what William's mother would say, if she were still with us, to see ... that.

WEDNESDAY

Well, now I'm joined by Gemma, who is one of Kate Middleton's oldest friends. Aren't you? Sort of. Yes. And have you spoken to her since this happy announcement? No? Well, I suppose she's got a lot going on! So when did you speak to her last? What's that? You've only spoken to her once? Ever? When she was eleven, and she bought something in your shop? Ah. And was there ... any sign then that she would one day be Queen? No? Fascinating. What a journey.

THURSDAY

Now, Julian, is it? You look quite posh. Ever been sick in a gutter? Well, I'm sure Prince Harry has, too. So how do you reckon he feels about getting a new sister? Sorry, no, let me stop you there, because we've just been joined by Clarissa, who owns the same blue dress that Kate wore to announce her engagement. I'm sorry? You don't own it? You just tried it on in the shop? And did you feel it was a dress fit for a ... No. Just a moment. I'm not crying. It's just the wind. In my eyes.

FRIDAY

And here I am, outside Clarence House. Still. And there you are, watching. Still. And I'm joined now by ... oh God, I don't know. Chris de Burgh? Kathy Lette? Eight people called Kate? I've been sleeping on a bench. I just have to keep talking and talking and there's nothing to say.

Excuse me, sir, but I'm told by my producer that you used to live in a house that looks a bit like the house that Kate and William lived in in St Andrews. Yes? Well good for you. Now f*** off. Or I'll knife you.

And now, as we cut back to the Newscopter, we can see that Buckingham Palace, which has been standing on that spot for more than 150 years, is still doing so. Yes. Costs more than I do, that thing. Never been in it. Not once. Bastards. Sorry. Back to the studio. I miss my wife. Thank you.

THE PRINCE OF WALES
11 MAY 2013

It's the week of the Queen's Speech. Buckingham Palace lets it be known that Prince Charles is to assume some of his mother's responsibilities. Meanwhile, the actress Helen Mirren has stormed off stage at a West End show to berate some noisy street drummers.

MONDAY

Mother has summoned me to Buckingham Palace. She and Papa are sitting on a pair of their more informal thrones, so I can tell this is going to be pretty intimate.

'Are you sure this is the right one?' says Papa.

'Yes, Philly,' says Mother.

Papa says he thought the bald one was the oldest.

'No, Philly,' says Mother.

'Will this take long?' I say.

'Watch yer lip,' says Papa.

'Philly, hush,' says Mother. 'Now Charles, look here. We are getting on. We have a good deal of help, but there are certain tasks which we begin to find tiring. So, we require your assistance.'

'Is this about programming the Sky box?' I say. 'Can't one of the footmen do it?'

'Royal we,' says mother. 'We refer to our regal duties.'

'Gosh,' I say.

Mother explains. It's nothing official; certainly not a Regency. But she doesn't want to do any more foreign travel and she'd like me to do a bit more at home, too.

So it's important, she adds, that I learn to be properly aloof, and to keep my views to myself.

'Bit rich,' I say. 'Chap in the paper had you outside a theatre the other day, screaming at some drummers.'

'That wasn't me,' says Mother.

TUESDAY

Mulling it over, I pop back in for an even more informal meeting with Papa. He says he knows why I've come.

'And there's no point bluddy sulking about it,' he says. 'The one with the ears is the heir. Simple as that.'

'I am the one with the ears,' I say.

'Oh,' he says.

I'm worried, I tell him, about this business of holding one's tongue.

'Suppose you're used to having a chap to hold your tongue for you,' snorts Papa. 'Eh?'

Seriously, I say. One has views. About the world. About foreign affairs. About everything. And one just can't imagine how one is going to travel to all these places, and speak to all these people, and never offend anyone.

'It's a knack,' says Papa.

WEDNESDAY

Today it's the Queen's Speech. Mother has asked me to come along, with the Duchess, and sit at her right hand. Bloody exciting. 'Reckon you can manage that?' she says, in the carriage on the way home.

Totally, I tell her. Only personally, I'd have stuck in some stuff about climate change and building regulations. And biscuits, maybe. 'But Charles,' says Mother. 'This is what we keep telling you. The government writes the speech. We only say it.'

Papa yawns. 'That's why all of her speeches are so boring,' he explains.

He's always suggesting jokes for the Christmas one, he says, but the buggers won't put them in.

'But Mother,' I say. 'Surely the government doesn't write the Christmas one, too?'

'Let it go,' says Mother, quickly.

THURSDAY

Harry is off to America. He pops round for breakfast, and to promise to drunkenly strip naked only in the company of extremely good friends.

'Ah,' I say. 'The fun you young ones have! I never did anything like that. And now I'm almost Prince Regent, I suppose I never will!'

'Come on, Dad,' says Harry. 'You had lots of fun back in the day. Dating Koo Stark, hanging out with dodgy oligarchs, *It's a Royal Knockout*, all that.'

'None of that was me!' I shout.

FRIDAY

Tea in the Palace. Smaller thrones still.

'Darling,' says Mother. 'We do hope you like the biscuits?'

One has no views about biscuits, I tell her. One may privately feel that Duchy Originals are a far superior biscuit, and grotesquely slandered for being overpriced and over-oaty. But I shall keep them to myself. No opinions here.

'That's my boy,' says Mother.

'But Ma'am,' says Camilla. 'Didn't you tell those drummers to fack orf?'

Wasn't her, I say.

'Bloody would have been me,' says Camilla.

'That's my gel,' says Papa.

ARCHBISHOP OF CANTERBURY
11 JUNE 2011

It's not all royalty, of course. Back when Rowan Williams was the Archbishop of Canterbury, he guest edited an issue of the New Statesman. *His editorial is deeply critical of cuts by the coalition government.*

MONDAY

It is with a deep and baffled sense of ennui that I rise in my chamber, summon my secretary, and notice that it is Monday again.

For as long as I can remember, it has always been Monday during this part of the week. This is clearly the result of a radical long-term policy for which no one voted. At the very least we must wonder about the message that the tireless recurrence of Monday is sending to our children.

For if Sunday is to be the day of rest (and the Anglican Communion must, of course, be open to those who seek to change this), then the ceaseless successions of subsequent Mondays must surely be a deterrence.

Of course, I do not suggest cynicism on the part of those authorities who permit Monday to...

'Christ,' says my secretary. 'Go back to bloody bed, already.'

TUESDAY

Nobody voted for Tuesday either, but never mind that.

This week, I am mainly editing a special edition of the *New Statesman*. Jemima Khan told me about it. We go to a lot of the same parties.

The real editor says he admires my grounding, and the way I so instinctively understand the concerns of real people.

'Thank you,' I say.

'No problem,' he says. 'Nice palace, by the way.'

'Do you have a good palace?' I ask him. 'I found Jemima's quite lovely.'

'Mine's a bit smaller,' he says.

WEDNESDAY

Hurrah! I have been trying all week to commission a piece by Philip Pullman, but he kept hanging up on me. This morning I finally get through.

'I'm really sorry,' says Philip. 'I genuinely thought you were Richard Dawkins, doing his Rowan Williams voice.'

Dawkins is an angry man, I say, sadly. One can only pray for him, and hope that the good Lord allows a little light into a life so characterised by bitter darkness.

'F*** off, Dawkins,' says Philip. 'You nearly had me for a minute there.'

THURSDAY

My issue of the magazine is published today. I won Philip Pullman over, in the end. I also have contributions from Richard Curtis and the Chief Rabbi. My leading article, in which I express disquiet at the coalition's mandate for cuts and the staleness of the so-called Big Society, has caused controversy.

John Sentamu, the Archbishop of York, calls in the morning.

'Rowan, my friend,' he says, gravely. 'I must question

the wisdom of such an overt foray into the political sphere.'

Don't think I don't know what this is really about, I say.

'You could have at least got me to do the TV review,' he says.

FRIDAY

The Prime Minister calls.

He's quite cross. He says he's no problem with me getting involved in politics, but I ought to say only things which are true, such as supportive comments about him being right about everything.

'For that is your right,' he says, 'and I would never begin to question it.'

I tell him I'm sorry if I have caused him difficulties, but I may only speak as my conscience tells me is fitting. And around this country, I have noticed, there is a real fear. Changes are being made, and nobody voted for them. It's like the whole Monday thing.

'For God's sake!' shouts the Prime Minister. 'Stop this nonsense! You know nothing about the real world! You live in a palace! Not even I have a palace!'

'You must,' I say.

'Well, I don't,' he says. 'It's Samantha's.'

RICHARD DAWKINS
18 SEPTEMBER 2010

Not completely sure Richard Dawkins belongs here. I thought about putting him in 'Literature', because he's famed for his books, and then about putting him in 'Celebrity' just to annoy people. But if the Archbish is establishment, I suppose he must be, too. This was written during a Papal visit to Britain.

MONDAY

This week, that absurd and stupid-faced popinjay Joseph Ratzinger visits Britain. Accordingly, I shall be spearheading a movement to 'Protest The Pope'.

Some people believe there should be an 'about' in that sentence. Pathetic. Grammar is nothing but a persistent meme perpetuated by the blind adherents of dogma. Objectively, there is no 'about', any more than there is a Tooth Fairy, or a Great Spaghetti Monster in the sky. QED, I'm right. Again.

I have teamed up with many of Britain's most prominent anti-papists including Peter Tatchell, Claire Rayner, Geoffrey Robinson and Ken Follett.

Sometimes people ask me how I can remain so resolute in my atheism, in such an uncertain world. What a stupid question. You try believing in a benevolent God after a dinner party with that lot.

TUESDAY

We're planning a big anti-Pope rally. A couple of the

organisers come round to talk preparations. I'm the key speaker, so they want to make sure people will see me.

'Maybe we could get some sort of special car?' suggests one, who is wearing a *The God Delusion* T-shirt. 'Something you can stand up in, and wave at people from?'

Sounds interesting, I say.

'Better still,' says the other, who is also wearing *The God Delusion*, 'how about some kind of tall, really shiny hat?'

WEDNESDAY

Of course, the Pope has always been leader of the world's second most evil religion and the dictator of a tinpot, Mussolini-concocted principality. But only recently has it emerged that he's also spent half a century sheltering paedophile priests across Western Europe and America.

Frankly, it's made my job a good deal easier. 'Thank God!' I'm sometimes inclined to say, before I remember that I really ought not to.

THURSDAY

Stephen Hawking has been muscling in lately. Irritating man.

There's a pecking order to this celebrity atheism lark, and I'm at the top, then Hitchens and Grayling, then Pullman. Then Pratchett, maybe. But along comes Hawking, with his planets and his equations, and barely any invective at all. You call that science?

Up in Scotland, the Pope has said that people who don't believe in God are more likely to do bad things than people who do. Seriously!

I mean, obviously I expected to hear some outrageous things from the man who considers himself God's pre-eminent messenger on Earth. But THIS?

FRIDAY

The anti-Pope rally organisers have come round. One's in a *The Blind Watchmaker* T-shirt. The other is wearing *The Greatest Show on Earth*.

'We were hoping to start with some music,' says the first. 'Somebody really popular. Although Susan Boyle's people aren't calling back.'

The event alone will be celebration enough, I say. An army of independent free-thinkers!

'I agree with everything you say,' says the other. 'We all do.'

I can't deny I'm quite excited. What an event! How dare the Pope come to our country, and tell us that without his antiquated belief system we cannot understand love, or forgiveness, or compassion?

'Damn right,' says *The Blind Watchmaker*. 'The old Nazi bastard won't know what hit him.'

PAUL BURRELL
19 JANUARY 2008

Remember Paul Burrell? He was Diana's butler, and her rock and swore he would never reveal her secrets. Then he wrote a book about this. This week, he appeared at the inquest into her death.

MONDAY

In the café near the Royal Courts of Justice, I order scones, jam and tea. The Princess loved tea. She used to drink it in a special way that only I knew. I will never betray her. It was our secret.

'Oh,' says the waiter, who has recognised me. 'You're that butler bloke, aren't you? The one with all them secrets?'

I was her rock, I agree. I supported the Princess of Wales, when all others had turned away, except for people like Elton John.

I knew everything. I had many secrets. And not just about tea. Also, about jam.

'Yeah? What was her favourite jam, then?' says the waiter.

I shake my head, solemnly. Diana's secrets will go with me to the grave. She trusted me. I will keep that trust. It is my duty. It is my bond.

'Go on mate,' says the waiter. 'I'll knock 50p off your bill.'

Oh, OK, I say. It was apricot.

TUESDAY

In court today, again. Truly, as the Queen once told me, there are 'dark forces' at work in this country. Of course, these were not her exact words. Those are a secret. To have quoted her accurately in my book would have been a betrayal. That is something I will never do.

For me, loyalty is paramount. It was loyalty which led me to surreptitiously copy Diana's correspondence behind her back and publish it in the form of two highly lucrative books that have subsequently made me a millionaire.

Some may protest that this makes little sense. There is a reason why it does. This is a secret, too.

WEDNESDAY

'So,' says the waiter in the café, 'that would be £7. But, seeing as you told me all them secrets about Diana's favourite size of sugar lump, Diana's preference for crispy bacon, and Diana's views as relates to Coke versus Pepsi, let's call it £4.50.'

Diana, I know, would have wanted me to remember her in this way. Like her, I am always inspired by my brushes with the common man.

Before returning to court, I doodle an idea for a new piece of Royal Butler merchandise.

Perhaps it is time to branch into kitchen utensils?

'He was her rock. This is her wok.'

THURSDAY

My wife Maria is at our home in Florida. I fax her with the wok plans. She calls back.

'Paul,' she says. 'Are you sure about this? I've never liked this rock thing. It's just, imagine if you were swimming. And you had a rock with you. Rocks are really heavy. It's not a great image. That's all I'm saying.'

I wasn't that kind of rock, I tell her. I was a safe rock. Solid. Firmly anchored to the ocean floor.

'The kind that sinks ships?' asks Maria.

FRIDAY

Of course, nobody else in the British Establishment could understand that a rock could be solid and reliable, spongy when boats hit it, but also floaty and totally fine to carry around while swimming. That was Diana's genius. I knew all about her views on geology, but I'll never tell. It was our secret.

As soon as I am back in America, I will have these woks made, and sold, in her memory. It is what she would have wanted. Maybe she even wrote me a note about it, which I copied, memorised, and then burned, to stop it falling into the wrong hands.

Oh hell, let's say that she did. I'll bung it in the next book.

MOHAMED AL FAYED
6 OCTOBER 2007

This next one was also during that inquest. After reading it, you'll want to read the next. Seriously. You really will.

MONDAY

Yes. There is Mohamed the Fayed, who is owner of Harrods shop and chairman of Fulham club and wearer of shirts like the wallpaper of Turkish brothel. And also, who is me. Ha!

Also I have little corner shop, which is also Harrods, for humour. By door number three, there is plinth and on plinth is fine, life-size waxwork of me, Mohamed of Fayed, who may look out and welcome the guests. Only sometimes, he is not waxwork.

Sometimes he is actually me. Ha! It is for relaxation. And also, to spot shoplift.

So today I am here for already three hours, studying customers and without the moving. I am in thought. Tomorrow begins inquest into murders of holy innocents by evil genius Prince Philip. Six months. And after six months, what will I do? The diary of Mohamed from Fayed, who is still me, and not waxwork who is now in cupboard with wobbly head, will be quite bare. Perhaps I buy second football club, or new shop like Mum Has Gone To Iceland. Who know?

As she pass by in after noon, blonde woman look up and stare at me. I wink at her.

Is polite. To do not would be quite mad. There is screaming.

TUESDAY

'I am Mohamed under Fayed!' I tell this English bobby, who is blocking my way with his fuggin truncheon. 'Stupid bobbert! I must get to this court!'

Mohamed Mr Fayed, who is still me (ha!) is running slightly late, due to argument with beautiful daughter about shirt which she alleged fashion crime. Is no good. First day today of the inquest into murderous royal bastard at Court 73 by Lord Justice Scott Baker, who I believe to be good man but may turn out, like many others, to be fascist stooge and numpty.

WEDNESDAY

Consultations today with senior staff, for smooth runnings of businesses. They look up, in Harrods foyer. I am on plinth.

'You!' I say, to my personal sculptor. 'Your statue. Of murdered innocents, by escalator. Is no good.'

He is pale. 'It is exactly what you wanted!' he say. 'Diana and Dodi dancing, while releasing a beautiful symbolic albatross!'

'Albatross?' I say. 'Fuggin' albatross? You fascist stooge and bribed, most likely, by royal bastard! I want bigger bird!'

He swallows.

'Bigger than albatross?' he says. 'What, an ostrich? A king penguin?'

'Bigger!' roars me from plinth.

'But Mr Fayed,' he say. 'They are dancing. They are releasing it. Which means, shortly beforehand, they were dancing, with it. There isn't even a cage. Which was already weird with an albatross. But with a penguin...'

He will be needing a new sculptor, Mohamed with the Fayed. Me.

THURSDAY

Diary still empty. Most likely inquest will be charade and farce, like other inquests. Although if not, how to spend the days? Cannot always be on plinth. Must seek other crimes for which Prince Greek royal bastard responsible, aside from murder of holy innocents and reduction of albatross. Perhaps he shoplift.

FRIDAY

Some annoyance for Mr Mohamed upon Fayed, who is still me without joke wearing thin. Ha! Bastard stooge sculptor has also stiffed me on waxwork with wobbly head.

Bloody head fall off in middle of day, hit customer on bonce. Gone for fixing.

Now all day must be spent on bloody plinth.

Perhaps, when six month pass, I spend all time up here. Find truth about royal bastard, look out for shoplift. Perhaps buy You Have it Your Way At BK.

Couple girls come by, staring up.

'That's really weird,' says one. 'Even weirder than the one with Diana and Dodi releasing that eagle.'

'Is fuggin albatross!' I say. More screaming. Perhaps I buy Milletts.

HUGO RIFKIND
(BY MOHAMED AL FAYED AND STAFF)
13 OCTOBER 2007

So. That went in the paper, and the following week I had an angry e-mail from a chap called Michael Cole, who handled press for Mr Fayed. It was quite long, but the gist of it was that I was a dreadful racist and shouldn't be, because I was Jewish and must have once had immigrant ancestors who spoke funny themselves, and how would I like it if somebody wrote something like that about me, and so on.

I replied, I think, nicely. Mr Al Fayed was welcome to write one about me, I said. Then Mr Cole replied and said he would, but he didn't know anything about me, and I replied again and said maybe he could have a crack at Google, then, like I had to do when writing about him.

To my astonishment, the below turned up in my inbox the next day. So, I took the week off.

The only minor complication was that everybody just assumed I'd written it myself, as some kind of curious meta-joke they didn't quite get.

MONDAY
Wake up. Stare at ceiling. Add up the number of beautiful women who had seen wonders in its snowy expanse while held in my thrall. Decided it is none. Feel depressed. Notice a spider's web on the cornice. I have never understood my fellow Scots' enthusiasm for Rabbie Bruce and his octoped. When I failed in my attempt to be a journalist,

I was delighted to fall back on the gossip columnist's red, plush divan. Notice cobwebs too. Memo to self: must get a cleaner. If she happens to be Portuguese and it turns into a rerun of my fave film, *Love, Actually* with me in the Colin Firth part, well, wow! I do miss Tony Blair. Wonder if that makes me secretly gay? Phone in the column. Turn over. Fall asleep.

TUESDAY

Bang! The sound of the tyre exploding on Sky TV (part-owned by the owner of this paper blah, blah, blah) wakes me at 11 a.m. The bus taking the Diana jury to the Ritz hit a bollard. I hate flat tyres. They remind me of my novel, *Overexposure*.

Was there ever a bigger misnomer? Must do something about the 15,000 copies in the spare bedroom. Perhaps I should put in a minigym? I am becoming a soft southerner in obvious places. Phone the office to complain about the useless showbiz pars in my column. Told I am responsible for buying them in. Memo to self: call the man in LA and tell him to stop lifting them from *Hollywood Reporter* and raid *Variety* instead. Phone in the column. Go for a walk. Must remember to switch off telly when I go to sleep.

WEDNESDAY

Yippee! Mail at last. A blizzard of white stiffies. The pick is the wedding of a niece of one of the Sugar Babes (*sic*) at a Harvester on the Basingstoke bypass.

I'm in! Go to the office. Wish I hadn't. Sitting in the gents, I hear the column unfairly characterised as 'pathetic, puny People', followed by sniggering.

Fortunately, it's only that fat sub-editor with a weakness for alliteration and the oik from the City desk who goes on about "edge funds'. What do they know? Memo to self: must mention Ian Hislop more often. He might get me on *HIGNFY*.

THURSDAY

Should I go to the Nigel Dempster memorial at St Bride's next week?

It would do no harm to be seen.

I might even pick up a story.

I cannot write about Boris Johnson all the time. Dempster used to get stories that ended up on the front page. And he knew all the people he wrote about. I am sure no one would make odious comparisons. I am not even in his league. England is so tricky. It is easy in Scotland. Edinburgh is 500 people who all know each other.

Memo to self: must get on television more. The novel gambit failed but I can become a media star. Keep saying it.

FRIDAY

I must get on television more. I could be like Richard Quest, of CNN, an acquired taste for those who like their erudition with a bit of eccentricity. I could do that. The other day I heard someone say: 'That Hugo Rifkind, he's a cult.' If I were on TV, I am sure my father would stop rolling his eyes when he sees me.

Trouble is he rolls his eyes most of the time. I see why successive editors dump the diary and bring it back in a new form. Hear rumour that the current one is thinking of outsourcing it to Bangalore. Resist urge to cry. Wonder how far my salary would go in rupees. The Peterborough column went from the *Telegraph* to the *Mail*, I could be transferred! And Dempster would not be there to hit me. Memo to self: look on the bright side. This is better than working.

DUKE OF EDINBURGH
3 NOVEMBER 2007

Funny how quickly royal scandals fade from the mind.
It took me ages to remember what this one had been.
Apparently the world's media was in a tizz because an
unnamed member of the royal family was being black-
mailed over a gay sex video featuring drug use and there
is much speculation as to who he might be. In the end, he
was named abroad as Viscount Linley.

MONDAY
'Well, I dewn't know who it bluddy is,' I grunt at the
wife, throwing the newspaper down on the breakfast
table. I take out my anger on a crumpet, ravaging it with
silverwear. 'Do you know who it is? I bluddy dewn't.'

'Phileeep...' says the wife, dangerously.

'Well, do you?' I ask her. 'Everybody else bluddy does.'

'I hehvn't really thought about it,' lies the wife.

She's tetchy. Bluddy Arabs turning up tomorrow, and
she's afraid I'll cause an incident.

'All right, all right,' I grumble. 'Yet another alleged
junky whoopsie in the family, and it's only muggins 'ere
who doesn't have a clue. That's all I'm saying.'

The wife fixes me with a look. Chilling. Great-great-
grandmother lurking behind the eyes. India got that look
once. Poor bluddy India. Never knew what hit it.

TUESDAY
We sent one of the boys to pick up the Arab from the

airport. Wotsisname. One of the ones with the ears. Now I'm waiting with the wife on Horse Guards Parade. The old chap peers about himself as he steps out of the car. Probably looking out for hands and bloodstains.

'Look at him,' I mutter, from the corner of my mouth. 'Smug blighter. I bet even he bluddy knows.'

'Phileeeeep...' hisses the wife. 'You aren't going to say anything, are you?'

I roll my eyes.

'Fear not, cabbage. Conversation pleasantries all the way, what?'

Before the wife can say anything back, the Arab is stepping up to say hello.

I grin, to put him at ease.

'What ho! Nobody told me it was fancy dress!'

The old battleaxe looks stricken, but the Arab seems unperturbed.

'My sympathies,' he says gravely, 'during a difficult time for your family.'

'Thenk you,' says the wife, and for a few moments we all stand in a dignified silence.

'Now look here,' I say, suddenly. 'It's not bluddy me, you know.'

WEDNESDAY

I find the wife in our private chambers, sitting on the floor with newspapers scattered all around. Honestly, these bluddy animals.

'Again?' I say. 'Can't you put the buggers in nappies?'

The old cabbage blushes. 'Oh Phileep,' she says. 'It's not the corgis! It's me. It's the alleged junky whoopsie. One simply must know who it is. Do help me. One is looking for hints.'

'You'd think somebody would just bluddy tell us,' I

mutter, leafing through *The Independent*. 'This chap they've arrested. He's friends with Freddie Windsor.'

The wife frowns. 'Is he the one with the ears?'

I shrug. 'Probably.'

THURSDAY

The ginger grandson comes around for mid-morning tea and scones. No whoopsie, he.

The wife waits until the servants have cleared the plates.

'Herry,' she says, triumphantly, 'is going to bring us a computer.

'Apparently one can find out what is what from the internet.'

He's something of a favourite, the ginger grandson. Normal ears on him.

'Should have been here on Tuesday,' I say with a wink. 'Had a bluddy Arab round, in a sheet. Chops fellers hands off for thieving, what.'

'And what's wrong with that?' says the ginger grandson.

'Good lad.'

FRIDAY

The wife and I stand around the ginger grandson as he taps away on a computer.

'Look,' he says. 'You just need to go to a website in Australia or somewhere. See? Oh.'

'Never heard of him,' I say, so the ginger grandson conjures up a photograph.

The wife reckons the ears ring a bell.

LORD BLACK
17 MARCH 2007

Baron Black of Crossharbour, otherwise known as Conrad, was once the owner of the Daily Telegraph. *Jailed for fraud in the US, his trial centred around the manner in which his wife, Barbara, was able to afford such an expensive lifestyle, and around something called 'non compete' agreements, paid to executives after bits of his various companies were sold.*

MONDAY

'In fact,' I muse, looking out over the Chicago skyline from my suite at the Ritz, 'much the same sort of ordeal was undergone by Socrates.'

Barbara, my wife, doesn't reply. She has thirty-seven different grapefruits lined up on a table, and is peering at them from different angles. A beauty, and a genius.

'Darling?' I say, sipping at my freshly ground coffee. 'Socrates? Don't you think? A visionary of impeccable conduct, ridden low by the ravening whoremasters of envy? No? Of course, I shall be fully vindicated of all aspects of this bilious and oafish defamation. And he was convicted. So I'm sort of cleverer than Socrates, aren't I?'

My wife collapses into an armchair, exhausted. Clearly, none of the grapefruits are up to standard. So be it. In recent years Barbara and I have learnt to live within our means. No breakfast for her today.

TUESDAY

I am in Chicago to undergo a major, utterly erroneous, yet frankly rather prestigious trial for fraud. Today we shall be visiting the court to see jury selection. My lawyer is anxious.

'Conrad,' he says, 'you gotta make this jury like you, yeah? You gotta problem. You got no connection with the common man.'

This fellow irritates me hugely. I tell him so. His impression of me is a monstrous caricature, based, not upon fact, but upon a bloated and fictitious image of my wife and myself. We are modest people. Our staff never stretched into triple figures, and the smaller of our two jets was very small indeed. I am as anybody else, merely richer, cleverer and better.

Furthermore, I tell him, I would prefer to be addressed as 'Lord Black'.

WEDNESDAY

Into court. Barbara and I passed the ranks of prospective jurors with scented handkerchiefs pressed to our noses.

'Yo, Black,' said one, an African-American gentleman. 'Too good for us, hey? Don't wanna breathe no germs from ordinary folk?'

I lowered my handkerchief and addressed him forthrightly. 'My dear fellow! We have nothing against the germs of ordinary folk! Perish the thought! It's your terrible stench that bothers us!'

He was quite won over by my logic. This trial will be a breeze. No connection with the common man, my ass.

THURSDAY

'Look,' I say to my wife. 'This lawyer. He wants us to change our clothes. Our taste is too refined. We must be

Roundheads, rather than Cavaliers. It's this damn city. It's Chicago. We must be as blue-collar as they are.'

'Well,' says Barbara, 'I do have a blue collar. It's part of a Hermes midnight-blue, pure silk ruff-effect blouse, with ruby buttons and a platinum trim.'

I shrug. 'Perfect.'

FRIDAY

Back in my suite at the Ritz, I survey the Chicago skyline once more. I am not due in court until Monday. Like Socrates, like Napoleon, like Jesus, I await my trial.

Barbara is out shopping. She has this clever financial system where she pays herself a reward for not buying all the things she wants to buy. Then, later, she uses that reward to buy them. Brilliant. I don't know where she got the idea.

For now, I am quietly furious. I have been wronged. I have been insulted. My reputation has been besmirched, and my name has been dragged through the mud. This is part of a long campaign of intimidation, defamation and degradation, and it shall not stand.

'I'm really sorry, Mr Black,' says the maid, who has come to collect the breakfast tray. 'I'm sure that the silver teaspoon fell into your pocket by accident. I didn't mean to suggest otherwise.'

'Get out,' I tell her, 'before I sue.'

THE PRINCE OF WALES
16 AUGUST 2008

Back to royalty. This week, I think, Prince Charles was worrying about genetically modified crops. And maybe I'd just seen The Little Shop of Horrors.

MONDAY

'OH CHARLES?' intones a baritone voice in one's Highgrove greenhouse.

'Yes?' one says, to one's eight-foot flesh-eating Venus flytrap. 'Yes, Master?'

One has had this plant since it was a sapling. One found it in the grounds, possibly after a meteor strike. It grew and grew.

One has always conversed with one's plants, and one was thrilled, initially, to meet one capable of speaking back. Initially, it would wish one a good morning, and we would discuss architecture, or the environment, or other matters of mutual interest.

Of late, alas, it tends to say: 'COWER, EARTHLING, BEFORE OUR ALIEN WRATH!' and snap, brutally, at one's head. It is dashed concerning. One has a steady supply of venison, obviously, but one is also running low on gardeners.

Today, the plant is concerned about the genetic modification of plant life.

'WE FEAR THE RISE OF INTELLIGENT EARTHLING BOTANY! YOU MUST STAVE OFF

COMPETITION! OR FACE OUR INTERPLANETARY FURY!'

One promises to see what one can do.

TUESDAY

An audience with Papa up at Windsor. He's standing in front of his mirror with a footman, being kitted out to go hunting something. I don't know what. It could be anything. It could be me.

'Gaaaaah!' he says, or words to that effect. 'Found yer mither's bluddy corgi yet, what? Not seen it since it blundered interr yer greenhouse!'

'No, Papa,' one says, and one shudders. One only found the collar and the teeth.

'Now listen here,' he says, 'Big Ears. I won't be around for ever. Need to stand on yer own two feet. Be a man. Time to make some bluddy gaffes, what? Show the buggers who's boss. Be rude about somebody.'

One clears one's throat and explains that one thought one might say something about genetically modified foods in the developing world.

Papa is silent for a while.

'Wogs, is it?' he says, eventually.

WEDNESDAY

What a blasted awful day. Because of the plant, one hasn't let Camilla near the greenhouse for weeks. She assumed that one was secretly growing pot, and let it slip to Harry. So in he went, on the rampage.

Dashed lucky he had his bayonet on him, really. Came out with his shirt ripped off his back and his arm already in a makeshift sling.

'Good s*** in there, Dad man,' he said, and went off up to his bedroom, to smoke one's coriander.

'YOUR BOTANICAL ALIEN OVERLORD IS MOST DISPLEASED!' intoned the plant, afterwards. 'THERE SHALL BE NO MORE DELAY! YOU SHALL ISSUE YOUR ANTI-GM STATEMENT IMMEDIATELY!

'MOREOVER,' it added, after a while, 'YOU SHALL NEVER AGAIN ATTEMPT TO FEED US A GINGER!'

So that's my plan to bump off Nicholas Witchell up the spout, as well.

THURSDAY

Papa is apoplectic. He calls early in the morning, having just read the *Daily Telegraph*.

'Am I the only person in this bluddy family who knows how to make a gaffe?' he roars. 'Multinational corporations? What's on yer mind? Are you mad? Is that how yer going to cause offence when I'm dead and gone? What about darkies? The disabled? What about whoopsies and Ruskies and the bluddy A-rabs?'

One wrings one's hands.

'It's one's blasted flesh-eating Venus flytrap alien overlord, Papa,' one explains. 'One fears its interplanetary wrath.'

Papa is irate. Sometimes, one is reminded that he spent many years in the Navy.

FRIDAY

Papa arrives in his hunting clothes, with his shotgun and a bag. He tells one to wait at the greenhouse door.

'COWER, EARTHLING!' shrieks my eight-foot Venus flytrap. Then there is a bang.

Papa says he is going to have it stuffed, and hung over his bed.

PRINCE HARRY
10 MARCH 2012

Harry time. Like I said, can't get enough Harry. This is him, on his state visit to Jamaica. Remember that? Everybody loved him, and he was clearly enjoying himself far too much.

MONDAY

I'm on a royal trip to the Caribbean, having breakfast with my minder from Clarence House.

'I assume you know where we're going today,' he says.

'Just a sec,' I say, and I wave at Miss Bahamas, across the foyer.

'Jamaica?' he says.

'Certainly tried, bruv,' I say. 'But she just wasn't up for it.'

My minder shudders slightly.

'Please sir,' he says. 'Do pay attention. Remember how concerned one's father was? That one might go on a raging bender and vomit upon a dignitary's shoes?'

'No chunder,' I say. 'Understood. And easy on the doobie.'

'Your Highness?' says my minder. 'Must I remind you that you are here as a representative of Britain? This is not a gap year.'

'Totes going to do a bungie jump,' I say. 'And I might get some dreads.'

TUESDAY

'Yo, Rastaman!' I say. 'Let's head on down to Trenchtown, and mak de fihuh light!'

'Huh?' says Usain Bolt. He's the fastest person in the world. Even faster than some of the chicks I know from Boujis. We're about to have a race. He says not to worry, because nobody expects me to win.

'Bloody hell!' I shout, pointing over his shoulder. 'It's a spaceship!'

Then I, like, totally peg it.

'That was a good joke, your Highness,' he says, catching me up.

'F*** off, Bolty,' I say. 'That was for real. Give me your medals.'

'Rematch,' he says.

'No,' I say.

WEDNESDAY

Today, I met Portia Simpson-Miller, the Jamaican Prime Minister. Lots of hugging.

'You know, Harry,' she says, as we walk on the lawns of her residence, 'you have impressed us deeply. I remain keen for my country to become a republic, but you have helped to remind us exactly what, in severing our close and historical ties, we have to lose. A charm. A quiet dignity. It has given us much to think about.'

Total PMILF.

'Anyway,' she says. 'I hope you have enjoyed your visit. But before you go, is there anything about Jamaica you'd still like to know?'

'Yah,' I say. 'Where can I get some weed?'

THURSDAY

Need to do some shopping.

Can't go home without a bong and a selection of ethnic bracelets.

From the embassy, I call Wills.

'Tree little birds,' I tell him, 'is by my doorstep.'

'Bastard,' he says.

Wills is jealous. He wanted to come here. At first, you see, Dad wanted to send me to the Falklands.

'Totty desert!' I objected.

'He's right, Charles,' said Camilla. 'Send Wills to the Falklands. He won't mind. Totty's no use to him now.'

'But I live in Wales,' said Wills, forlornly. 'You're sending me to the Falklands from Wales?'

'I suppose Harry could go to the Caribbean,' mused Dad, 'with me.'

'Over my dead body are you going to the Caribbean,' said Camilla. 'He'll have to go by himself.'

'Cheers Mum,' I said. 'Gizza fag.'

FRIDAY

In Brazil now. Rio de Janeiro. Totes awesome bottomage. Phwoar.

In the afternoon, we've got a photo-op down at the Copacabana with this chick, who is showing me how to play beach volleyball.

'Sir,' says my minder, looking worried. 'You will keep your eyes on her face? There are cameras everywhere.'

'She's got a face?' I say.

'You're a public figure!' he says.

'So is she,' I say, admiringly.

'Your Highness!' he shouts. 'Remember why you are here!'

'Dude,' I tell him. 'I don't even remember where I was this morning.'

'Jamaica!' he shouts.

'Give it time,' I say.

*This was my version of the best man's speech I expected
him to give at the wedding of the Duke and Duchess of
Cambridge. Wonder if he nicked any of the jokes?*

The best man.

Bruv! What a day! I know you aren't supposed to
say it at a wedding, but, phwoargh! Wotta sexy stunna!
Talk about fit for a queen! I mean, I know a lot of your
birds have been top totty, especially that one from Kenya
(Yeah. You. Table Four. Stand up. Woof!), but, I gotta say,
this one takes the Duchy Original. Can't stand them, by
the way. Yeah. Way too oaty.

But bruv! Where was I? Kate? Tidy piece, my man,
tidy piece. I'm thrilled. Couldn't be more thrilled. Me
and Kate go way back, don't we? Remember when
we first met? When I came up to St Andrews for the
weekend? And I was wearing your see-thru dress? God,
that was a laugh. Did you ever get my chunder out
of that rug, by the way? Didn't even remember eating
broccoli. Always the way, innit?

So, yeah, don't mean to go on about it, but good pull.
And I don't reckon she'll go bad, either. Coz there are
some birds, aren't there, who are hot when they're young
but wind up looking like Rod Hull. Know what I mean,
Dad? Yeah.

But Kate's mum ... well, I don't want to sound inap-
propriate, but I totally would. In fact, when I came up to
Berkshire for a few days, I sort of tried to. Sorry about
that, Carole. You know how it is when you've had a
few. Did you ever get my chunder out of that rug, by the
way? No?

Anyway. The stag. That's what you all want to hear
about, isn't it? Personally, I reckon fancy dress would

have been a great laugh. Not sure why it got vetoed. Still, we had a good one, didn't we bruv? Me, you and the rest of the lads. And the *News of the World* was wrong about the stripper. Totally, she was eighteen. Believe you me, up close, you could tell that ... what's that? Wrap it up? Bloody hell.

OK, look. A toast. Let's leave it with that, yeah? So please, Gran, Dad, little people, crazy aunt, charge your glasses and join me in toasting the beautiful couple. Couldn't ever have asked for a better bruv, and now I couldn't ask for a better sis, either. Sis? Can I call you Sis? What's that? You'd prefer Ma'am now? All right, don't push it. F***ing oik.

*And, while we're on Harry, here's something I wrote
for* Tatler, *after somebody in Canada suggested that the
Canucks might fancy a royal line of their own and put
him to good use.*

Dear Bruv,

Greetings from the Kingdom of Canada! Good, eh?
Hope you like my new royal crest. Those are hills on it,
by the way, like the Rockys we have in the West. Hills,
yeah. With nipples on them.

But look, bruv, you're bound to be wondering. 'How
come the Harrymeister's suddenly a king? He's not even
the heir! He's the spare!' And you're not wrong, my
man, not at all. Thing is, these Canadian folk – who are
like Americans, but ours – have decided they wanted a
king of their own. Maybe you read about it in the *Daily
Mail*. So, given that I was going spare, they asked me.
Well, it wasn't going to be Uncle Andy, was it? He'd have
brought the aunt. Bankrupted the place.

They told me there were a lot of mooses here, but
not from where I'm sitting. Know what I mean? Woof!
Reckon I'm going to be having my own Royal Wedding
pretty soon. Not sure who with, but she's gonna have to
be fit for a Queen. Hell, between us, she's going to have
to be fit for a Victoria's Secret model. Shouldn't be hard.
Man, I'm going to have the hottest court you ever saw.
It's going to double as a beach volleyball court. Hubba.

You should send that bridesmaid of yours out here. And
her mum. Not being disrespectful or anything, but I totally
would. Both of them. At once. I mean, I've tried before,
obviously, but I reckon I'd have more luck now. Last time I
asked Carole to slip away and join me in the throne room,
it was sort of a euphemism. But now I've got one.

Oh bruv, it's amazing here. It's bigger than Britain, but don't feel bad coz there's not much in it except for stuff to shoot. I should get Granddad out here. He'd have a whale of a time. Like, literally. They've got sunlight almost 24 hours a day in the summer, and apparently British Columbia is really fertile. Great for growing the old Duchy Original. Know what I mean? I'll totally have to legalise that.

You reckon I can pass laws? I'm deffo going to try. One of the lads at Boujis once told me about droit du seigneur. That sounds well rude. Especially as I'm the seigneur. Apparently the clubbing here is boss, too. They set out on boats every spring, and do it out on the islands. It lasts for months. I've seen photos. Talk about blood on the dancefloor. Mental.

Only bummer is, I've probably got to learn French. There's this whole bit out East where they don't speak anything else. It'll be quite cool ruling over French birds, though. They're well saucy. I met one the other day. 'Bonjour King 'Arry,' she said to me. 'Vous must come visit Quebec, and see the Arctic bear.' Sounds like a weird tradition to me, but I'm up for it if she is.

Yeah, it's going to take me a while to get to know the place. Can't believe it's been in our family so long, and I've never really paid it any attention. Looking at the map, though, there's this huge region up in the North West that doesn't seem to be mine at all. Just this morning, I asked a courtier what that was about, and how come Gran never owned it.

'Alaska,' he said.

'Don't bother,' I said. 'I'll ask her myself.'

Skype soon, dude,

King Harry I of Canada

RICHARD III
15 SEPTEMBER 2012

And finally, here's a long-dead royal. They dug him up in a car park in Leicester. Remember? It was the week after the Paralympics.

MONDAY

Now is the long winter of my lying quite happily in the dark, made into a slightly jarring summer of being under a crappy marquee while some boffin dusts my ribs with a toothbrush.

'Look at his spine!' shouts an academic. 'It's definitely him!'

'Rudely stamp'd!' agrees another. 'Deform'd, unfinish'd, not shaped for sportive tricks!'

You want to try lying in a hole for five hundred years, chum. See how straight your spine is. Believe you me, when I announced, 'plots I have laid' in that speech Shakespeare wrote up, I never expected to have to add, 'in'.

I wonder what it looks like up there these days? If only I had some suitable transport for carrying a dead body.

A hearse, a hearse! My kingdom for a hearse!

TUESDAY

By means of ghostly mind-reading, I've been trying to find out who won the War of the Roses. Some people seem to think it was a tie between Michael Douglas and Kathleen Turner. Others suggest Quality Street. No idea what that's about.

My kingdom today seems much changed. Only last week a great contest finished, during which the country realised that people born with disabilities can achieve great things. This was a surprise? What was I? Chopped liver?

There's a different family on the throne now. My favourite is the heir's brother, a warrior prince whom everybody has seen naked in the newspapers. Somehow I've got this horrible feeling I'm going to know how he feels. Although at least he's got, you know, skin.

WEDNESDAY

The archaeologists have the radio on. Seems it's causing quite a buzz that I've spent 525 years in a Leicester municipal car park. According to jesters on Twitter, I'll owe millions in fines and am liable to get clamped.

Another source of great intrigue is the two princes I had locked up, whom nobody saw, ever again. Inasmuch as I can make out, this is still a popular strategy for dealing with people who are politically embarrassing. The current Prime Minister is said to have done something similar with a chap called Oliver Letwin.

THURSDAY

So apparently the plan is to chip off a bit of one of my bones to take it away for testing to establish whether or not I really am Richard III. Because I could have been any one of a number of high-born hunchbacks who died in battle near Bosworth Field in the late fifteenth century, couldn't I?

There's also a debate raging about what should happen to me if it turns out I am me after all. Some people think I should be taken to Westminster Abbey. Most reckon I should stay in Leicester. Because 525 years in Leicester isn't enough, is it? Oh no. They've got the National Gas Museum here, you know.

FRIDAY

Life doesn't seem to have got much easier for royals. I mean, sure, I had to deal with conspiracy, murder and getting my head staved in by some huge Welsh bloke with a poleaxe. But at least I could freely sunbathe topless in France. And I did.

Seems the British press aren't willing to publish pictures of a naked duchess, though. Lucky for some. Bet they don't put so much as a bikini on me. Might complain to the PCC.

BOB DIAMOND
30 JUNE 2012

Finally, a pair of bankers. The first was the head of Barclays when the Libor-rigging scandal hit. 'The what?' you ask. Exactly. The same week, the papers had exposed Jimmy Carr, the comedian, for some energetic tax avoidance.

MONDAY

Our PR guys reckon it's a problem, the way I've got the surname 'Diamond' and am one of the richest bankers alive. Still, as I meet today with my fellow senior bankers Maxwell Cash, Neville Bullion and Sir Reginald Firkin-Minted, we've got bigger things to worry about.

'This Libor business,' says the head of PR. 'Is it going to cause problems?'

It might not. For one thing, nobody understands it. And if they did, they'd realise it wasn't dodgy at all. So we fibbed a bit about how much it costs us to borrow money? Big deal.

'The public has no right to be upset,' says Sir Reginald. 'After all, it's not like banks didn't let them lie when they wanted to borrow money, for years. And they never complained about that.'

'All the things we've done,' says Bullion, 'and this is the one that makes them cross?'

'People without impressive surnames,' I say, 'have unimpressive minds.'

TUESDAY

All the same, I decide it's probably worth doing some pre-emptive damage limitation before news of our fine breaks. So I call David Cameron.

'Just wanted to check,' I said, 'after the Jimmy Carr thing. You aren't going to go on a moral crusade about this Libor business?'

'I have literally no idea,' says Cameron, 'what you are talking about.'

'Libor,' I say. 'You know. Libor.'

'Is that a kind of mint?' says Cameron.

'Never mind,' I say.

WEDNESDAY

This time tomorrow, the world will know about e-mails in which bankers ask each other to manipulate Libor, and say things like, 'anything for you, big boy,' in response. Fortunately we haven't yet disclosed that other cache, which includes messages like, 'Yo yo yo, let's rape Greece' and 'Wassup, beeyatch, let's GARP the NASDAQ's ass.'

But it's only a matter of time, so I call Ed Miliband.

'You aren't going to go big on Libor, are you?' I ask him.

'New Liebor?' says Miliband. 'B. Liar?'

'What?' I say.

'What?' he says.

Sometimes, I wonder how it can be that the political establishment has failed to crack down on casino banking for so long. But usually, I really don't.

THURSDAY

Well, it's out. Barclays has been fined £290 million and lots of people are calling on me to resign. As a gesture of how sorry I am, I have decided to forgo one of my bonuses.

'Or,' says the PR guy, 'and I'm just floating this, you could forgo both of your bonuses.'

'The name's Diamond,' I remind him. 'Not Bob Cubic Zirconia.'

FRIDAY

Sir Mervyn King, David Cameron and George Osborne are all attacking me. The latter two bother me less, for reasons already explained.

All the same, I give the PM a call.

'You're being completely unreasonable,' I say. 'It's only Libor. How can everybody be so angry about something that nobody understands?'

'This is a very serious matter,' says Cameron. 'You have questions to answer.'

'Well ask them, then,' I say.

'I would,' says Cameron, 'but I don't know what they are.'

SIR FRED GOODWIN
4 FEBRUARY 2012

This guy was the old head of RBS. This week, he lost his knighthood. You remember. Stephen Hester was the new head of RBS. Meanwhile, Chris Huhne (the Climate Secretary) was facing accusations of dodging speeding points, and John Terry (the England captain) was facing accusations of racism.

MONDAY

I'm just waking up underneath my Edinburgh garden in the gold-lined bunker in which I've spent the past year and a half, burning money to stay warm, when the diamond phone rings. It's one of the PR guys from RBS.

He's never forgotten the way I invested £25 million of shareholder cash into his venture to use igloos to solve the housing crisis in Chad. Weird how that never worked out.

'Bad news,' he says. 'We've just heard. They're taking it away.'

The millions I earned in charge of RBS?

'No,' he says.

My £16 million pension pot?

'No,' he says.

My collection of classic cars? My beautiful enormous house full of oil paintings of me and diamond-studded sculptures also of me?

'No,' he says. 'Your knighthood!'

'I'd totally forgotten I had a knighthood,' I say.

TUESDAY

Stephen Hester calls. I suppose you'll be wondering where to buy a golden bunker, I say.

'Don't be daft,' says Stephen. 'We've all got golden bunkers.'

In fact, he's calling to offer his sympathies and thank me for becoming the main banker that everybody hates, again.

'You've had it worse,' I tell him. 'You lost actual money. I can always buy another knighthood.'

Stephen says you can't actually buy knighthoods. His wife once looked into it, for their anniversary.

'We're being made into scapegoats for the whole damn system!' he says. 'It's an outrage, Fred!'

Sir Fred, I remind him.

'Not anymore,' he says.

This is starting to hit home.

WEDNESDAY

George Osborne has been on the telly, crowing about my misfortunes. I call him on the diamond phone.

'Hello Fred,' he sniggers.

This isn't fair, I tell him. I've been convicted of no crime. This is cruel and populist bullying.

'I disagree,' says Osborne.

Then he says it's actually a powerful demonstration that, contrary to popular belief, our titular system is a transparent, democratic process, which doesn't just encourage archaic deference to an Establishment elite.

'But your own father is a Sir!' I shout. 'What if somebody wanted to de-honour him?'

'Completely different,' sniffs Osborne. 'That's a baronetcy.'

THURSDAY

Spent all day in my platinum bed, shivering. That smell of burning taxpayer cash just doesn't warm me like it used to.

I always thought I'd have another job by now. I'm the guy who lost £26 billion. That's not easy. You'd think those skills would be transferable. Maybe I could work at the Ministry of Defence, or run the NHS.

I have to do something. They might come for my 'Fred' next. That'd hurt. I've had it for ages.

Then my 'Goodwin'. I'd be a man without a name! I'd have to pick a symbol, like The Artist Formerly Known As Prince!

'£' maybe. Hmm. Yeah.

FRIDAY

This morning, I spend a while trying to get through to Energy Secretary Chris Huhne and England captain John Terry. Both of them are in the same boat as me. What if we all lose our names? We'd all be total nobodies, with only millions and millions of pounds to console us. What a fate!

Still, no sense in moping. In the afternoon I put on dark glasses and a woolly hat, and sneak out to cheer myself up at my favourite swanky Edinburgh steak house.

'I'll have my usual, please,' I say to the waitress. 'The sirloin.'

'I'm sorry, Mr Goodwin,' she says. 'But for you, it is just a loin.'

PART VI

GOING
SPARE

THE MAN FROM THE ABATTOIR
16 FEBRUARY 2013

Sometimes, the person of the week is nobody in particular, or not even a person at all. Oddly enough, these tend to be my favourite weeks of all.

This week, traces of horse had been found in beef products across Britain.

MONDAY

OK look, I say to Bob, the foreman. This is all kicking off. We need to be able to prove that all of our beef is really beef.

'Just tell 'em,' says Bob, 'that once you get the feet, head and saddle off, all of these animals look pretty similar.'

'Don't say saddle,' I say.

'But it's a bit of meat,' he says.

'Which sometimes has a buckle,' he adds.

I rub my eyes. 'I'm pretty sure pigs are the pink ones,' I tell him. 'Cows are the big ones and chickens are the ones with wings. And anything with metal feet technically shouldn't be here. Look, where's that fat floor manager of ours? He understands this stuff.'

The foreman says he hasn't seen the floor manager since this morning, when he went to clean the sausage machine.

'Bit odd, actually,' he says. 'Started shouting about something, and then just wasn't there.'

'So unprofessional,' I say.

'Did a good job, though,' says Bob. 'Production is way up.'

TUESDAY

A man from one of the supermarkets has come to see us. He says that non-cow DNA has been found in some of their burgers.

'We've traced it back through our agents in Holland and their sub agents in Murmansk,' he says, 'via suppliers in Latvia and a haulage company based out of Burkina Faso. And the buck stops here.'

We take this extremely seriously, I tell him. No stone shall be left unturned in our investigations.

'Got any leads?' he says.

'Hundreds,' I say. 'They're all out the back, still mainly attached to collars. Why?'

WEDNESDAY

Today it's a team of inspectors from the Food Standards Authority.

'So,' says the one in charge. 'Do you have much of a problem with vermin?'

Bob says he wouldn't call it a problem, as such.

'I mean, it's all protein,' he says. 'Isn't it?'

'But inspector!' I say, hurriedly. 'How's your complimentary hotdog?'

'Good,' says the inspector. 'But ... is this a fingernail?'

'Claw,' says Bob.

'Claw?' says the inspector.

'Hoof,' I say.

'On a pig?' says the inspector.

'Beak, then,' says Bob.

THURSDAY

'Why the long face?' says Bob.

Lots of reasons, I say. The supermarkets are probably going to cancel their contracts, and the FSA might shut us down. Plus, I've gone right off my food. And I still can't figure out what sort of animal Quorn is supposed to come from.

'I actually meant on that cow,' says Bob.

I don't think that is a cow, I tell him.

'Might be on the inside,' says Bob.

FRIDAY

I'm in the mutton section when Bob finds me and says the FSA just called. They've lost one of their inspectors, and want to know whether we've seen him. Big guy, apparently, with spiderweb tattoo on the back of his neck.

'Like the ones you get on lamb chops?' I ask, watching the conveyor belt.

'Never noticed them before,' he says.

After a while I tell Bob I might give vegetarian sausages a shot.

'Nah,' says Bob. 'Never know what's in them.'

EVERYBODY
29 DECEMBER 2012

It's Christmas. Downton Abbey *was on. It was rubbish, and the main guy died.*

MONDAY
A yard of Jaffa Cakes! That's clever. I'll get three. Now. Two more presents and I'm done. But what can I get them? Napkin rings? Do people still use napkin rings? Maybe if I give him that corkscrew and her the book I was going to give my aunt then ... oh God, this is awful. Why didn't I do this on Amazon weeks ago? Shopping! Today! I'm never going shopping again. It's like a jungle. Is it normal to want a machete when you're shopping? Wait. A machete? Will she want a machete? What if I give him the machete, and I give her the corkscrew? Actually, no! She's an alcoholic! Isn't she? Or does everybody just think she is? I want a drink.

TUESDAY
Happy Christmas! Should we start cooking? A yard of Jaffa Cakes! How funny!

Look, me too. Oh. It's just lots of normal boxes in a big tube. Oh well.

And Baileys! Shall we...? Oh, wait, you don't. Oh sorry! You do! Well, let's!

What a lovely jumper! No, I'll wear it tomorrow. And, well, I mean, it's not an iPad, obviously, but it's almost as good. No, I don't know how you turn it on. When's the Queen? And *Downton Abbey*? I feel sick. Well, it's not really a breakfast food, is it? Only four and a half yards to go. When are we eating? Hell, I thought you were cooking it.

Won't it? Well, chop it in half! Hold on. You know this is still frozen? We need a machete! It's funny, but I nearly bought you a ... never mind.

Look, let's not argue. She's just drunk. No, I didn't want a f***ing iPad.

Really, I'm very grateful. When are we eating? Four hours? We've almost missed the Queen! What is she wearing? Don't be stupid, of course I'm not standing up. You stand up. I'm starving. Keep your f***ing Jaffa Cakes. You do this every year.

Finally! Well, we can just have it on our laps in front of *Downton*, can't we? No, I don't remember who he is. Wasn't she the one who died? This is a bit dull, actually. Isn't there normally more shagging? Oh, sod this, I'm going to bed.

WEDNESDAY

He died? How? Why? Oh, never mind.

I'll watch it later, on the iPad. No, I know it isn't an iPad. Really, it's fine. I didn't want one. I promise. No, I haven't found the 'on' button yet. Shall we go for a walk later? Wow. We ate three yards of Jaffa Cakes? That's, like, two feet each. I want some fruit. No. Not an orange. Not an orange. Oh, OK. Fruit cake.

I can't believe we missed *EastEnders*. Seriously? We didn't miss *EastEnders*? I don't remember that at all. *Miranda* wasn't great, either. All that standing around in front of a Christmas tree, droning on about the Olympics. What? Oh. Well, she was looking a little grey. Yeah, you're right. Probably the Queen.

THURSDAY

What day is it? No, I mean, I know it's the 27th, but what day? Is it, like, Tuesday or something? I'm definitely going for a walk today. No, I haven't tried the jumper on yet. Oh, it's a bit small. Tell you what, let's go shopping. There aren't any parking restrictions today, are there?

FRIDAY

I had the strangest dream. There were these Jaffa Cakes, but they were massive, and they were chasing us down the high street. I think we might have been naked. I wonder what it meant? Seriously? Five feet of Jaffa Cake left? Oh, go on then. Actually, they're OK with turkey, aren't they? We should tidy up.

None of my clothes fit any more. What's gout? Is this gout? I'm sorry about the parking ticket. I just thought, well, you know. Maybe we can appeal. I'll look it up on my iPad. Yeah, actually it is an iPad. I changed it yesterday. Sorry. Have a drink. No, go on. It's almost New Year.

GOOGLE'S TAX ADVISER
25 MAY 2013

Google, the internet giant, is facing criticism in both the US and the UK for cleverly avoiding tax by basing itself in places where it has hardly any employees. HMRC doesn't seem that bothered.

MONDAY

'Right,' I say to the three guys from Google. 'This is what you need to understand. None of us are here. This meeting is not taking place in London.'

The guys from Google all have side-partings, special rimless glasses, and the same green polo shirt with 'DON'T BE EVIL' printed on it. It's quite hard to tell who is who.

'Are you, uh, sure?' says one of them.

'Definitely,' I say. 'See, I've arranged a conference call through an internet telephony app. So, even though we're all sitting here together, this conversation will technically be happening in your virtual office in the Cayman Islands.'

'Anyway,' says one of the Googlemen. 'How much corporation tax are we paying this year?'

Well, I say, I've had your boffins sort out an app for that, too. It uses predictive technology to estimate this year's bill, based on last year's bill.

'So almost none, then?' he says.

'Yup,' I say.

TUESDAY

Today I'm mediating in a summit between Google and HMRC. We had planned to do it virtually, via a chat service, but the guys from HMRC still have BlackBerrys. It's sort of tragic.

'This has to stop,' says the taxman.

The Google guys don't say anything.

'You owe us tax,' he continues. 'Lots and lots of tax.'

The Google guys still don't say anything.

They're only here corporally, I explain. Thanks to new, implanted Googlechips in their brains, intellectually they're all at the company's HQ in low-tax Ireland.

'Prove it,' says the taxman.

'Mine's a Guinness,' says one of the Google guys, quite suddenly.

'No further questions,' says the man from HMRC.

WEDNESDAY

Today, Ed Miliband is giving a speech at the Google Big Tent event. It's quite long. He's talking about how Google should be paying more tax, because the founders made a big deal about not being evil, and not paying tax is a bit evil, actually. Row upon row of identical Googlemen in the same glasses and clothes watch him speak. And at the end, nobody applauds.

'Hmm,' says Miliband. 'I suppose they're all intellectually at the Google HQ in Ireland, thanks to these brain-implant Googlechips I keep hearing about.'

'Actually,' I tell him, 'I think they're just asleep.'

THURSDAY

Obviously, I also have other tech clients. This morning I met with three guys from Apple, who are all bald and wearing polonecks. My advice is that they should relocate their headquarters either to a planet nobody has ever visited, or to somewhere on the visible spectrum somewhere between violet and aquamarine. They're totally thinking about it.

Later I'm seeing three guys from Facebook, who all have really bad curly hair and no social skills. Right now, they're in the process of dramatically lowering their tax liability by rapidly losing users and money. I call this the Friends Reunited Approach. Never fails.

FRIDAY

I'm brainstorming with my assistant when two Google guys turn up at my door. I've literally no idea whether they're the same ones I've met before. Apparently there's a problem with the whole Cayman Islands thing.

'We've struck a deal to make literally everybody who lives there wear a webcam on their head literally all the time,' explains one of them. 'So if we're going to pretend to have an office there, we might actually have to build one.'

My assistant rubs his chin and says he knows of another island we can use instead, which doesn't come up in a Google search, so basically doesn't exist.

'So how do you know about it?' asks one of the Google guys.

My assistant says it's actually incredibly easy to find, but only on Bing.

'So basically doesn't exist,' I repeat.

AN ORDINARY MEMBER OF THE PUBLIC
22 DECEMBER 2012

Andrew Mitchell, formerly the International Development Secretary, is accused of calling police protection officers 'plebs'. An e-mail from a member of the public seems to confirm this. But then it emerges that this so-called 'member of the public' was a policeman, too.

MONDAY

Exiting my abode at 0830 HOURS and passing down LETSBE AVENUE in the usual manner, it came to my attention that many of those I passed were under the MISAPPREHENSION that I was AN OFFICER OF THE LAW.

''ALLO, 'ALLO, 'ALLO,' I said, to a passing MILKMAN. And I asked him to explain how this outrageous MISUNDERSTANDING had come about.

'BECAUSE OF YOUR TRUNCHEON?' he suggested. 'AND YOUR HAT?'

Is this what our country is coming to when a PERFECTLY ORDINARY MEMBER OF THE PUBLIC is confusioned in this respect. At 0832 hours I made it clear that he was mistaken in this presumption. Then I asked him to stand aside, so I could get to my car.

'THE ONE WITH THE BLUE FLASHING LIGHTS ON TOP?' he asked.

But I am not sure why he felt this was relevant.

TUESDAY

This is not the first time I have been misidentified as one of Britain's HARDWORKING POLICEMEN who ONLY EVER DO EVERYTHING RIGHT. Some months ago, I was approached by a SENIOR MEMBER OF THE GOVERNMENT. Having a keen interest in politics and the Conservative Party, I immediately identified him as NOBODY ANYBODY HAS EVER HEARD OF BEFORE.

He told me he was investigating an e-mail.

'WOULD I BE CORRECT IN ASSUMING YOU ARE A POLICEMAN?' he said.

I told him he would not. 'BUT YOU ARE WEARING A UNIFORM,' he said.

This could be the uniform of a POSTMAN or a TRAFFIC WARDEN or even a SAILOR, I told him. Or maybe I am merely a fan of INSTITUTIONAL TAILORING.

'GOOD ENOUGH FOR ME,' he said and went AWAY.

WEDNESDAY

According to MR ANDREW MITCHELL – the Member of Parliament for Sutton Coldfield who has outraged ALL RIGHT THINKING PEOPLE by addressing POLICE OFFICERS as 'PLEBES' – a police officer has fabricated evidence by pretending to have witnessed something he did not, while pretending to be A PERFECTLY ORDINARY MEMBER OF THE PUBLIC such as you or I. Imagine my horror at this clearly baseless accusation.

After hearing of it, at 1300 HOURS I visited Central London with my nephew from Hong Kong to do all the usual site seeing. One of the sites we saw was the INSIDE OF SCOTLAND YARD into which PERFECTLY ORDINARY MEMBERS OF THE PUBLIC can, of course, wander at will. And none of the HARDWORKING and HONEST OFFICERS there could believe it either.

THURSDAY

Today, as of 1130 HOURS, I am standing next to a BROKEN TRAFFIC LIGHT waving my arms around for NO PARTICULAR REASON at all.

'EXCUSE ME, OFFICER,' says a passing MOTORIST.

'I AM ACTUALLY A PERFECTLY ORDINARY MEMBER OF THE PUBLIC,' I tell him. 'AS ANY OF THESE WITNESSES HERE PRESENT, SOME OF WHOM ARE FILMING, WILL ATTEST.'

The MOTORIST says there aren't any other people around, though.

'THAT'S NOT WHAT IT SAYS IN MY NOTEBOOK,' I tell him.

FRIDAY

Not being A POLICE OFFICER in ANY WAY, I am of course completely impartial in this fight that A DIRTY LYING TORY is having with DECENT HARD-WORKING PUBLIC SERVANTS.

But, as I find myself telling the MILKMAN on LETSBE AVENUE, I can quite understand their fury at being called 'PLEBES'.

'WHAT IS A PLEB, ANYWAY?' says the MILKMAN.

An ordinary person, I tell him.

'LIKE YOU?' says the MILKMAN.

'GET IN THE BACK OF THE VAN,' I say.

A TAX LAWYER
23 JUNE 2012

Jimmy Carr, a comedian, heads a long list of public figures revealed to be zealously avoiding paying much tax.

MONDAY

The day starts with a meeting with a very famous comedian. No, not that one. Another one.

'From now on,' I say to him, 'you get paid in toast.'

'Toast?' he says.

'Not bread,' I say, 'because then we couldn't claim back the VAT. Toast. And the other great thing about toast is that it starts depreciating in value from the moment the toaster goes pop. So this creates a loss, which we can offset against everything else.'

'And here comes the clever bit,' I say.

'There's a clever bit?' he says.

'Absolutely,' I say. 'You see, toast, as a legal term, is actually quite broad. At a stretch, it also includes other aspects of the "toast" snack, such as jam, and marmalade. And, provided these are sealed in suitable jars, these don't lose their value at all.'

'But we're talking £2 million of toast here,' he says. 'Will the taxman accept it's all for personal use?'

'Provided you eat some of it,' I say, 'we'll be fine.'

TUESDAY

I've got a meeting today, with the entirety of HMRC's

celebrity tax division. He's fifty-eight, and he's got Sellotape holding together his spectacles.

'Sorry I'm late,' I say. 'I tried to call, but your mobile wasn't working.'

'We couldn't pay the bill,' he says. 'Vodafone cut us off. It's sort of ironic.'

Anyway, he says. He wants me to help him to understand this business of Jimmy Carr's taxes.

'Have I got this right?' he wonders. 'Some guy convinces 1,000 people that if they give him all their millions, and let him keep 18 per cent of it, he'll lend them the rest back?'

'Yup,' I say.

'But I could have done that,' he says. 'Anyone could have done that. I'm in the wrong job.'

'At least the money's good!' I say.

'I'm wearing a string belt,' he says.

WEDNESDAY

David Cameron has described Jimmy Carr's tax affairs as 'morally wrong'. Lots of my showbiz clients are calling, in a panic.

'Calm down,' I say to a pop star with an OBE. 'This is an opportunity, not a crisis.'

'I don't see that,' he says.

'Look,' I say. 'Public displays of immorality are a liability, right? So we offset them. The very act of aggressively avoiding taxes damages your public brand to the tune of, what, £1 million a year? £2 million? It's a tangible loss. And some people will pay good money for one of those.'

'But people will hate me even more than they do now,' he wails.

'Ker-ching!' I say.

THURSDAY
A quick call from my man at HMRC, who wants to know about some of the film-making schemes that my top clients have invested in this year.

'I'd better be quick,' he says, 'because I'm in a phone-box. I just need to be sure that these are real films, which are actually going to be made. So I want to know the titles. Right now.'

'There's one called *Winging It*,' I say, quickly. 'And another called *Expedient Duplicity*. That's a thriller. Also a comedy called, um, *Another Thing I Just Dreamt Up On The Back Of An Envelope*.'

'That last one sounds ace,' he says.

FRIDAY
My comedian client comes round again. He looks exhausted.

'I don't want to do this any more,' he says. 'I don't care about the money. Or the toast. I feel like I'm selling my soul!'

'At least it's gone down in value,' I say, 'so there's no capital gains.'

UNDERCOVER AGENT Z
<u>15 JANUARY 2011</u>

*Various undercover policemen are revealed to have infil-
trated various protest groups over the course of the past
decade. Some have had relationships and even children.*

<u>MONDAY</u>

Hey. How's it going? Nice posters. Well, not 'nice'. You
know. Poor little doggies. And rabbits. I love animals,
me. Die for them. Got any of battery hens? They're my
favourite. Just want to hug them. Sometimes I wish every
hen in the world was a battery hen. Wait. I didn't mean
that. Did I? No.

Anyway, good to meet you. My name's Warlock. That's
a weird name? You aren't all called things like 'Warlock'?
Oh, OK then. It's Dave. What do you think about the
environment? I love the environment. Yeah. Bloody coal.
You need any help? I'd be really useful on demos. I've
got loads of experience of how policing works. For some
reason. And I've got a van.

Nice dreadlocks, by the way. I should get some of them.
Look, do you want to come back to my place and smoke
some marijuana cigarettes? Listen to some music with
a repetitive beat? You'd love my flat. I've got loads of
posters with aliens on them, and the whole place smells
really, really bad.

Hey, when's the next Climate Camp? We should do

it somewhere warm next time. Majorca, maybe? I think easyJet goes there. Guys? Guys?

TUESDAY

Sarge? It's me. Can't talk long, but I'm in. We're all going to check out a power station tomorrow. I'll need a van. Yeah, it was quick work, wasn't it? It would seem that my experience as a serving police officer has given me organisational skills far superior to those of the average activist. I know. Astonishing. It must be the drugs.

WEDNESDAY

Yo! Comrades! How do you like the van? What's that? Don't be silly. Of course it isn't. It was an ice cream van, I think. They all have those orange stripes down the sides, don't they? And the lights on top? Which flash? Bright blue? Course they do. Look, don't worry about it.

Have another spliff.

So what are we going to do when we get to this power station, then? Hang around outside, you say, waving banners? Hmmm. You're not tempted to break in, at all? Smash it up? Perhaps plant some sort of bomb? You don't know how to make bombs? Jesus, what's wrong with you people? Haven't you heard of the internet? Right. Fine. Just the banners, then. What's that? You haven't even finished nailing the poles on yet? Oh, for heaven's sake. I think there's a hammer in the back. Yes, that's it. The thing shaped quite a lot like a truncheon.

THURSDAY

Sarge? Me again. Listen, great news. I've totally penetrated the activists' inner circle. They trust me. I'm one of them. And so I'll be needing some condoms. To use as paint bombs. Or something.

FRIDAY

All right, comrade. Good of you to pop round. Come on in, make yourself comfortable. On the bed, if you like. I tie-dyed that myself. Loving the nose-ring, by the way. Got to say, that stained day-glo bandage dress really looks good on you. And speaking of which, how do you like the dreadlocks?

Of course they're real. Of course I'm not just wearing a novelty Rastafarian hat I bought at the Notting Hill Carnival. Stop it. Don't tug.

But look, I'm glad you came round. Between you and me, there's a thing, isn't there? The rest of these monkeys couldn't organise an organic mead piss-up in a collectively occupied brewery, could they? That's right, darling.

Not like us. We do all the work, don't we? We pay for the leaflets, and we drive them around, and we come up with all the ideas. Without us they'd be no threat at all to the capitalist ... hold on. Your voice sounds slightly familiar. It's not ... Sarge?

A COMMONWEALTH VILLAGE CONCIERGE
25 SEPTEMBER 2010

It's the Commonwealth Games, in Delhi. Facilities are somewhat grim.

MONDAY

Welcome, sir, to your room in new, luxury, state-of-the-art Delhi Commonwealth Games Athletes' Village! As you will be seeing, it is exceeding luxurious. You have found a complimentary chocolate? On your pillow? Ah, no, sir, I would not be eating that. Too late? Well, you will be finding some complimentary worming pills in the bathroom cabinet. Indeed, sir. Next to the more obvious complimentary excrement.

And you will notice from my shiny suit and Bluetooth headset, sir, no expense has been spared! I beg your pardon? You would rather they had spent it on actually painting the walls? Imminent, sir. Likewise the light-fittings. And yes, that bit of the floor.

Now, I shall leave you to settle in. But if you have any further queries ... the elevator, sir? Oh, I assure you. Again, any day now it will be fixed. Come now, my friend! This is only the seventeenth floor! Are you not supposed to be a marathon runner?

TUESDAY

And hello, madam, and let me say how happy we are to have you here. Please, hand your suitcase to that porter.

Child labour? Oh no, madam! He is, in fact, almost thirty, but just looks much younger.

Twenty-five years younger? Yes. Thereabouts.

You are worried about terrorism? No need, no need. Fortunately, we have displayed a state-of-the-art RDRD security system. You are not familiar with the acronym? Random Deployment of Rabid Dogs, madam. There are many of them, inside and out. See how that one there has taken hold of our porter, by the face, and is shaking him? They are very diligent.

Also, there is the outbreak of dengue fever, which is quite a deterrent for evildoers! In fact, that alone would keep anyone but an idiot as far away as possible! Well, here we are, madam. Sleep well.

WEDNESDAY

Not English? Not Welsh? Scottish! Well, these are your rooms and ... what's that you say? Unfit for human habitation? Simply disgusting? Quite unlike anything you have ever seen? Oh, sir, I cannot believe this is true. After all, I have been to Dundee.

THURSDAY

Oh, whatever. Come on in. For your comfort, we have bulldozed the homes of thousands, and bussed them out to camps.

But doubtless you wish to complain about the smell. Or the stains on the wall. Or the fuse box, which, I must admit, does not look as though it was put in by your Prince Philip.

Look, I am sorry. This is India. We are aware we are far from perfect. But I swear to you. Delhi's Chief Minister has sworn that all of this will be fixed by tomorrow, or her name is not Sheila Dikshit.

And it is. No, really, it is. I know. But it is.

FRIDAY

Hello, sir! Or should I say, g'day, mate! Welcome, anyway, to the new, shiny, spangly Athletes' Village. Observe the hole-free floors. Observe the sturdy ceiling. No, sir, I could not swear that is a chocolate on your pillow, but hell, today I reckon it is worth a punt.

You are gravely disappointed? You had heard this would be a Third World hellhole, and you were hoping for some shocking photographs to send your wife? Well, sir, in that case let me take you to one of the British residences. Indeed, sir. It is just our little post-colonial joke. Don't let on, but everybody else's are absolutely fine.

PAUL THE PSYCHIC GERMAN OCTOPUS
10 JULY 2010

He predicts foootball results. He's an octopus. He's psychic and German and called Paul. What more do you want?

MONTAG

Guten Morgen, unt velcome to my tank. It is little known, but in fact ve octopuses are alvays psychic. Ve have to be. Ze humans are all 'on the one hand, on the other hand' but for ze octopus it is rather more complicated.

Since hatching from egg, I haff been vundering. How to turn ze psychic octopus ability into psychic adwantage? Is very hard for octopus to land job with Deutsche Bank, regardless of skills at predicting bond market. And, vhile I can perform many dexterous tricks inwolving jam jars, those little pens in Ladbrokes are altogether too fiddly. I do, of course, have my own ink, but my sac-writing is terrible.

So. In collaboration vith my keeper, I am devising cunning plan to predict ze results of ze Vorld Cup football games.

My accuracy is formidable, and yet there remain many sceptics.

'I can't believe everyone is going so nuts for this,' says my keeper. 'They want to send in TV cameras next time! There are just so many suckers in the world.'

Indeed, I am tzinking. I myself haff several hundred.

DIENSTAG

Today I am called upon to predict ze outcome of semi-final match between Deutschland und Spain by eating shellfish off flag of victorious nation.

Zis is operation conducted under maximum security. After I predicted ze Argentine defeat last week, there are many who vish me harm. Some say there is ze contract out on my head. Others are unsure whether I haff one.

Until now, ze most traumatic call of all was ze Deutschland vs Ingerland match of last veek. For I myself was hatched in Weymouth. As secret Inglander, I haff much emotional conflict.

Ze day after I predicted zat Cherman victory, a British fan was in my aquarium. 'I was going to put a lot of money on this match,' he said, sadly, 'but you've convinced me it's just a six quid bet.' I am not sure vot he thought was wrong with me.

MITTWOCH

I haff eaten my mussel from flag of Spain and am now guarded day and night by crack team of snipers.

I am not sure vhy they are bothering. I predict I will be fine.

Of course, I haff many imitators. In Singapore there is a psychic parakeet. In Argentina zey haff mystical dolphin. Elsewhere here in Chermany ve haff spiritual hippo. Only ze parakeet has my respect. All true psychics haff a beak.

DONNERSTAG

Needless to say, Spain vins a resounding wictory.

Now that my fame has spread far and wide, there are many who come to me for predictions of another sort. For example, *Bild* has asked me to use my psychic powers to decide which of ze many potential photographs depicts ze secret mother of Cristiano Ronaldo's baby. Alas, I do not haff enough legs.

Also, this morning, a detachment of Britishers visited, seeking guidance as to who would be ze first person to drop out of ze Labour Party leadership race. I'm not sure I did such a good job. There were complications. Would you want to eat your dinner off ze face of Ed Balls?

FREITAG
The Vorld Cup Final is this weekend. Vith attack helicopters flying overhead and surrounded by ze men in sunglasses with earpieces, I haff predicted that Spain vill beat Holland.

This, despite ze rogue Dutchmen sneaking through security and vhispering 'sushi!' at me, over and over again. Is easy to ignore, as I probably don't haff ears.

Vottever happens, anyhow, I am now ze bonafide celebrity. Indeed, I predict I vill soon become ze most famous octopus since the *Octopussy* octopus. I haff new agent. Britisher television has been in touch, pointing out zat many people would rather vatch me talk about football than James Corden.

Unt, best of all, John Terry has sent ze SMS to see if I want to go on ze secret date. Psychic or not, I genuinely did not see that one coming.

THE TOYOTA HELPLINE
6 FEBRUARY 2010

Toyotas across the world are being recalled due to a spate of defects.

MONDAY

Good morning! The car in front is a Toyota! What's that? You'd rather not be quite so far in front? No need to shout, madam. Sir? Not madam? Forgive me, it's just that your voice is so very high. Screaming terror? I see. Moving at some speed? Well, I do hope you're on speakerphone. Sir? Thought we'd lost you there for a moment! Now, what seems to be the problem? Your accelerator? It's sticking? Funny. We seem to be getting a lot of calls today. Is this a flash mob thing? No need to get shrill, sir. Well. Shriller.

What I need from you, sir, is your engine number. It's on the block, under the distributor. No, not very convenient, sir. You might need a torch. Hmm? Still driving? Towards the end of a pier? Ah. Well, let's see. First, I'd suggest winding up the windows.

Now. Are we still moving? Quite a long pier? Jolly good. In which case, my next suggestion would be to get down on your hands and knees – perhaps your daughter can steer? – and tug at the accelerator. It worked? Just in time? Your front wheels are over the edge? Phew! Good job Toyota has such excellent customer service, eh sir? Sir? Well. How rude.

TUESDAY

Good afternoon. The car in front is a ... oh. You, too, eh? Well, yes, madam. Of course it points to a flaw. A flaw in feet. People just don't know how to use them. I suspect that yours are unusually big. Or small. Or perhaps just a funny shape. I understand that the situation may be different in America, but here in Britain the problem is evidently your big clodhopping feet.

Oh. Hold on. I'm just getting an e-mail. Ah. Forget everything I just said. Turns out it absolutely is our fault, in Britain, too. So what you should do, madam, is bring in your car immediately. You know where we are? Splendid. When you come into our car park, there's a big glass kiosk dead ahead. Right? Well, when you come in, if you feel like accelerating, please point your vehicle somewhere else, because that's where I sit. Have a nice day.

WEDNESDAY

Morning. The car being towed in front is a Toyota. How may we help you? Pedals, is it? Oh? Not pedals? The mirror? It makes your face look funny? Wider than it is long, like the baby out of *Family Guy*? Oh. No, I don't think that's a recognised flaw with the Toyota Aygo. But, what the hell. We're recalling up to eight million vehicles worldwide. A couple more won't make any difference. Your sister's Corolla has a funny smell? Yeah, bring it along.

THURSDAY

Oh, hello. The car wrapped around the lamppost up ahead is a Toyota. Only kidding, madam. Just our little topical joke. May I ask your particular reason for calling to shout at us today? Accelerator? Brakes? Did we forget to fit enough wheels? No, don't tell me. It's the seats, isn't it? Are they facing the wrong way? No need to be sniffy, madam. Could have happened in this company. Could have happened from Seoul to Idaho, and we'd never even know. Oh, bring it in. Or as close as you can. The car park is getting full.

FRIDAY

Good morning. The worst job in the world is this one at Toyota. What do you want? My chair? My desk? What's that? Unresponsive? Not pointing in the right direction? Seems to keep disappearing? I'm sorry, sir, but I didn't quite catch which part of your Toyota you were talking about. Oh, I see! You work for Toyota! You're talking about Akio Toyoda, the company president! Sure, send him in. I dare say we can persuade some of the lads in the workshop to give him a going over, too.

THE GOD PARTICLE
13 SEPTEMBER 2008

In Switzerland, they turn on the Large Hadron Collider.
The BBC sends Andrew Marr.
   It's bloody clever this one. Not sure if it's very funny,
but it's clever as hell.

MONDAY

'I bet you're excited,' says this proton I've been working
with. 'Any day now you'll be revealed to the world!'

'Get away with you,' I retort. 'You think I've got time
to be excited? Who do you think it is who does all the
heavy lifting around here? Muggins, that's who. Bit of
force here, bit of mass over there. "Does my bum look
big in this?" Blame it on the boson.'

The proton looks a bit nervous. Maybe I'm ranting.
Or maybe it's because his favourite electron is wandering
off. She's a right slapper, that one. Lusty eye. Slip her a
handful of photons and she'll bond to anyone.

'I just thought you might welcome the recognition,'
he says, miserably. 'My electron thought you'd be off on
those reality TV shows. Lecture tours and whatnot. She
reckons you'll be on *Newsnight Review* in a month or
two, opposite the Archbishop of Canterbury.'

'I'm not one to judge,' I say, archly, 'but the pair of you
seem a little unstable.'

The proton sighs.

'It's her fault,' he says. 'She's just so terribly negative.'

TUESDAY

Of course, I'm just being coy. Actually, I'm very excited. That's why I'm here in this tunnel under Switzerland, limbering up for the big run. This is my big moment.

I've a lot to prove. According to a bunch of sniggering quarks I just met sharing a fag by one of the electromagnets, Professor Stephen Hawking doesn't believe I exist.

I'm not really sure what that means. Hawking, in case you haven't heard of him, is a hypothetical entity proposed by scientists in order to explain the existence of all the pages in *A Brief History of Time* after chapter one. You see, science is convinced that they are there, even though nobody has ever actually read them. Ergo, Hawking.

Personally, I think 'Hawking' might be a far too neat and convenient way of answering a very complicated question. But maybe I'm just bitter.

WEDNESDAY

I'm not convinced about this 'Andrew Marr' business, either. Maybe this really is a universe in which a major national broadcaster would send a politics journalist to cover the largest science experiment in the history of the world, for the radio. But I prefer to think that we live in a rational universe. A universe that, one day, we might actually understand.

THURSDAY

A full day of whizzing round and round this giant pipe, and still nobody has noticed me. I feel a bit like the bits of the British cycling team who aren't Chris Hoy. And I'm not sure what else I can do. Grow a beard? Wear sequins? Go on *Switzerland's Got Talent*? Without wishing to buy into my own hype, I am supposed to be the

GOD particle, you know. Doesn't my mass count for anything?

That wasn't a pun on mass, by the way. Although maybe it should have been.

FRIDAY

Another few hundred circuits this morning and I bumped into my old friend the nervous proton. There was no black hole, but our conversation did have some awkward voids. Eventually I asked him what had happened to that slutty electron of his.

The proton looked downcast.

'She's gone,' he said. 'Left me. Said she wanted to experience new attractions. Said I made her feel unbalanced.'

'How ionic,' I remarked. That one was a pun. I was rather proud.

'Mmm,' said the proton. Then he brightened up. 'But it's not like I'm alone. I've made friends with a neutron. After a few more circuits I thought we might ditch this merry-go-round and go and explore the world. Some reckon it's grey goo out there by now.'

'And what does your neutron think?' I asked.

The proton shrugged. 'He has no inclination either way.'

A SUITCASE FROM TERMINAL FIVE
5 APRIL 2008

A new terminal has opened at Heathrow. Everybody's luggage is lost.

MONDAY

It started after a flight back from Florence. Ooh! What a week! I'm only black plastic, a bit battered. Most of the time I'm up in an attic in Croydon with that mouldy teddy and that tedious old pram. But not this week. This week I've seen the world.

The flight back was nothing special. I was on top of this dignified old gent, a pre-war Samsonite with a strap. Been around the block. He was telling me about seaplanes. Time was, apparently, you used to get a bit damp. Think he was showing off, to be honest. There were a couple of sweet young wholesale Italian cake boxes next to us in the hold. They were totally listening. Little tarts.

When we landed, that was when it all went strange. They came at us on the runway, like they always do, but this time they didn't seem to know what they were doing. Hands everywhere. All of us bustled along on shoulders. Loads of shouting. I'm off one way, the tarts another, and that proud old Samsonite a third.

'Tell my matching hatbox I love her!' he cried, and then he was gone. I never did see him again.

TUESDAY

By now, I knew something was wrong. I was still in the airport. I was in this weird storage warehouse with a grumpy-looking bag of skis.

'Why the long face?' I said to him, as a bit of a joke.

He didn't get it. In a right mood, actually. Poor bloke was only from Putney, just down the road. Me, I reckoned I was on an extended holiday. Him, he was on his way out. Furious skis inside him, who had reckoned they were going to be on the slopes by now. Still, he was one of the lucky ones. There was a little red trolley bag next to us, stuck midway from Marseilles to Manhattan. He didn't look well at all. Turned out he was full of Brie.

WEDNESDAY

And suddenly, we're on a truck to Milan. Why Milan? Don't you pass Croydon, on the way to Milan? Wrong direction entirely for the Brie trolley bag. Makes more sense for the ski bag, I suppose.

I was buzzing. Literally, buzzing. Somebody dropped me. Always embarrassing. Nobody ever believes it's just an electric razor.

Mind you, there's worse things than buzzing. Stinky trolley had little rancid guffs coming out of his vents. Even sports bags were edging away. There was this locked medical icebox, which was totally panicked because it was worried it might have somebody's lung. And this young rucksack over from South America in the corner, all fretful and mysteriously quiet.

THURSDAY

And the next day, back to London. This time, I was on a FedEx plane. Back in my warehouse, I found myself stacked beside a very snooty Gucci suitcase, who was saying nothing to anybody. Apparently it belonged to Naomi Campbell, who was on her way to Los Angeles.

Nobody is thinking straight. Somebody should have asked her to take the cheese.

FRIDAY

Today I'm being sent to Manchester. Which is nice. Never been to Manchester before. I don't think it's on the way to Croydon, but I'm beyond caring. Buzzing stopped. Battery must be dead.

No idea what happened to the others. According to rumours, ski bag is still in Milan, organ box was being taken south by a Bedouin camel train, and Naomi's suitcase is being carried around the world at random in the belly of a giant whale. These celebrities, eh? Always with the special treatment.

'It's ridiculous,' says a mail order short plank, who is strapped to another short plank. 'Why do we have to go to Milan? Why can't we just stay here, until somebody comes to get us?'

The other plank agrees. I do, too.

It's funny. I always assumed that the bosses of BAA were cleverer than two short planks. But maybe not.

MARGARET THATCHER'S HANDBAG
20 APRIL 2013

The big news this week was the funeral of Margaret Thatcher.

MONDAY

We are a handbag. We saw it all.

'Where there is discord,' said the Lady, 'may we bring harmony. Where there is error, may we bring truth.' And where there are any of these things, she went on, we shall bring our handbag. But nobody reported that bit.

This past week, we must say, we have felt a bit neglected. We were one of the first handbags in the House of Commons, you know. And, while there had been other handbags in Downing Street, they had never called the shots. It was we who put the fear of God into François Mitterrand. We, who smote the Argentinians, miners and trade unionists. Albeit, not literally. Well, sometimes literally.

We were her constant companion. We were the only one who never left her, or betrayed her, or decided that we'd have more fun on the arm of John Major. And we never got lost in the desert. Although once in a closet. But not for long.

TUESDAY

It is peculiar, but nobody has ever asked for our secrets. We are regarded as a mere appendage. Nobody questions the things we have seen, or held inside. Nobody asks if George Osborne was actually found in us, abandoned at Victoria Station.

Nothing like that. Instead, people bring their preconceptions. For some, without us, Britain would today be a bleak wasteland, ruled by men who were either Welsh or wore donkey jackets. For others, we are held responsible, still, for turning the North of England into a place where people rarely own decent handbags at all.

By far the strangest, though, are those elderly gentlemen who have suddenly piped up to say that they always found us sexually attractive. That's weird, that. We didn't see that coming. That creeps us out.

WEDNESDAY

Today was the funeral, and we were pleased to see how many women attending paid tribute to our style. We weren't sure about Samantha Cameron's whole get-up, though. We felt that to be somewhat taking the piss.

Of course, we haven't been getting out lately, and it was nice to see all the old faces. Norman Tebbit hasn't aged, has he? He still looks just the same; not a day over 132. And wherever has the rest of Nigel Lawson gone? Even Michael Heseltine was there.

He was the Lady's great rival, you know, both in her job, and in her large and magnificent hair. But he never had a handbag. And he hated that.

Everybody knew.

THURSDAY

Like all the best handbags, we have no patience with internal divisions. There is inside and there is out.

And we have no patience with wets. For they would ruin our lining, and perhaps stain our leather exterior.

'Treat us well,' we always said to the Prime Minister. 'For you cannot give us an iron, Lady.'

Alas, we didn't make it to the wake. We always missed the parties, you know. The Lady's husband loved them. She, less so.

'There is no such thing as sobriety!' he used to say.

'But there is a tapestry,' she would reply. 'On the couch,' she'd add. 'Which you can sleep under. If you don't come home now.'

FRIDAY

To be honest, even we are a bit bored with reading about Margaret Thatcher now. It wasn't all her, you know.

Yes, she slept only three hours a night, but who was in charge then? Us, that's who. Ruling the world, along with Reagan's Brylcreem and that strange mark from the top of Gorbachev's head.

Finally, though, some recognition! According to today's news, our sales have rocketed in the last week. We are flying off the shelves!

It is what she would have wanted. The legacy shall not die. We are still a handbag. And we shall go on and on and on.

A PIC'N'MIX SHOVEL
13 DECEMBER 2008

And finally, this was the week that Woolworths closed. Remember Woolworths? They had a big sale. Some people blamed the Conservatives, because they'd been moaning a lot lately about kids eating chocolate.

MONDAY

We had that David Cameron in here yesterday. He steered clear of me, obviously. Probably wants me to shovel fruit or something. Fruit! What do I want with fruit? Cherry cola-cubes and chewy strawberries, yes please. Real cherries and real strawberries, no thank you. Bring me out in a rash. Or potentially, a mould. I'm not sure.

What happened to politicians like Ken Clarke? That's what I want to know. There's a man who knew his chocolate mice from his pink, foamy mushroom-shaped things. A real man.

A Woolworths man.

That's what the country needs.

Trust me on this. I'm on the aniseed balls now, but I've worked every section on the Pic'n'Mix from flying saucers to those things that look like Mini Eggs. I once spent four months buried at the back of a compartment of jelly rings so I've known hardship, but I've never seen anything like this.

TUESDAY

Here's what we're all wondering. When they say 'everything must go', do they mean us, too? That's always been the existential question of Pic'n'Mix life – are we for sale? Could a punter use one of us to shovel up a bag of the rest of us and cart us off to the sticky scales by the cash desk? Would we be 69p for 100g, too?

Because we don't weigh much. We certainly weigh less than those beige cubes that pretend to be fudge. We'd be a bargain.

Actually, I tell a lie. The existential question of Pic'n'Mix life is how they got those little hundreds and thousands to stick to the curvy bit of the chocolate buttons but never to the flat underside. I suppose we'll never know.

WEDNESDAY

There are 815 Woolworths shops in Britain, with about 25,000 staff. By my reckoning, there must be at least 30,000 of us shovels. Why does nobody care about our futures? Is it because we aren't unionised? Scooping is the only life I've ever known. Man and boy.

Spade and spoon? Whatever. I'm the soul of Woolworths. Backbone of Britain. That's me. Well, maybe not the backbone. Another bit. The roof of the mouth, maybe. What else can I do? What else needs scooping? There are rumours about a deal with Pet World. I don't like to think about it.

THURSDAY

So get this. There were 100 people queuing outside the door at 9 a.m. They came in and swarmed.

They took the computer games. They took the Wiis and the Xboxes. They took the bumper-sized Dairy Milks and the plug adaptors and the ironing-board covers and the toilet roll dispensers.

They took the cuddly toys and the plastic toys and the washing lines and the adjustable ratchet screwdrivers and the tiny bayonet light bulbs. And yet, as I now rest in my echoey, empty compartment amid grains of sugar and slivers of stuff that smells like absinthe, I can't help but notice that the next compartment still remains full of those apparently edible, faux-pineapple cubes.

What does that tell you, eh?

FRIDAY

Well, we know what it tells you. To be honest, I've had my doubts about the whole Pic'n'Mix concept for a while. We all have. It's not just because pineapple chunks look like they come from the bottom of a urinal.

It was the fried eggs that did it. What the hell is that about? Chocolate eggs, hmm, weird concept, although tradition counts for a lot. But fried eggs? Made of jelly and not tasting of anything? Not even eggs? It's madness. All the shovels knew it, but you wouldn't listen to us, would you? That's the £385 million of debt right there. The fools.

WITH THANKS TO...

1. *The editors and Saturday editors who first let me start writing this column and then let me keep writing it, and then, at various vital times, refused to let me stop writing it. They are, respectively, Robert Thomson, James Harding and John Witherow, and George Brock, Eleanor Mills and the brilliant Nicola Jeal.*
2. *Many, many sub-editors.*
3. *The readers who have e-mailed me, continuously, to ask why these weren't compiled in a book, and Jeremy Robson at Robson Press, for allowing me to now reply by saying 'they are'.*
4. *The people who work in PR who e-mail me, almost as continuously, to pretend that they love the column, and to ask whether I'd fancy interviewing their client for it. This never stops being funny.*
5. *Fran, my wife, who has the best and most important laugh in the world.*